BLOODROOT

BLOODROOT

A MARTHA'S VINEYARD MYSTERY

CYNTHIA RIGGS

MINOTAUR BOOKS
A THOMAS DUNNE BOOK
NEW YORK

A THOMAS DUNNE BOOK FOR MINOTAUR BOOKS.
An imprint of St. Martin's Publishing Group.

www.thomasdunnebooks.com
www.minotaurbooks.com

Library of Congress Cataloging-in-Publication Data

Names: Riggs, Cynthia, author.
Title: Bloodroot : a Martha's Vineyard mystery / Cynthia Riggs.
Description: First Edition. | New York : Minotaur Books, 2016. | Series: Martha's vineyard mysteries | "A Thomas Dunne book."
Identifiers: LCCN 2015050414| ISBN 9781250058683 (hardback) | ISBN 9781466863095 (e-book)
Subjects: LCSH: Trumbull, Victoria (Fictitious character)—Fiction. | Martha's Vineyard (Mass.)—Fiction. | BISAC: FICTION / Mystery & Detective / Women Sleuths. | GSAFD: Mystery fiction.
Classification: LCC PS3618.I394 B58 2016 | DDC 813/.6—dc23
LC record available at http://lccn.loc.gov/2015050414

Our books may be purchased in bulk for promotional, educational, or business use. Please contact your local bookseller or the Macmillan Corporate and Premium Sales Department at 1-800-221-7945, extension 5442, or by e-mail at MacmillanSpecialMarkets@ macmillan.com.

First Edition: May 2016

10 9 8 7 6 5 4 3 2 1

FOR DIONIS COFFIN RIGGS
POET
1898–1997

BLOODROOT

—

CHAPTER 1

After the last guest left, the four Wilmington grandchildren gathered on the front porch, Heather and Susan on the swing, Scott in an Adirondack chair facing the view of pasture and the wide sweep of ocean beyond, and Wesley on a porch rocker.

"Glad that's over," said Wesley, a redhead and the youngest of the four. "My face hurts from smiling."

It was a fine June afternoon and all four were barefoot, the two women in ragged cutoff jeans that just covered what needed to be covered, Wesley in equally ragged but longer jeans, and Scott in neatly pressed chinos.

"Well," Wesley continued, "it's good to be with you guys again. You know, we ought to get together more often."

"Not here." Heather shook her head and her blond ponytail swung across her back. "At least not while she's around." She jerked her head at the house behind them. "Once every ten years is just fine."

"How did Grandmother talk the rest of you into this so-called annual visit?" asked Wesley. He leaned forward in the rocker. "I went along only because she said all of you were coming."

Scott, the eldest of the four, dark-haired and heavyset with a full beard, was resting his feet on the porch railing. "Threats," he muttered. He looked over his shoulder at his brother and sisters. "Mildred said if I didn't show up for her 'annual visit' "—he made quote marks in the air with his fingers—"she'd cut me out of her will."

"What?" Susan leaned forward in the swing. Her hair, unlike her younger sister's, was cut short and curled around her face. "She said that? And stop calling her Mildred. It's disrespectful to Grandmother."

"Oh yeah? She deserves our respect?" said Wesley.

"To answer your question, Sue, the implication was clear." Scott turned back to the view. "Glad the fog cleared."

"She must be feeling mortal or something," said Heather. She and Susan were both tall blue-eyed blondes and both needed to lose a bit of weight.

Wesley pushed his foot against the porch floor, setting his rocking chair into motion. "I got the same message. The old lady sent me a lavender-scented note, 'The others will be here. If you value your future, you'll be here, too.' Like that, only more subtly worded."

"Speaking of lavender scents, Heather," said Scott, looking over his shoulder again, "what's that perfume you're wearing? Nice. Smells like money."

"Thanks. It's Dior's Midnight Poison."

Wesley laughed. "You suppose we could give a bottle to Mildred?"

"There must be something cheaper." Scott turned back to the view.

"This is all very funny, you guys, but I have to live with her," said Susan.

"So leave," said Heather.

"Oh, sure," said Susan.

"How can you stand it?" Heather asked.

Susan shrugged. "I manage."

Wesley's chair clicked rhythmically over the uneven floorboards. "How's about us getting together someplace else next time? Not in another ten years. We may all be dead by then."

"Like, where?" asked Heather.

"What about your place, Scott?"

"You talking to me?" Scott glanced back over his shoulder "Me? After Bitch-Ex cleaned me out, I'm living under the railroad bridge in a cardboard box drinking Ripple."

"Ripple's long gone," said Wesley. "Get with it, bro."

"What happened? Did you give her the house?" asked Heather. Scott looked affronted. "The Honorable Ms. Judge did so."

"At least you got to keep half," said Susan.

"Surely you jest." Scott placed his hand over his heart. "I've barely got my skin."

Wesley turned to Heather. "Be fun to meet in LA."

Heather got the swing going with a push of her foot. "I live in one upstairs room in a house with about twenty druggies. And a shared bath. And a hotplate."

"How can you afford Midnight Poison?" asked Scott.

"The magic of plastic cards." Heather turned to Wesley. "What about you, Idea Man? Oklahoma City sounds like a fun town."

"Could be," said Wesley. "I'm never there."

"Cops after you again?" asked Scott without turning his head.

"I ain't afraid of no cops." Wesley gave another push with his foot.

"That bad, eh?" Scott grinned. "Poor investments?"

"You could say that."

"Looks like Grandmother's place is it," said Susan.

"We could all meet under Scott's bridge," said Wesley.

"Share his neighbor's Ripple," said Heather.

"Probably nicely aged by now," said Wesley.

"If I can put up with her for ten years all by my lonesome," Susan put in, "you can deal with her for a week."

3

"Miz Sue, if I have to be around that woman for another week, either she'll be dead or . . ." Scott didn't finish.

Wesley laughed. "Is that a promise?"

"Ouch!" Victoria Trumbull winced. It was two days after Mrs. Wilmington's reception for her visiting grandchildren. Victoria was standing by the sink, where she'd bitten into a slice of apple.

Elizabeth, her granddaughter, was passing through the kitchen on her way to her car. Elizabeth was as tall as her grandmother, who was almost six feet tall.

"That tooth again, Gram?" Elizabeth was dressed in khaki slacks and white uniform shirt for her job at the Oak Bluffs harbor.

"Only a small slice of apple," said Victoria, her gnarled hand up to her jaw. "I'd even peeled off the skin."

"Is the dental clinic open? Want me to call for you?"

"I'll call." Victoria reached for the telephone. "I suppose I'd better act mature about this."

"If you can get an appointment now, I'll take you. I don't have to be at work for a while." Elizabeth picked up the slice of apple that Victoria had dropped and put it in the compost bucket. "The upcoming presidential visit means the harbor is crazy busy."

Two hours later, Victoria was at the clinic, listening intently to her dentist's tale of how she'd extracted the eyetooth of a lightly sedated Bengal tiger. Victoria had dressed in her gray corduroy slacks and turtleneck shirt with tiny rosebuds printed on it. She was reclined in the chair, her mouth full of cotton. A paper bib covered her chest and she didn't want to dwell on what Dr. Demetrios was about to do. Dr. Ophelia Demetrios seemed far too attractive and much too young to know what she was doing.

Victoria clenched the tissue she'd been given. It had become a tight damp wad in her perspiring hand. "Lightly sedated," Dr. Demetrios repeated, pulling her mask down below her chin. "The zoo thinks a *tiger* is more valuable than *I* am!" She touched her chest with a gloved hand, rolled her large, moist dark eyes, and pursed her mouth into a pink rosebud. "The keepers warned me—there were four of them—that if the tiger should open his eyes . . . !"

"Umpf," said Victoria.

Dr. Demetrios returned to her patient. "Just a slight prick, Mrs. Trumbull, then a gentle tug. Is your jaw numb enough yet?"

Not knowing how numb it should be, Victoria shook her head.

"Just think, Mrs. Trumbull, here you are, ninety-two," Dr. Demetrios said brightly, "and you're growing a wisdom tooth." She patted Victoria's shoulder. "That means you are very wise."

Victoria, annoyed by the condescension, was about to protest when a scream from a cubicle down the hall made her sit up.

Dr. Demetrios dropped the instrument she'd been about to poke into Victoria's mouth. She planted both gloved hands on the top of her head, mussing her shiny blue-black hair, which had been pulled back into a tidy bun.

Victoria spat gauze and cotton into the nearby basin and swiveled around. "What was that?" She set her feet on the floor.

"I knew that would happen." Dr. Demetrios ran her latex covered hands down her elegantly carved cheekbones. "He should never have hired that, that ignoramus, that, that *malakas*."

A second scream echoed down the hall, weaker than the first.

Victoria stood up. The paper bib twisted over her shoulder. She tossed her wadded up tissue onto the chair and brushed past Dr. Demetrios into the hallway that led to the reception area.

Patients, bibs askew, popped out of rooms on either side.

Dr. Horace Mann, the clinic's director, burst out of his office door and hurried toward the cubicle from which the sound was coming.

"What the hell?" A large middle-aged man popped out of another cubicle, tore off his bib, and threw it on the floor.

A series of lesser screams subsided into a series of coughs. Then retching sounds.

In the cubicle there was the sound of raised voices, feet rushing back and forth, metal instruments dropping on the floor.

A young woman Victoria recognized as Susan Wilmington, one of the four Wilmington grandchildren, was in the waiting room, standing, frozen, her hands up to her mouth, a magazine splayed at her feet. She was wearing a blue denim skirt and sandals and had sunglasses perched on the top of her short blond hair.

"Oh, my dear God!" Mrs. Hamilton, an acquaintance of Victoria's, who had been sitting in the reception area, rushed over to Victoria and grasped her arm with both hands. "Oh, Mrs. Trumbull, what shall we do? What was that?"

"I'm sure everything is under control, Mrs. Hamilton," Victoria assured her, not certain herself that everything was under control.

When Dr. Mann dashed out of his office, he'd left the door wide open. He now stood in front of the cubicle from which the screams had come, blocking it from view. His forehead was beaded with sweat. He was a tall, slender man in his early forties with light reddish-brown hair, wearing an open white lab coat. From the sounds that came from the room, two people were rushing back and forth. Dr. Mann turned to the people gathering around him. Under his lab coat he wore a blue shirt and a tie with blue and white stripes. He adjusted the tie nervously. "There's been an accident," he said. "Please go back to your rooms."

Susan stumbled over to him. "My grandmother? Is that my grandmother?"

"The ambulance is on its way. Please go back to your seat."

"What happened?" Susan stared wide-eyed at him.

"Has someone called 911?" asked Victoria.

"Yes, yes." Dr. Mann wiped his forehead with a blue bordered handkerchief he'd snatched out of his pocket. "The ambulance is on its way. Everyone, please! Go back to where you were!"

The large man headed for the door. "I'm outta here." He clumped down the outside steps leaving the door open, muttering over his shoulder, "I sure as hell don't want someone messing around in my mouth after that."

"I have to agree," Victoria said to Mrs. Hamilton. "Surely, no one will have a steady hand after such a commotion."

From the small room came the sound of moans. Susan grasped Dr. Mann's arm. "Please! Is it my grandmother?"

He shook her hand off his arm. "We're taking care of everything."

A siren wailed to a stop in front of the clinic. Two EMTs, a slim blond man and an equally slim young woman, carried a stretcher up the steps and into the cubicle two rooms from where Victoria had been. She recognized them as fellow West Tisbury voters, Jim and Erica.

More sirens whimpered down, and both Edgartown and West Tisbury police arrived. Two Edgartown officers hurried into the building, closely followed by West Tisbury's police chief, Mary Kathleen O'Neill, also known as Casey, and Junior Norton, her sergeant.

Casey glanced quickly around the reception room. When she saw Victoria she stopped abruptly. "How did you get here before we did?"

Victoria was Casey's police deputy. After Victoria had backed into the Meals on Wheels van Casey confiscated her license. When she offered to give Victoria a ride whenever she needed, Victoria climbed into the shotgun seat and that was it. Casey soon discovered how valuable Victoria's knowledge of the Island was and presented her with a hat that read WEST TISBURY POLICE DEPUTY in gold stitching across the front.

Before Victoria could answer, Casey demanded, "What are you doing here, Victoria?"

"I was having some dental work done."

"Are you all right?"

"Yes, I'm fine. It's a patient down the hall who doesn't sound all right. It may be Mildred Wilmington."

"I'll talk to you later. We're up to here"—Casey brought a hand up to her chin—"with the presidential visit. I don't need this." She left to join the EMTs and others in the cubicle.

Victoria's jaw felt quite numb.

She thought of the screams. She thought of Dr. Demetrios's shaking hand. She thought of that troublesome wisdom tooth, and she thought of having to go through this entire process again. Getting up her nerve to call for another appointment. The countdown to the day, the hour. The sitting in the waiting room with its array of outdated magazines, listening to the receptionist make appointments for other sufferers. The desultory conversation around her that she could never focus on. The sound of the drill . . .

She thought of the poor patient two cubicles from hers, the screams and retching. What dental procedure could cause such a reaction? Perhaps she could put up with that troublesome tooth.

And she thought of Susan Wilmington worrying about her grandmother. She went to her and put her arm around her. "You came with your grandmother?"

Susan, eyes bright with tears, nodded. "I don't know for sure that it is my grandmother, but she hasn't come out. Dr. Mann won't tell me anything."

Victoria handed her a saved paper napkin she'd taken from her pocket and Susan wiped her eyes.

"I don't believe there's anything he can tell you just yet."

The EMTs wheeled the stretcher out of the cubicle as they worked on the patient.

Casey, at the rear, looked up briefly and nodded at Victoria. "I'll call you later, okay?"

The stretcher was whisked down the steps and into the ambulance.

Victoria went over to Dr. Mann, who was still standing by the small room. "Is it Mrs. Wilmington?"

Startled, he swiveled. "What?"

"Susan Wilmington came here with her grandmother. Is it Mildred Wilmington? If so, you need to tell Susan. Or I'll tell her."

He wiped his forehead. "Mrs. Wilmington. Yes."

Victoria returned to Susan. "It is your grandmother. You'll want to drive to the hospital to be with her."

Victoria returned to Dr. Demetrios's room to collect her cloth bag containing her wallet, poetry book, notebook, and police hat.

Dr. Demetrios, standing at the door of her cubicle, moved aside to let Victoria pass. "I knew it," she said. "Dr. Mann should never have hired that woman."

CHAPTER 2

"Why shouldn't Dr. Mann have hired that woman?" asked Elizabeth when Victoria explained why her appointment had been cut short. "And who's the woman Dr. Demetrios was talking about?"

Elizabeth had left work to pick up Victoria at the clinic, which was located in the airport business park. The top on her convertible was down and the bright June sun picked up gold highlights in her sun-bleached hair.

"The 'she' is a dentist Dr. Mann hired a few months ago, a lovely young woman. A graduate of the Harvard dental school."

"But what had she done?" Elizabeth asked again, looking both ways before turning right onto Barnes Road.

"I can't imagine. The EMTs were hovering over the patient with bottles and tubes while Casey and Junior Norton accompanied the stretcher out to the ambulance." Victoria glanced at her granddaughter. "The patient was Mrs. Wilmington. Her granddaughter Susan was in the waiting room."

"That doesn't sound good," said Elizabeth. "I'll drop you off at home and then I gotta get back to work."

At the emptied-out clinic, Dr. Mann had recovered some of his color and was holding a weeping Dr. Aileen McBride against his chest.

"She's getting your clean jacket all wet, Dr. Mann," said

Dr. Demetrios, who'd come upon the tender scene. She stood with her fists on her hips. "Mascara stains don't wash out."

Dr. McBride pushed herself away from the arms of Dr. Mann and blotted her eyes with a handful of tissues she'd snatched out of the box on the receptionist's desk. Her hair hung in a long auburn braid down her back. Damp tendrils curled around her pale face. Mascara streaks ran down her cheeks from large green eyes that were magnified by tears.

"Mrs. Wilmington, wasn't it?" asked Ophelia Demetrios. "I doubt if she and her grandchildren will be back. Harvard? Paugh!"

Aileen wiped her cheeks and examined the black smears on her tissues. "I didn't do anything." Her sobs had subsided into hiccups. "I didn't do anything."

"That figures." Ophelia turned to Dr. Mann and asked in a gentler voice, "Will Mrs. Wilmington be all right?" She brushed an auburn hair off the front of his white coat. "Were all of her grandchildren here?"

"Susan was here," said Dr. Mann. "I didn't see the others."

"Too much was going on," said Ophelia. "Exactly what occurred?"

Dr. Mann looked down at his lab coat and smoothed a hand over the front of it. "We're not sure yet what happened, Ophelia." He seemed to notice for the first time the staff members who'd been working on patients: Dr. Sam Minnowfish, who had been about to do a root canal on the large man, and two of the three dental assistants, one who was cleaning a young bearded man's teeth and one who was taking X-rays of Mrs. Hamilton's jaw. The one who had been assisting Dr. McBride with Mrs. Wilmington's usual checkup was missing. The three stood mutely by the doors to their respective operatories.

Dr. Mann turned to Dr. McBride. "Where is your assistant?"

"In the lavatory. She's isn't taking this well."

"Like you think the rest of us are all happy?" asked Dr. Minnowfish.

"It's an awful mess," said the assistant who'd been taking X-rays.

"We'd better clean things up," said Dr. Mann, taking charge. "Where's Vivian?"

The receptionist scurried into the corridor from the waiting room. "Yes, Dr. Mann?"

"Please bring us the cleaning supplies."

"Certainly, Dr. Mann." Vivian hurried to the broom closet at the end of the hall.

"You want all of us to clean?" asked Dr. McBride.

"All of us, dearie," said Dr. Demetrios. "You heard him."

"The place is a mess," Dr. Mann said. "We also need to work off the adrenaline generated by this, this"—he swallowed—"unfortunate incident."

Vivian returned, wheeling a cartload of plastic bottles, brushes, buckets, and rags, and the clinic's staff got to work.

They mopped floors, emptied waste into the incinerator behind the clinic, rinsed bottles and glasses and put them through the autoclave, took linens and uniforms to the laundry near the airport, and wiped down all surfaces with bleach.

When they were finished, Dr. Mann announced, "Come into my office. You, too, Vivian." He nodded at the receptionist, who was fanning herself with a copy of the *Island Enquirer*. After scrubbing floors on hands and knees, she'd collapsed into one of the padded waiting room armchairs, where she sat slumped, her sandaled feet flat on the floor, her floral-printed skirt draped between her spread legs.

Dr. Minnowfish and the two technicians, Arthur Morgan and Roosevelt Mark, lugged chairs into Dr. Mann's office. Dr. McBride's assistant, Jane Douglas, a young woman with silver-blond hair and a stunned look, who'd been helping with Mrs. Wilmington, had come out of the lavatory and was hovering in the background, her face almost as pale as her hair. She murmured, "Horace," and with that she fainted.

Mann moved toward her, but Roosevelt was already at her side and caught her as she fell. He lowered her onto the floor and knelt beside her. Her face was ashen. She was perspiring. Roosevelt looked up. "Someone get a blanket." He pulled off his navy blazer, rolled it up, and put it under her feet. "Shock," he said. "Small wonder."

Mann bent over her. "Jane?"

No answer.

Ophelia Demetrios had returned from the linen closet with a blanket and tucked it around Jane.

"Brandy, do we have any brandy?" asked Sam Minnowfish. Sam was a Wampanoag from Gay Head (Aquinnah).

Swathed in the blanket, Jane opened her eyes. "I'm all right." Her voice was weak. "Really. Quite all right. Please. I'm fine." She eased up to a sitting position on the floor, clutching the blanket.

Aileen McBride, who didn't look great herself, appeared with a mug of hot tea from the staff room down the hall and handed it to Mann, who held it up to Jane's mouth. "I put a couple of spoonfuls of sugar in her tea, Horace, to elevate her blood sugar."

Jane took the mug from Mann. "Thank you. I'm sorry to be such a bother." She took a sip. "How is Mrs. Wilmington?"

"Mrs. Wilmington will be fine," he said.

Minnowfish raised his eyebrows.

Arthur Morgan, a husky guy with thick black hair and a pock-marked face, helped Jane into a nearby chair. He shook out Roosevelt's blazer and returned it to him.

"Would you like me to take you home, Jane?" he asked.

"No, no. Please. I'm fine." Jane held the mug in both hands and sipped, eyes closed. She looked as though she'd been rescued from drowning. Her face was gray. Her beautiful silver hair hung in damp strands around her face. She clutched the gray wool blanket around her.

"Everybody okay now?" asked Mann.

"Hardly," said Minnowfish. "But go ahead with whatever you have in mind, Mann."

Dr. Mann returned to his office, the only room with a window, and sat behind his desk. The others pulled up chairs in a semicircle before him.

The phone at the reception desk rang. Vivian left her seat by the door to answer.

Dr. Mann leaned back in his chair and cleared his throat. "Thank you for your fine work."

"What I paid to go to dental school for," said Minnowfish, "mopping up Mrs. Wilmington's vomit."

"Don't say that, Sam," said Ophelia Demetrios.

"We're all concerned about this upsetting incident." Dr. Mann glanced around at his staff.

"Incident," repeated Minnowfish. "I like that."

"Sam, please!" warned Dr. Demetrios.

Vivian tiptoed back to her seat. Her glasses had slipped partway down her nose and the sour odor of perspiration drifted in with her.

"As we know," Dr. Mann continued, "Mrs. Wilmington has a weak heart. And she's not as young as she used to be."

"She's considerably younger than Mrs. Trumbull," said Dr. Demetrios, defending her patient.

"Not everyone is a Mrs. Trumbull." Dr. Mann ran a hand over his hair and straightened his tie. "I'm closing the office for the rest of the day. Vivian, please cancel all appointments."

"Certainly, Dr. Mann." Vivian seemed about to cry.

"By the way," he said, "What was the call?"

"Oh, Dr. Mann . . ." She looked up through bangs that almost concealed her eyes. "It was just a friend of mine who works at the hospital."

"Yes, Vivian?"

"That call, Dr. Mann." She pushed her glasses back into place with a forefinger. "She wasn't supposed to say anything."

"Well?" asked Mann, showing a bit of impatience.

"Mrs. Wilmington—" Vivian stopped. "Mrs. Wilmington has passed away."

CHAPTER 3

Within minutes of the time they'd received word of Mrs. Wilmington's death, Sergeant John Smalley of the state police and Trooper Tim Eldredge showed up at the dental clinic. Smalley was proud of the fact that he weighed only ten pounds more than he had when he played football in college. Tim Eldredge had recently graduated with an associate degree in criminal justice.

It was shortly after noon. The staff meeting had just broken up and Dr. Mann met them at the door. "Hello, John. Tim."

"What d'ya say, Red," said Smalley. The two shook hands. "Bad news, I'm afraid."

"If it's about Mrs. Wilmington, we heard."

"Can't believe you got the news before we did."

Mann grimaced. "Island grapevine at work. Privacy laws be damned. Come on in. I was about to let everyone go home."

"Where are they?"

"In the staff room getting their belongings together."

Smalley stepped into the doorway and was greeted by the smell of bleach. "I hope to hell you haven't cleaned up."

"Of course we did. The stench was overwhelming. Everyone got busy the minute Mrs. Wilmington was carried out." Mann waved a hand to include the entire dental area. "Nervous energy. Scrubbed everything down."

"You have to be joking." Smalley stood stock-still.

Mann looked blank. "What do you mean?"

"Evidence."

"Evidence of what?"

Smalley sighed. "Death of undetermined causes."

"I don't know what you're talking about." Mann leaned against the reception desk and crossed one ankle over the other. "She had a weak heart." He folded his arms over his chest.

"Undetermined causes," Smalley repeated. "You've destroyed potential evidence."

"Oh, for God's sake," said Mann.

Smalley strode into the clinic and paced the spotlessly clean hall with its sanitized operatories on either side. "I can't believe he's such a fool," he grumbled at Trooper Tim, who was following him around.

"Maybe he's not, sir."

Smalley paused and glanced at Tim. "We don't need this shit right now. With the president due next week we're short-handed."

"Thought he was coming in August."

"His daughter's getting married. June wedding."

When they reached Dr. McBride's cubicle, Mann joined them. "This was where Mrs. Wilmington had her attack," he said.

"What did you do with the wastebaskets?" asked Smalley.

"Usual waste such as paper bibs and towels, that sort of thing, we emptied into the incinerator. That included the rags and towels we used to clean up the mess. Then we rinsed out the containers with a bleach solution. Standard procedure."

"The incinerator?" asked Smalley.

"High tech, state of the art, green. Low emission," Mann said with pride. "We're the first facility on the Island with this type of on-site incinerator."

"Where the hell is it?" asked Smalley, shifting impatiently.

"Behind the clinic." Mann waved in the general direction. "The black box, looks like an office refrigerator."

"Is the waste still accessible?"

"It's already been fired up. Nothing but clean ash in it."

"Damnation, Red." Smalley sighed and turned away. "What did you do with the medical waste?"

Mann indicated a new and empty red plastic bag suspended from a metal frame. "Anything with blood or body fluids goes into a biohazard bag. Everyone wore gloves, of course."

"I'm afraid to ask. You empty out today's waste?"

"Good heavens, yes. Today's med waste has already been taken to the medical waste disposal unit."

"God damn it," muttered Smalley. "Where's the normal Island inefficiency when you need it?" He stood, feet apart, fists on his hips. Tim waited silently behind him.

Mann nodded. "We had to clean up."

Smalley moved away from Mann and marched into one clean room after another, getting angrier and angrier.

"Sorry," said Mann. "But I could see no reason for not cleaning the mess."

"Christ," said Smalley. "You get an A plus for cleanliness."

"Thanks," said Dr. Mann.

"I'm supposed to secure the entire place as a potential crime scene."

"What are you talking about? There was no crime, John."

"The forensic team will be here shortly to collect evidence. You made sure they won't find any, didn't you?"

"What in hell are you implying?"

"Evidence," said Smalley. "Destruction of evidence carries a stiff fine and a jail term."

"I didn't think for a moment that—"

Smalley interrupted him. "That's for sure."

"You don't have a problem with my dismissing my staff for the afternoon, do you, *Sergeant*?" Mann asked with more than a touch of sarcasm.

Smalley ignored him and went to the reception area where staff members had gathered.

"Do you all live on Island?" he asked.

Nods all around.

Smalley turned to Mann. "Go ahead. Dismiss them. You stick around, though."

Mann saluted and turned on his heel.

Arthur Morgan, one of the technicians, had been watching Jane Douglas, who was still pale. "You don't look so good. I'll drive you home."

"Thank you, Arthur. That's nice of you. I really don't feel like driving myself."

After Dr. Mann dismissed the staff, Vivian Parsons, the receptionist, sat in her car, shivering, her arms wrapped around her stomach. Her face was blotched from weeping. Her eyes were red-rimmed and swollen.

Roosevelt Mark, one of the dental technicians, came out of the clinic and walked over to where she was parked. He was a small, neat man with steel-rimmed glasses, short white hair, and a tidy white mustache that contrasted nicely with his dark skin. He tapped on her window. "You okay, Viv?" Roosevelt, in his fifties, was a good ten years older than she was.

Vivian tried to fit the key into the ignition to start the engine so she could lower the window, but her hand was shaking so badly she couldn't find the slot.

He opened her car door. "Move over. I'll drive you home."

Vivian shook her head.

"The gear shift is blocking you," he said. "Go around to the passenger side. I'll drive. We've all had a rough day." Even after a morning of scouring the clinic, his khakis looked pressed, his shirt unwrinkled, his tie in place. His blazer, which had been rolled up under Jane Douglas's feet, was tidy.

Vivian started to hand him the keys but dropped them instead. She looked blankly at where the keys had fallen onto the floor mat. A half-dozen keys and a brightly cheerful Mickey Mouse dangled from the keychain. The mouse was stepping forward, welcoming arms extended, big round ears alert, a happy grin on his mouse face.

"I should have realized," she murmured.

Roosevelt picked up the keychain by its ears and looked at it. "I would think all these protuberances would get caught up in your purse."

She didn't respond.

"I'll stop at the Tidal Rip on our way to your place."

"I don't want to stop at a bar," said Vivian.

"Passenger seat," he repeated, beckoning with both hands. "We'll talk about it on the way."

Vivian tried to swing her legs to the side.

"Easier if you unfasten your seat belt," said Roosevelt.

Vivian, tears welling up again, unbuckled her seat belt, eased herself out of the car, and stumbled around to the passenger side.

Roosevelt watched. "You really are in a state."

"I'm sorry," murmured Vivian.

"About Mrs. Wilmington, yes." He nodded. "Unfortunate."

"I shouldn't have answered the phone." Vivian tugged a tissue out of her purse and blotted her nose.

"There was nothing wrong with that."

"You know where I live?"

"Off Wing Road. You'll have to show me where. But we'll get something to buck us up, first."

20

"I don't want a drink." She held the tissue to her nose.

"Well, I do. A necessary medicinal dose."

He pulled out of the clinic's parking lot and turned left onto Barnes Road toward Oak Bluffs and some conviviality. Vivian was shaking so hard the car seemed to vibrate in time with her.

Roosevelt followed the one-way streets in Oak Bluffs until he got onto Circuit Avenue going the right way and there, in front of the Tidal Rip, was a parking space. He pulled into it.

"I've got the touch," he said with pride. He switched off the ignition and handed her the keys.

He turned to her. "This is our stop."

She shook her head.

"Look," he said, "you're not the only one suffering because of Mrs. Wilmington's demise. Think of what Dr. McBride must be feeling right now. And her assistant, Jane."

Vivian remained seated.

"Come on, don't be shy."

"I don't want to go in there," she said.

"Okay, give me the keys again. I'll drive you home. But I'm stopping at the liquor store first for my own sake."

She fished out the chunky batch of keys and handed them to him. "All I want is to go home."

Roosevelt drove to the far side of the Oak Bluffs harbor. The liquor store parking lot was almost full, but he found a place and pulled into it.

He glanced at Vivian. She was breathing rapidly and her face was white. "Do you have a blanket in your car?"

She nodded.

He found a plush throw on the backseat and tucked it around her. "I'll be right back. Everything will be okay, Viv."

She nodded.

CHAPTER 4

Arthur Morgan escorted Jane Douglas to his pickup, opened the passenger door, gathered up empty chips bags and used coffee cups and tossed them behind the seat, along with a ratty towel. "My dog's favorite place," he apologized, helping her up into the seat. Arthur was a quiet, stocky man in his mid-thirties, about ten years older than she. He'd changed into jeans and a yellow knit collared shirt. His chin had a shadow of dark beard, although it was just past noon. He fastened his seat belt. She fastened hers.

Jane had changed out of her green scrubs into black slacks and a white cotton blouse, had combed her hair, and put on a touch of lip gloss. Her face was pale.

"What kind of dog do you have?" she asked politely.

"He's a Heinz Fifty-Seven," Arthur said, and grinned. "Fifty-seven varieties of dog. My buddy."

"How nice," said Jane, who wasn't fond of dogs.

"Heard Roosevelt tell Vivian he was going to stop at the Tidal Rip for a drink. You interested?"

"No, thank you," said Jane.

"I don't know exactly where you live," he said, glancing at her. "I know it's Vineyard Haven, but where, is what I mean."

"Off Main Street," said Jane. "I hate to impose."

"No imposition," said Arthur. "I been looking for an excuse to get to know you better. I mean, us being coworkers and all."

Jane turned away from him and looked out the window.

Arthur turned right, out of the business park onto Barnes Road toward the Edgartown Road.

"Aren't you going the wrong way?" asked Jane.

"I know you haven't lived here year-round. Thought I'd show you West Tiz." He paused, eyes on the road.

"I've spent all my summers since childhood on the Vineyard, Arthur. You really don't need to show me around."

Arthur kept his eyes on the road. "You must feel terrible. Mrs. Wilmington being your patient and all."

"It wasn't a pretty sight." Jane stared out the window.

"Her granddaughter, Susan, was there at the clinic."

Jane nodded.

"I heard the other three were there, too, the two grandsons and granddaughter. I didn't see them, myself."

"I wouldn't know them," said Jane.

" 'Course you wouldn't. They were all patients before they left home. Long before you arrived on the scene." He opened the window. "Well, the two guys kept in touch with a couple of us after they left. They're here, now, visiting Granny."

"Her death will be a terrible blow to them." Jane leaned her head back against the seat.

"I doubt it," said Arthur.

A small plane zoomed over their car and set down smoothly at the end of the runway to their right.

"I wonder why they mow such wide swaths on the sides of Barnes Road here," said Jane, changing the subject away from Mrs. Wilmington. "It's not in keeping with the Island."

"Emergency landing strip," Arthur answered.

"Thank you."

"No problem." Arthur nodded. "About Mrs. W. Tough on all of us, but you were there I mean. And she was your patient. No wonder you passed out."

"I'm embarrassed about that." Jane examined the pale pink polish on her manicured fingernails.

"No need to be. Anybody going through what you went through would've acted worse," said Arthur.

"I feel sorry for her granddaughter." She looked over at Arthur. "But I really don't want to talk about Mrs. Wilmington."

"Yeah, I understand. She wasn't the nicest person in the world." He braked at the stop sign where Barnes Road ended and turned right onto the Edgartown Road. "She's been coming to the clinic a long time."

Jane turned to face him. "We shouldn't discuss patients."

Arthur barked out a laugh. "She ain't no patient no more."

Jane stared at him. "That's not at all funny."

"Sorry." Arthur flushed. "Mrs. W was no fan of Dr. McBride's, you know. I guess it was pretty clear to everybody that McBride was playing up to Mann." He glanced quickly at her. She had her eyes closed. "We all knew Mrs. W had a thing for Mann, too. Jealous, I guess."

"Please, Arthur. I don't want to talk about it. I want to get home." Jane folded her arms over her chest.

"Sure. No problem." Arthur pressed the accelerator and the pickup sped up.

He was quiet for a few minutes. Then he said, "She's been seeing Mrs. W's grandson, too." He took a hand off the steering wheel and rubbed his thumb and third finger together. "McBride can smell money a mile off. Mrs. W was worth a bundle, you know. McBride is scouting around for a rich husband."

Jane turned her head away from him.

24

"Sorry. I know you want to get home quick."

They passed the airport and reached the outskirts of West Tisbury before she spoke again. On their left was a weathered gray shingled house. "I've always wondered who lives in that house," she said twisting to look back. "It must be one of the oldest on the Vineyard."

"That's Mrs. Trumbull's place. She was there today."

Jane nodded.

"House is older than she is." He turned to her again. "I'll stop at Alley's and buy you a cup of coffee. Perk you up."

"No thanks." Jane looked at her watch.

"No problem." Arthur slowed up as they came to a house with a small building leaning against it, about to collapse. "That used to be an ice cream parlor and the house used to be Gifford's General Store."

"I didn't know that," said Jane.

"Grandkids own it now. They had a yard sale couple years ago. I bought a bunch of old stuff."

"Really? What sort of things?"

"Bottles. I collect old bottles. Sulphur matches. You could still light them. Old man Gifford never threw anything out. Before my time. I never met him." He sped up again. "There's the police station on the right. Garden Club on the left. Used to be a mill. The Mill Pond on the right."

"Yes, yes, I know all this," said Jane.

He turned right after the pond and they passed the cemetery and Whiting's fields and the new Ag Hall and the arboretum.

Jane looked at her watch.

When they reached Vineyard Haven he said, "I'd sure like to treat you to a sandwich and a beer at the Black Dog. It's lunchtime and we haven't eaten."

"I'm not hungry, Arthur. Please, I want to get home."

"Yeah. Sure. Of course."

He turned onto Main Street. They passed CB Stark Jewelers and Bunch of Grapes bookstore.

"I'm beyond Owen Park on the right toward the water."

"High rent district," said Arthur.

"Yes, it is." She stared out the window. "It's lucky I make a high salary at the clinic."

"Yeah," said Arthur. "Minimum wage. How'd you end up here?"

"An inheritance."

"Yeah?" asked Arthur.

She didn't answer.

They reached the entrance to a narrow lane. The harbor spread out below them. "You can drop me off here," she said. "I need the walk."

Arthur grinned. "Great place to live, you and your baby girl. Nice view."

She stared at him before she opened the door. "Thanks for the ride." She got out and shut the door firmly behind her.

She walked down the lane, shrugging her shoulders as if to rid herself of an unwanted load, which was exactly how she felt. Arthur had a crush on her and she'd avoided him. How had he known about her baby? She was obsessive about her daughter's privacy.

She took a deep breath of the sea air, turned left onto a brick path between boxwood hedges, and started down a set of steps that led to her house.

An elderly Jamaican woman with closely cropped gray hair, barefoot and wearing a brightly colored flowered muumuu that fell almost to her ankles greeted her at the wide glass door. "Missy. What're you doing home at this hour?"

"It's a long story, Abigail," said Jane. "Has Davina been a good girl?"

"She's playing in her sandbox. Only family I know has a sandbox on the beach." Abigail was taller than Jane, ageless and reed thin. Her skin was the color of coffee with cream, and she'd been Jane's nanny when Jane was a child.

Jane went to the large window overlooking the beach. The little girl was seated in an area bounded by old railroad ties, pouring sand from a plastic measuring cup into a red plastic bucket, and singing to herself. From where Jane stood, her daughter's head was framed by a red-gold halo of baby-fine hair.

"Sure is a pretty child," said Abigail.

Jane smiled. "One of my earliest memories was playing in a sandbox Grandfather made for me in that same spot. I remember picking up shells and taking them to you for you to admire. It was my very own special place."

"Nothing like boundaries for a little one," said Abigail. "You look worn out, Missy. Have you had lunch?"

"I can't eat anything." Jane turned away from the window.

"Cup of tea, then."

"That's just what I want. Thank you." Jane kicked off her sandals and seated herself on the couch where she could watch her daughter. "Fix yourself a cup, too, and I'll tell you all about the most awful morning of my life, if you're interested."

After Arthur Morgan dropped Jane Douglas off, he backtracked to Oak Bluffs. He was thinking about the phone call the receptionist took. Someone at the hospital was going to be in big trouble, letting out information on that woman's death. There was something else, though, about that call that upset Vivian. What was it?

He checked his watch. Past lunchtime. He'd head back to Oak Bluffs, get a bite to eat at the Tidal Rip. He drove down the hill overlooking the Oak Bluffs harbor and when he saw the liquor store, decided to stop. Get himself a six-pack of Bud. As he drove into the crowded parking lot he recognized the two Wilmington grandsons. They were just entering the building. He wasn't sure he wanted to see them after this morning, so he drove slowly through the parking lot and then spotted the receptionist's car. Seems like everyone's here, he thought. Roosevelt and the receptionist were probably in the store. He'd get the beer some other time.

The forensic van from off Island arrived at the dental clinic and three investigators came into the reception area—a black guy with a shaved head, who seemed to be in charge; a young white guy with thick glasses; and a young woman with spiky green hair. They slipped into clean white scrub suits before entering the clinic itself.

"Do I need to stay around for this?" asked Dr. Mann.

"Yes," said Smalley. "Get yourself a cup of coffee and wait in your car. The forensic team is likely to have some questions."

The team pulled covers over their shoes, bouffant caps over their hair.

"I hate to tell you, Doc," said Smalley, "but these assholes cleaned the place after the victim was carried out."

The principal investigator, Dr. Joel Killdeer, was chewing gum. "Don't worry, John," he said. "We'll find something. They never do a real thorough job."

Smalley looked dubious. "Good luck." He went out into the parking lot and joined Tim in the police car. Tim produced a thermos of coffee and poured it into two cardboard cups.

"Where's Mann?" Tim asked. "Car's gone."

"Getting coffee, I imagine," replied Smalley, blowing on his own coffee before taking a cautious sip.

CHAPTER 5

Dr. Horace Mann climbed into his car, offended, angry, and humiliated at his shoddy treatment at the hands of Sergeant John Smalley. Smalley had known him since high school and certainly didn't need to treat him as though he'd committed a crime by cleaning his clinic. Of course he was going to clean the place.

He'd changed back into his tan slacks and brown and green madras shirt.

Damned if he was going to wait around, though, sitting in his car drinking coffee while the forensic team inspected his clinic. Of course they wouldn't find any evidence. What evidence did they expect to find?

He had to check on Vivian. Something about that phone call had upset her. Something more than the news of Mrs. Wilmington's death. What had the friend said to her above and beyond the death? After the staff meeting he'd contacted the hospital to report the call. Vivian's friend had disregarded strict privacy laws.

He headed toward Oak Bluffs, his window open, his radio tuned to some talk show. Damn Smalley. Proper hygiene demanded the clinic be clean. He was gripping the steering wheel so tightly his fingers were numb.

The straight road soothed him. The state forest on his right had bright new undergrowth of huckleberry. On his left, a small plane roared overhead for a landing at the airport. He came to the dip in the road where a rutted road led off to the state forester's place. He thought about turning in there. A peaceful place canopied by tall pines. He could park in the shade and calm himself.

But he had to find Vivian. What had that friend told her?

By the time he reached the roundabout, he'd regained some of his equanimity.

Jane. He should never have hired her as Aileen McBride's assistant. That was a mistake. Aileen disliked Jane on the spot, but he'd insisted and Aileen had no choice. And Jane was good. Patients loved her.

He smiled when he thought of Jane staggering toward him after Mrs. Wilmington's attack this morning. She had called out his name.

Aileen had watched with that odd expression. Then Ophelia came out with her comment about mascara stains. What was there about women and him? Women gravitated to him. And, he admitted, he liked their attention. Probably too much.

He reached Oak Bluffs, wound his way through the one-way streets, and stopped for coffee-to-go at Nancy's Snack Bar. Cream, no sugar. Back in his car he drove slowly past the harbor. Sailboats rocked on moorings. Power boats were lined up along the seawall. He came abreast of the liquor store parking lot. Lots of cars, but no people around. Vivian's gray Suzuki was parked there. He stopped.

What was her car doing here? He wanted to talk to her. Then he remembered that Roosevelt was driving her home. She was either in the store, or in the car, waiting.

He looked at his watch.

Roosevelt had taken Vivian's car keys with him while he went into the liquor store leaving Vivian, with whatever terrors she had, alone in her car. He didn't want her driving in her condition.

The store was crowded. He greeted several people he knew and two men who looked familiar. They'd been patients at the clinic years ago, but he couldn't quite place who they were. He pushed his way through to the hard liquor shelves and picked up a bottle of Glenlivet, then made his way to the counter. He waited patiently in the line at the checkout. Someone had won fifty dollars on a lottery scratch card, and there were exclamations and congratulations. A small celebration was about to take place, but he didn't want to wait for it. When he filled out his check, the clerk needed his driver's license. He tugged his wallet out of his back pocket, thumbed through the pack of cards, and handed it to her.

The entire transaction took much longer than he'd expected. He checked his watch. Half an hour. Hope she's okay, he thought.

When he came out, carrying the paper bag with his bottle of Scotch, he glanced through the windshield, but didn't see her. Good, she was probably lying down. He opened the door. She wasn't in the front seat. Or the back.

"Damnation," he muttered. He should never have left her alone. He glanced around. The road was clear all the way to the other side of the harbor and, looking back, all the way to the top of the hill. No sign of her.

I suppose someone offered her a ride home and she accepted, he thought. Tired of waiting. Should have let me know.

Then, with an uneasy feeling, he thought of the way she'd been acting. And he thought of the harbor near where he'd parked.

She'd been more upset than he would have expected.

What happened in the clinic today was enough to upset anyone. But she was a sensitive woman, might have been worse on her.

He was wasting time. Still clutching his paper bag with its precious Scotch, he dashed across the asphalt toward the bulkhead that edged the harbor.

A stiff breeze was blowing off the water. Sailboats rocked on their moorings. Steel halyards slapped rhythmically against aluminum masts like tolling bells. A gull flew overhead, mewling. The breeze lifted a piece of paper and flung it against his leg. He didn't notice.

He reached the bulkhead and leaned over, hoping he would see only floating detritus swept by the wind to this side of the harbor. His glasses had slipped. He pushed them back with his finger and held them in place while he looked down.

The wind had shoved a swath of flotsam to this side. Bottles. Cups. Sticks. A dead gull. Seaweed. Plastic bags.

And there she was, facedown in the debris, her flowered skirt ballooned above her like an inflated plastic bag.

He stood up straight and looked around the parking area for someone, anyone. "Help!" he cried out. The paper bag slipped out of his hand, dropped to the pavement, and the bottle of Glenlivet shattered, spraying Scotch and shards of glass around him. "Man overboard! Help!"

He turned, tugged off his shoes. Pulled off his tie. Shrugged out of his blazer and dropped it on the ground. "Help!" he shouted again and plunged into the murky harbor water.

He surfaced, shook his head to clear his eyes, and reached out to her. He tried to turn her over, but she was too bulky. He tried to lift her face out of the water, but he couldn't get a purchase on her head, her hair, her chin.

"Hey, down there, buddy! Trouble?" A man leaned over. "Jesus Christ! I'll get a line to you."

"Call 911!" someone shouted.

"What happened?" Another voice, another man. Too blurry to make out. Roosevelt's glasses, gone.

Back at the clinic, Killdeer opened the door and pulled off his bouffant cap. His shaved head was shiny with sweat. Then he pulled off his booties, one after the other, then shed his coverall. Underneath he wore pressed stone-washed jeans and a black T-shirt printed with a white osprey in flight.

The woman with the green hair said, "We're getting a ride to the boat, Doc. See you at the lab tomorrow."

"Right," said Killdeer. "Thanks, both of you."

"Anytime," the other tech said. "Pleasure."

"Yeah, sure," said Killdeer.

"I'd like to hire those dental guys to clean *my* house," said the woman. "Bye."

Killdeer called out to the state police. "Come on in."

Smalley joined him in the reception area.

"Never seen anything like it." Killdeer snapped his gum. "Place got cleaned up, and I mean cleaned up. No fingerprints. No trace of body fluids. No partly used containers." He gathered up his shed protective clothing. "Nothing."

"Yeah," said Smalley.

"Take medical offices. We usually find something." Killdeer shook his head and chewed steadily. "This is like an operating theater." He tossed the shoe covers and cap onto one of the padded chairs and folded his coverall.

"The clinic director claims the victim had a weak heart."

"You better hope it was natural death. Zero evidence here."

Smalley said, "I'm off duty as soon as we're through here. Care for a beer?"

"Sounds good." Killdeer went to the door and looked around at the parking area. "Where's Mann? Needs to sign some papers. He can open the clinic now, far as I'm concerned."

Smalley looked, too. "Damn that guy. I told him to wait." Smalley reached into his pocket for his phone, looked at the display, and flipped it open. "State Police, Smalley." He frowned. "Ambulance on the way?" He glanced over at Killdeer. "Be right there. Ten minutes." He closed up the phone. "So much for the beer. Just fished some woman out of the harbor."

"I'll take a rain check on that beer," said Killdeer. "Enough action around this place. Be back before long."

"I hope not," said Smalley. "Not that I don't like seeing you around." He climbed into the passenger seat of the cruiser and Tim drove to the Oak Bluffs harbor.

"Everything happens at once," grumbled Smalley in the cruiser. "We're full out with the presidential visit. His daughter's wedding makes it twice as complicated. And now this. Unexplained death and a woman pulled out of the harbor."

"Dead, sir?" asked Tim.

"Probably." Smalley gazed out the window at the state forest on either side of them.

When they reached the liquor store, the first person Smalley confronted was a soaking wet and bedraggled Roosevelt Mark. "Seems to me I just saw you at the dental clinic."

"A million years ago," said Roosevelt, shivering.

A group of people had gathered by the harbor, watching while EMTs tried to resuscitate Vivian. The EMTs loaded her into the ambulance and took off toward the hospital, siren going.

As Smalley questioned him, Roosevelt was wet, filthy, and shivering.

"Afraid I can't tell you much about Vivian," Roosevelt said. "I'm disoriented without my glasses. All I can see are indistinct images."

"Where does she live?" Smalley looked up from his notebook.

"Oak Bluffs off Wing Road somewhere. I offered to take her home in her car. She was too upset to drive."

"Understandable," said Smalley.

Roosevelt hugged himself. "I wanted a drink. She didn't. So I stopped here to get a bottle of Scotch for myself."

"Go on," said Smalley.

"The liquor store was crowded and it took me a while." Roosevelt's dark skin showed through his translucent wet sleeves. "When I came out, I didn't see her. Figured she'd gotten a ride home with someone else. I delayed. And, well . . ."

Smalley turned to the trooper standing by. "Call the clinic and get her address. Killdeer is probably still there."

"Maybe they cleaned out their address records, too," Tim said, and added, "sir."

Smalley turned back to Roosevelt. "She married? Children? Next of kin?"

"I don't know much about her. She's from the Island. That's all I know." Roosevelt shivered. "Sad. I don't know if she's married or single, gay or straight. She's a private person."

Smalley continued write. "She socialize with anyone?"

Roosevelt shook his head. "The others hardly notice her, since she's only the receptionist." He touched his mustache, picked out a bit of seaweed, looked at it, and dropped it to the ground. "At office parties she sits at her usual place behind the desk. I'm the only one who talks to her." He looked up at the tall sergeant. "Afraid all I can see of you is a blob of a face in a blue garment."

"That about describes me," said Smalley, with a grim smile.

CHAPTER 6

Once she got home, Victoria took off her shoes to ease her sore toe, and sat by the cookroom window, watching cardinals and blue jays at the feeder.

After she'd rested for a few minutes, she remembered that Casey had said something about the presidential visit. But when she called, the police station phone was busy. So Victoria put her shoes back on, slung a gray moth-eaten cardigan over her shoulders, collected some dried bread crusts and put them in a brown paper bag, picked up her lilac wood stick, and set off for the police station. She could use a walk to rid herself of the mental image of the episode from this morning that kept running through her mind. And the ducks, geese, and swans that lived on the Mill Pond would like the bread.

When they saw her coming, the fowl gathered around. She shook out the last crumbs from the paper bag before she went up the steps into the station house.

Casey was still on the phone, and she wiggled her fingers at Victoria while she talked. "I need to know the number of guests and their names. Home addresses and contact information, too." A pause. "Yes, I know. I agree."

She set the phone down. "You wouldn't believe the details we have to check." She ran her fingers through her hair. "We're supposed to know who's visiting and where they're staying and their life histories." She leaned back in her chair.

"He *is* the president of the United States," said Victoria.

Casey sighed. "And the West Tisbury police force is only me and three guys." She sat up straight. "You should have called. I'd have picked you up."

"You have the president to worry about," said Victoria. "How can I help?"

"I wish," said Casey. "Everyone connected with this visit has to have some kind of security clearance that you don't have. I'm stuck with making these stupid phone calls." She leaned back in her chair. "I ought to be spending my time taking care of our town's problems."

"I'll think of some way to help," said Victoria.

While Victoria was at the West Tisbury police station, Roosevelt was at the Oak Bluffs harbor trying to answer Sergeant Smalley's questions. All he wanted was to retrieve his dropped clothing and get home. Shower. Find his pair of spare glasses. Put on clean, dry slacks and shirt, and pour himself a drink. He thought of the sound and smell of his bottle of Glenlivet smashing on the asphalt paving. He sighed.

Smalley shut his notebook and put it into his pocket. "You said you drove her car here?"

"The gray Suzuki." Roosevelt patted his wet pants pocket. He still had her keys. Not likely to slip out, with the Mickey Mouse hands, feet, ears, and tail sticking out like a burr. He handed them to Smalley, who took them.

"We'll take care of her car. Where's yours?"

"At the clinic. I can't see to drive."

Smalley nodded. "I'll give you a ride home in the cruiser."

"I'm afraid I'll get the seat dirty."

"Not a problem," said Smalley.

On the way to Roosevelt's house, the cruiser's radio crackled on and a voice announced something cryptic.

"Ten-four," answered Smalley, and hung up the mike. He turned to Roosevelt in the backseat. "Afraid the lady you rescued from the harbor didn't make it. Dead on arrival."

CHAPTER 7

Sam Minnowfish and Ophelia Demetrios sat at a small table next to the window at the Tidal Rip.

Both had changed out of their clinic whites into something more suitable. Ophelia had on skinny black pants and a bright scarlet silk shirt with a necklace of large red and orange beads and dangling earrings to match.

Sam lifted his sweating beer mug. "Cheers. You look pretty good in civvies." Sam was wearing an L.L.Bean chamois shirt.

"And you are quite handsome in that Native American attire."

"Wampanoag, not that PC Native American shit. *We* didn't come up with the name America."

Ophelia lifted her glass of Chardonnay. "Cheers to you," she said, "you big handsome Indian."

"What a morning." Sam took a swig of beer and set his mug down. "I can't remember when anything tasted better." He blotted his mouth with a paper napkin.

"What do you think of Jane and Horace?" Ophelia ran her finger around the rim of her glass making it squeak.

"What about them?"

"She called out, 'Horace,' in that little-girl-hurt voice?"

"Didn't notice. There was too much going on," said Sam.

"Would you please order something for us to nibble on, Sam, potato chips or nuts? It's past lunchtime and I'm hungry."

Sam got up and returned shortly with a bowl of tortilla chips in one hand and salsa in the other. He glanced out the window before he sat. "Wonder where he's going."

"Where who's going?"

Sam set the chips and salsa on the table between them. "Arthur Morgan just drove by."

"Oh?"

"He was taking Jane home to Vineyard Haven about the same time we left," said Sam, and shrugged.

"Perhaps he forgot something at the clinic," said Ophelia.

"With the police still there, he won't get in." Sam sat down again. "You were saying about Horace and Jane."

She leaned toward him. "When Jane fainted Horace rushed to her side."

Sam swigged his beer and set the glass down again. "Someone faints, you help."

"I think there's more to it than that." She sat back and sipped her wine. "You know, Horace recommended Jane for the job. To work with Aileen. He knew Jane from before, I am sure."

"That figures. He must have known her if he recommended her."

"Horace and Jane have something intimate going on between them, Sam. Aileen didn't want to work with Jane, but had no choice. You know that, don't you?"

"She could have let Jane go after a trial period."

Ophelia dipped a chip into the salsa and munched it. "Oh, my! Hot!"

"Want some milder stuff?"

Ophelia shook her head. "No, I like it." Her eyes were watering. "Our Greek cuisine is not so spicy." She wiped her eyes. "I was about to say, Aileen is not able to let Jane go." She fanned her mouth with her hand. "Jane works hard. Patients like her. Aileen dislikes her because of Horace." She took a sip of wine and added after a pause, "Jane knows more about dentistry than this girl from what they call Haa-vahd."

"Now, now," said Sam. "But you've got the pronunciation down just right."

The waitress, a thin woman in her forties, stopped by. "Need anything, folks?"

Sam held up his mug. "Refill for me. Want more wine, Ophelia?"

Ophelia looked up. "Please. When I finish this."

The waitress stuck her pencil behind her ear. "Beer, Chardonnay," she said, and left.

Ophelia sipped her wine.

In a few minutes the waitress returned with drinks and picked up the empty glasses. "You folks want to order something to eat?"

"I don't know," said Sam. "What've you got besides chips?"

"Pizza, four-cheese, pepperoni, and de-luxe."

"Any good?" asked Sam.

The waitress shrugged. "Not really. Frozen and nuked."

Sam looked at Ophelia, who shook her head. "No, thank you."

The waitress left.

"Jane lives in a house on the Vineyard Haven harbor," said Ophelia. "Why does she work at a clinic where she makes so little money when she lives in such an expensive house? Does she have money?"

"She inherited her grandmother's house." Sam started on his second beer. "Doesn't mean she has money. Who knows why she works."

"Perhaps it is to keep an eye on Horace."

"Keep an eye on him? She doesn't even seem to care much about our Dr. Mann."

"Appearances are deceiving," said Ophelia.

"With a house on the water she probably has to work to pay the taxes," said Sam. "That is, unless she inherited a fortune to go with the house."

Ophelia lifted the fresh glass of wine. "He is at least fifteen years older than she is." She took a sip.

Sam laughed. "Mann's a year or two older than me, and I'm forty. She's mid-twenties, I'd guess."

"She is twenty-five," said Ophelia. "I thought Aileen and I were going to be rivals over his affections. I didn't know he liked such very young women."

Sam raised his eyebrows.

Ophelia thought for a few moments. "You know, Sam, this Island is like towns in Greece. Different social strata. Native Islanders don't mix with the rich and famous visitors, summer people don't mix with new residents. I don't know anything about Horace's life. Was he married at some time?"

Sam laughed. "He's damned careful about not giving away his secrets. He's been married to the same woman for twenty-some years."

She set her glass down. "He *is* married?"

Sam nodded. "Sure is. Two kids, sons."

"He wears no wedding ring."

"Dentists and doctors don't usually wear wedding rings. They work around too many implements that might get caught on the ring."

"He doesn't act like a married man."

"He married his high school sweetheart," said Sam. "She was in my class. They got married right out of high school. Like I said, they have two sons. He went to college and she worked to put him through dental school."

"His wife did? I had a feeling his family was wealthy." Ophelia turned her wineglass around and around. "I thought our Dr. Mann had money."

"You don't know our Dr. Mann." Sam drained his glass and set it down. "His adoptive parents disowned him because of some college scandal. Boys will be boys. Even married boys. Ready for another? You need to catch up here."

In the house overlooking Vineyard Haven harbor, Jane told Abigail, Davina's nanny, about Mrs. Wilmington's collapse and death.

Outside, the little girl stood up in her sandbox and lifted her arms toward the house.

"About time for her nap." Abigail gathered up the skirt of her muumuu and stood. "I'll bring her in. Maybe a snack first. You'll want a few minutes with her, Missy."

"Thank you. I do." Jane stood and started to collect the tea things. She cocked her head. "I hear someone at the door."

"You get your baby, I'll see who's there," said Abigail.

Jane set down the tray, slid open the back door that led onto the beach, and picked up her sandy daughter. The baby stuck a thumb into her mouth and laid her head with its red-gold hair on her mother's shoulder as her mother went back into the house.

"It's all sandy, Davy," said Jane, tugging the thumb out of Davina's mouth. The baby started to wail. "You can have it back as soon as I wipe off the sand you haven't eaten." She was intent upon brushing off the small thumb and didn't notice the caller at first. Thumb released, Davina popped it back into her mouth and nestled her head against her mother again.

Jane looked up with a start. "What are you doing here?"

"I had to make sure you're all right."

"Did you, now." Jane stroked her daughter's back. "Why the sudden concern?"

"It's been a rough day." He held out a hand. Jane backed away. "Please, Jane, don't be like that."

"I didn't ask for your help, Horace."

"You called out my name."

"That was inadvertent. A mistake." She snuggled the baby tightly against her pink blouse and a scattering of sand fell onto the floor.

"She's beautiful," said Mann. "A redhead. Don't you think it's about time you let me get to know her?"

"No, Horace. I don't."

"She's mine, too." Mann moved toward Jane, hands reaching for the baby.

Abigail, who'd been standing quietly to one side, arms folded, stepped forward.

Jane, holding the baby tightly, turned away. "You have no claim to my daughter, Horace."

"She's got my hair, my coloring. Her genes are mine."

Abigail said, "Time for her nap, Dr. Mann." She pried Davina gently out of Jane's arms and disappeared.

"Be reasonable, Jane. I have my rights."

"No, you don't." Jane folded her empty arms over her chest. Another dusting of sand dropped onto the floor. In a distant room she heard the crooning of a lullaby. "Get out, Horace."

"If you hate me so much, why did you take the job?"

"That's why," said Jane, with a smile.

Mann laughed. "Working with a dentist you can't abide and who can't abide you, either. Assisting with patients like Mrs. Wilmington who demean you. Working with creeps like Arthur who lust after you? You'll do that to get even with me?"

Jane turned her back on him and faced the window overlooking the sandbox.

"Please, Jane. All I want is to see my daughter occasionally. Be a part of her life."

Jane swung around, her ivory face no longer pale. "Be a part of

44

her life? You?" Her voice rose. "How can you possibly be so arrogant, so egocentric, so blatantly stupid?"

"I accept all that."

"You, promising me we'd have a life together, and I believed you. Marriage. A honeymoon on a chartered yacht. And all the time you had, and still have, I believe, a wife and two children. And then I find out your wife put you through dental school. I never suspected you were such a monster. And here I was, wondering why you kept putting off our wedding."

"Jane," said Mann, holding up his hands to stop her flow of fury. "Please, calm down."

"Calm down!" sputtered Jane. "You, who went ballistic when I told you I was pregnant? Who insisted I get an abortion? Arranged for the abortion despite my protests? Paid in advance, tried to shanghai me to the doctor's? How can you possibly lay claim to my daughter. Or to me? I vowed to make life miserable for you, and, by God, I will." She strode past him, flinging over her shoulder, "Your poor wife. Does she know what you are?" She went to the door and slid it open with a flourish. "Get out. Don't you ever show up again at my daughter's and my house."

"Jane—"

"In thirty seconds I'm calling the police. One . . ."

Mann backed out of the door, and Jane slammed it shut so hard it bounced in its track.

"Baby's asleep," said Abigail, coming back into the living room. "Nice chorus you and the doctor were singing."

"Oh, Abigail!" Jane threw her arms around her nanny and burst into tears.

"There, there," said Abigail, patting her on the back, "There, there. Sit down, Missy."

She led Jane to the couch and gently pushed her onto it. "A cup of hot chocolate with rum. That'll fix you up good. You need something in your belly. Never you mind about that Dr. Mann."

Jane looked up, her eyes blurred with tears. "I despise that man. I loathe the ground he walks on."

"You listen to me," Abigail said. "I know what's best. Known you since before you was Davina's age. You keep up your strength. We'll set things right, you and me. I'm calling Mrs. Mann right now and inviting her to tea to meet her husband's daughter."

Jane brought her hands up to her face. "Oh, my God, Abigail! No! Don't do it."

"Wait and see, Missy. Things will turn out all right."

CHAPTER 8

Mann drove from Jane's to Morrice the florist and picked out a bouquet of yellow roses. A dozen of them.

"Yellow roses mean a broken heart," said the florist, an attractive woman who looked like Jane, but with dark hair instead of platinum. "I hope that's not the case."

"No, she just loves the color yellow." He didn't believe in that language of flowers nonsense. He didn't think Jane did, either. He wrote out a check and the florist assured him they'd be delivered that very afternoon.

"Have a pleasant evening," she said with a knowing smile.

"Mrs. Mann?" Abigail asked the voice that answered the phone.

"Yes. May I ask who's calling?"

"My name is Abigail Baker. You don't know me, but I work for a lady employed at your husband's clinic."

"Oh, no!" A voice of alarm. "What's happened?"

Her reaction set Abigail back for a moment.

"I didn't mean to alarm you, Mrs. Mann. I'm the nanny for the lady's baby and she wanted me to invite you to tea so she could meet you."

A long silence and Abigail thought at first that she had been disconnected. "Mrs. Mann?"

"Yes, yes, I'm still here." Another pause. "It's just that . . . I don't know. Something apparently happened at the clinic today. I've gotten several calls telling me an ambulance was there and asking me why, and I don't know the answer. I haven't seen my husband all day."

"Yes, ma'am. That must be unsettling." Abigail decided it was not up to her to explain about Mrs. Wilmington's death and about her husband's visit to her lady. "I wish I could tell you, ma'am. My lady is Dr. McBride's new assistant, Jane Douglas." Abigail wondered if Mrs. Mann would recognize the name.

Another pause.

"Dr. McBride," Mrs. Mann repeated. "Isn't she the new dentist?"

"Yes, ma'am, she hasn't been there a year yet."

"And her assistant. She must be fairly new, too. What did you say her name is?"

"Jane Douglas, ma'am."

"I don't know much about my husband's work or the people who work for him. He prefers to keep work and home separate." Another pause. "You have a lovely voice, Abigail. Are you from Jamaica?"

"Thank you. Yes, ma'am."

"And you say you're Jane Douglas's nanny?"

"I'm now her baby's nanny, but when Ms. Douglas was a baby I was her nanny, too."

"Wonderful. What did Ms. Douglas want of me again?"

"She'd like to invite you to tea, ma'am. She wanted to meet you, but it's not easy for her to leave the baby. Except to go to work."

"My children are old enough to be left alone now, so I would be available to accept her invitation. I'm free almost any day." She paused. "It's time I got to know some of the people my husband works with."

"Would Thursday be convenient, ma'am? At four thirty?"

"I think so. Let me check my calendar."

Abigail waited.

Mrs. Mann returned to the phone. "Thursday at four thirty would be lovely. Will others be there?"

"No, ma'am. Just Ms. Douglas and you."

"You'll have to tell me where you live."

Abigail gave her directions and told her where she could park near the house.

"That's right on the harbor, isn't it?"

"Yes, ma'am."

"I look forward to meeting Ms. Douglas and the baby. How old is he?"

"She's a girl, ma'am, almost two years old. Her name is Davina and she's a pretty little thing. Very bright."

"You must be proud of her."

"Yes, ma'am, I am."

"I'm sure you're a good influence on Davina."

"I hope so, ma'am. Thank you."

"What can I bring?"

Even though she'd been with Jane's family for at least twenty-five years and had spent much of that time on Martha's Vineyard, Abigail had never become accustomed to the Vineyard tradition of potluck everything. Invite someone to dinner and they say, "What can I bring?" and you tell them, "Either salad or dessert." Or main course. Or mashed potatoes. Should she suggest something Mrs. Mann might bring? Perhaps something for Davina.

So she said, "Davina loves those little boxes of animal crackers."

Mrs. Mann laughed. "That's what I'll bring. Thank you so much."

"We'll see you on Thursday, then, Mrs. Mann."

Abigail had just headed from the kitchen phone to the downstairs bedroom to tell Jane Mrs. Mann had accepted the invitation for tea when there was a knock on the door. She answered and accepted the florist's bouquet in a tall glass vase.

"She's not going to like this one bit, Dr. Mann," Abigail murmured to the flowers. "You don't know my little girl." She cradled an opening bud in her hand. "Pretty, though."

"Who was that, Abigail?" Jane appeared from the bedroom. She'd changed into her black watch flannel bathrobe and was brushing her hair.

Abigail offered her the vase of flowers without a word.

Jane plucked out the card, read it, tossed her hairbrush aside, and tore the card into pieces. She threw the pieces onto the floor and stamped on them. She lifted the roses out of the vase and flung them into the wastepaper basket. "The nerve of him. Yellow roses? Is he that stupid?"

Abigail picked the roses out of the trash. "Not the flowers' fault." She straightened a bent stem. "Mind if I keep them?"

Jane turned and the hem of her robe made an angry swish around her. "Take them away. I don't want to see them." She swiveled back again. "You know what yellow roses mean? Do you?"

Abigail shook her head. "Don't believe in that stuff."

"Well, he couldn't have sent a plainer message. Yellow roses for infidelity. Yellow roses for betrayal. How about that?"

Abigail buried her nose in the flowers. "They'll surely look pretty on my dresser."

She would wait until later to tell Jane about Mrs. Mann and their engagement for tea.

Arthur lived on Snake Hollow Road, where he'd built a cabin on a small fenced lot. Two rooms, one a bedroom, the other a combination kitchen and living room with a toilet and shower off to one side.

As he pulled up to his place, a large dog greeted him with a basso profundo bark, paws up on the chain-link fence, tongue out. He was a huge dog of an indeterminate mix, maybe shepherd, husky, boxer, collie, Lab.

Arthur opened the gate, bent down, and ruffled his fur.

"Hey, Dog. Home early."

He went into the house and got a leash, which he didn't fasten to Dog's collar, and the two went for a long walk on a path that ran behind his place. He tossed sticks that Dog fetched until Arthur tired of it and sat on a fallen log beside the path. Dog chased squirrels and searched for game until he, too, tired of it and lay down next to Arthur.

"What do you think, Dog. Gave Miz Douglas a ride home. How about that?"

Dog thumped his tail.

"First time she noticed I was alive, Dog. Glad enough for me to give her a ride home." He bent down and picked up a small stick. Dog's ears perked up and he lifted his head. Arthur broke the stick in half, then in half again, and dropped the pieces.

Dog laid his head back down on his paws.

"Pretty rough on a lady like her watching someone die in front of her eyes."

Twigs snapped and last fall's dead oak leaves crackled on the path. Arthur and Dog both looked in the direction of approaching footsteps.

An older man, tweed hat, plaid shirt, walking with a cane. "Howdy, Arthur. Hey, Dog. How're you two doing?" He stopped and leaned on his cane. "Off from work this early?"

"What d'ya say, Mr. Tabor. Too nice a day to be at work," said Arthur, not wanting to go into details of his morning.

"You can say that again." John Tabor reached into his pocket and brought out a treat. "Always prepared to run into you and Dog. Okay with you if I give him this?"

"Sure. Be his friend for life."

John Tabor held out the biscuit to Dog, who sat up and wolfed it down. Then he stood up as straight as he could, stretched, and took a deep breath. "Roses, honeysuckle, and the sea." He let out his breath. "Best perfume in the world. Taking my noon constitutional. Not enough days in the world like this."

"Right," said Arthur.

"Be seeing you two." John lifted his hat and shuffled off down the path.

Dog lay down again.

The footsteps died away. Arthur picked up another dead twig and snapped it in half. Aside from his ears perking up again, Dog didn't move. He snapped the twig pieces in half again and tossed them aside, got to his feet. "I'll keep an eye on her, Dog. Make sure she's safe."

CHAPTER 9

On the way home in the police car Roosevelt was thinking about the line between life and death. Would Vivian still be alive if he hadn't stopped for his bottle of Scotch? If only he'd spent less time at the liquor store. If only . . .

"Mr. Mark." The police officer driving interrupted Roosevelt's thoughts. He looked him straight in the eye in the rearview mirror. "I know what you're thinking. Don't go there." He looked back at the road. "There was nothing you could have done differently. You did your best."

Once home, Roosevelt stripped off his wet clothes and took a long hot shower. After he toweled himself dry, he found his spare glasses and dressed in clean slacks and shirt. He fixed himself a Scotch on the rocks from PJ's bottle of Dewar's, since his own bottle lay in shards by the harbor, and settled into his recliner.

He needed desperately to tell his partner about his horrendous morning. Two deaths. But PJ would be seeing patients for the rest of the day and Roosevelt didn't want to disturb him.

Indelibly printed on Roosevelt's brain was the sight of Vivian's flowered skirt billowing up out of the murky water, a gigantic jellyfish, an inflated plastic bag floating amid the harbor's rubbish. Such an undignified end.

He sipped the Dewar's, then held the stubby glass up to the

window. The Scotch intermingling with ice ranged from pale gold to robust amber. He swirled the glass to watch the shifting shades of color, then set it down on a napkin on the end table.

Why had she killed herself?

Was it possibly an accident? Had she gotten out of the car for a breath of fresh air, wandered over to the harbor to view the boats, had a dizzy spell, and fell?

He sipped his Scotch. What had gone through her mind?

Of course she was upset about Mrs. Wilmington's death. The entire staff was. Think how Mann must feel. Dr. McBride, whose chair Mrs. Wilmington was in. Jane Douglas, McBride's assistant. If anyone on the clinic's staff could be called fragile, it was Jane. Think what it must be like now for her.

He felt a momentary anger at Vivian for the inconvenience of it all. His lost glasses, his wet clothes, his useless attempt at life-saving, his Glenlivet. What had she been trying to prove?

And what had she meant by her last remark? Something like if only she hadn't answered the phone. Strange.

He stood up. Past lunchtime. He usually ate promptly at noon, sometimes with Sam Minnowfish, driving the short distance from the clinic to the restaurant at the airport.

He had no idea what was in the fridge. That was PJ's bailiwick. He picked up his glass and sipped the last drops. Ice bumped against his mustache and he blotted his mouth with the napkin.

Someone would have to notify her next of kin. He supposed the police would take care of that. He had no idea who her next of kin might be, or whether they even existed, for that matter.

He thought about pouring another drink and decided he'd really better eat something.

The sound of Mrs. Wilmington's screams echoed in his brain and would, he knew, for a long time. The screams were like a tune he couldn't stop hearing. The screams and the sight of her being hustled out on the stretcher. Was that a reason for Vivian to kill herself? Was she that sensitive? He didn't think so.

He rattled the ice cubes in his empty glass and glanced out the window at the view that always soothed him. His and PJ's house was situated on a cove of Sengekontacket Pond with a view that encompassed vast beauty. Above the pond the wide sweep of sky produced ever-changing weather. Hawks, gulls, terns soared and dipped. Along the barrier bar that separated the pond from Nantucket Sound he could see cars, tiny in the distance, heading toward Oak Bluffs or Edgartown. On a clear day like today he could see the thin band of the mainland.

What had possessed her to give up this Island's beauty?

He went into the small kitchen, opened the refrigerator, and stared at the food within. What did he want? Nothing. He shut the door, poured himself another glass of Dewar's, and sat back in his recliner, turning to face the view.

That was where PJ found him when he came home hours later, asleep in the chair, mouth open, eyes closed, one arm flung across his chest, the other almost touching the floor, and the bottle of Dewar's on the table next to a full glass.

PJ, tall, blond, blue-eyed, leaned over Roosevelt. "I gather you had a rough day," he said softly. When Roosevelt didn't stir, PJ covered him with a light blanket and went quietly into the kitchen. Roosevelt would wake up to the smell of dinner. In the meantime, let him sleep.

Elizabeth came home from the harbor early that afternoon, clearly upset. "I was listening to the news, Gram. Mrs. Wilmington died."

Victoria had been thumbing through seed catalogs. She pushed her chair away from the cookroom table. "Have they determined the cause of death?"

"Not yet. By the way, how's your tooth?"

"It only bothers me when I eat," said Victoria. "Her poor grandchildren."

"Her soon-to-be rich grandchildren," said Elizabeth. Then, seeing her grandmother's expression, she changed the subject. "Isn't it late in the season to be going through seed catalogs?"

"I lose myself in them," said Victoria. "It was such a dreadful morning. I was hoping to forget Mildred."

Elizabeth sat across from her grandmother and picked up the catalog Victoria had been studying. "You've marked bloodroot?"

"I've been meaning to grow it for some time," Victoria explained. "I found a seed company that offers plants. They won't ship it until fall."

"Bloodroot sounds like the Wilmington kids and their grandmother . . . or a dental procedure."

"Actually, it is used in dentistry," said Victoria. "To reduce plaque buildup."

Elizabeth set the catalog down on the table. "When I was in college we went on a botany field trip to the Smoky Mountains. The bloodroot was in bloom all over the mountainside. We pulled up a plant to see its roots and the sap did look like blood."

Victoria pushed aside the stack of catalogs. "Everything I do today recalls Mildred Wilmington. Dentists, bloodroot." She glanced at the stack of seed catalogs on the table. "I can't throw them out. I always imagine my gardens will look like the ones pictured, but they never do."

Elizabeth indicated the lush flower garden pictured on one of the catalogs. "I prefer yours to those."

Victoria pushed her chair back and stood. "I think I should make a condolence call on the Wilmington grandchildren."

"Right now?" asked Elizabeth.

"Tomorrow would be better."

Elizabeth checked her watch. "I'll see if there's anything else on the news about Mrs. Wilmington." The radio they seldom listened to was on the lower shelf of the bookcase. Elizabeth switched it on.

But the only news was of a woman drowned in the Oak Bluffs harbor. The victim's name was being withheld pending notification of next of kin.

"How sad." Victoria headed to the kitchen. "I wonder if she's someone we know?"

The fragrance of biscuits baking and the sounds of dinner cooking awakened Roosevelt. He hadn't remembered putting the fleece blanket over himself. The view of sky and sea was velvet black, punctuated by stars and the long-thrown headlights of cars moving along the barrier bar. It took him several moments to recall what had happened that morning.

He tossed off the blanket and got to his feet.

PJ looked up from the stove and greeted him. "Morning, sleepyhead." He opened the oven door, brought out a pan of biscuits, and set them on top of the stove. "It looks like you had quite a day. Went for a swim, judging by the heap of wet clothes in the bathroom. And a pre–five o'clock drink? A *nap!*"

Roosevelt sat down at the table. "You won't believe it," and he told PJ about Mrs. Wilmington's seizure and the drowning of the receptionist. "And to top it all off, I broke my bottle of Glenlivet."

"A thoroughly disagreeable day," PJ said. "I was listening to the radio on my way home. Your Mrs. Wilmington died."

"We heard." Roosevelt set his elbows on the table, lowered his head onto his hands. "The way she sounded. She sounded like death."

PJ patted his partner's back. "A good meal will help."

Roosevelt shook his head. "I don't think I can eat a thing."

PJ set a platter of chicken thighs baked over a bed of rice on the table along with a bowl of broccoli, a salad, biscuits.

Roosevelt looked up at him and smiled. "Well, maybe a bite or two." He folded his hands on the table and said grace.

"You think it was accidental?" asked PJ, opening his napkin.

"Mrs. Wilmington? Or Vivian?" Roosevelt looked down at his plate. "If I hadn't lingered so long in the liquor store—"

"Don't go there," PJ warned.

"That's what the police officer told me."

"He was right."

"She was upset." Roosevelt smoothed his napkin on his lap. "I should have taken her directly home."

PJ pointed the tines of the fork at him. "Stop that."

Roosevelt nodded.

"Eat up," said PJ. "I put half the herbs in the garden in. Not sure I can duplicate it. Did you have any lunch?"

"I didn't feel like it." Roosevelt chewed. "Thyme? Lemon?"

PJ nodded. "And salt and pepper. But back to your drowning victim. Could someone have given her a push?"

Roosevelt set his fork down and patted his chest. Swallowed a mouthful of water. "On purpose? Why? She was an inoffensive woman. Quiet." He cleared his throat.

"The quiet ones are sometimes the deepest ones. Still waters, you know." PJ leaned his elbows on the table. "Two people from the same office, same day, dead under less than normal circumstances? I don't believe it."

Roosevelt cleared his throat a few more times. "Mrs. Wilmington apparently had heart problems."

"From your description her reaction doesn't sound like myocardial infarction," said PJ, jabbing his fork into the broccoli. "Someone poisoned her. The number one motive is money. Did she have any?"

"She lives, lived, in Chilmark, the big house overlooking the Atlantic. Yeah, she had money."

"Uh-huh." PJ nodded. "Any children?"

"Grandkids," said Roosevelt.

"Grandkids are more likely to be desperate for money than their parents. And they figure Granny has lived long enough."

Roosevelt shook his head. "You can't think Mrs. Wilmington's death is connected with Vivian's."

PJ set his fork down. "Damn right that's what I think. One of those grandkids poisoned her and one of those grandkids gave your receptionist a push, for some reason. Won't be the first time."

"What reason would they have for killing Vivian?"

"She knew something," said PJ.

Roosevelt sipped his wine. "People are frightened of dentists. Couple that with a weak heart. Mrs. Wilmington died a natural death."

"How long were you in the liquor store?"

"About half an hour."

"Plenty of time. Vivian got out of the car and went to the harborside for a breath of air. Someone was following you. That someone saw an opportunity and gave her a shove."

"I can see her getting out of the car," agreed Roosevelt. "But I can't see someone pushing her. Too much of a coincidence." Roosevelt scraped up the remaining grains of rice. "Maybe it was an accident. The wind was splashing water up on the bulkhead. She could have slipped and fallen."

PJ pushed away from the table. "Dessert, anyone?"

CHAPTER 10

It was the morning after the incident at the dental clinic and even though it was early June the day was warm enough to put the top down again on the convertible, a top held together, like most Vineyard cars, with duct tape. Elizabeth had taken the morning off and this was the day they planned to pay their respects to Mildred Wilmington's four grandchildren.

Elizabeth dressed in somber black slacks and a black turtleneck topped by a white blazer that helped to break the solemnity. Victoria had on the green plaid suit she usually wore to church.

"You'd better bring a heavy sweater," Victoria cautioned her. "Chilmark weather can be chillier than West Tisbury's."

"Right," said Elizabeth.

According to Victoria's definition of weather it was a typical Vineyard day. The sky was an intense, almost fluorescent blue. The air was scented with wild roses and honeysuckle and the light breeze carried the smell of the salt sea. Ira Bodman was haying the Doane's field across the lane from Victoria's pasture and the sound of his mower waxed and waned as he drove up and down the rows.

"The morning is too lovely for such a sad errand." said Victoria. "A dripping sea fog would be more suitable."

"They're probably rejoicing. Those Wilmington kids are pit vipers," said Elizabeth.

"What is it you have against those children?" Victoria had put on a straw hat she'd taken from a peg in the entry. She'd tied a scarf around it to keep it from blowing off and was holding both ends of the scarf. "They seemed perfectly fine to me when we went to the reception. It doesn't seem as though it was only three days ago that we were with Mildred."

"Gram, those kids are all self-centered and disagreeable. You don't know them the way I do."

"Their grandmother took them in after their parents died in that tragic car crash. They must have been grateful to her."

"Well they weren't grateful at all. Mrs. Wilmington was a controlling, resentful woman who didn't understand kids. Susan was her pet, so the others picked on her. Heather was a handful as a teenager, and Mrs. Wilmington was nasty to her." Elizabeth tightened her hands on the steering wheel. "I hated going to their house. They were always bickering. The very air was hostile."

"We needn't stay long," said Victoria.

They drove on, both silent.

After passing Alley's they continued on South Road into Chilmark. The gently rolling fields of West Tisbury gave way to low hills clothed with oak and beech. The hills, a jumble of rocks and boulders covered by a layer of soil, were a reminder of the glacier that had formed the Island twenty thousand years ago. Sheep farmers had cleared stones from their fields to form walls to fence in their animals and mark the boundaries of their land.

Victoria broke the silence. "I love seeing the different styles of stone walls," she said. "You can tell that each farmer had his own distinctive way of putting one stone on top of another." She pointed to one of the stone walls they were passing. "Some are almost too tidy. You can just imagine a farmer thinking of a creative way to deal with the stones he'd cleared out of his field."

"Now it's an art form," said Elizabeth. "Isn't there a Vineyard poet who builds lace stone walls?"

Victoria nodded. "He's in one of my poetry groups. He told me the openings let the breeze blow through."

Shortly after they passed the Chilmark cemetery the view of the Atlantic opened up across the fields of the Allen Sheep Farm, a brilliant, breathtaking blue touched with bright sparkles of sunlight. Elizabeth slowed. White, brown, and black sheep grazed on the June-green grass.

Victoria took a deep breath to absorb as much of the beauty as she could hold.

"Only a half mile farther," said Elizabeth.

"Let's stop at Chilmark Chocolates and buy a box of candy to take with us," said Victoria.

At the small shop, they luxuriated in the fragrance of chocolate and spices. They picked out a selection of chocolates for their gift box, ones Victoria liked herself.

The dirt road leading to Mildred Wilmington's was only a short distance from the chocolate store.

Victoria opened the white cardboard box to examine their purchase. "Why don't we each have a small piece. I don't think two pieces will be missed."

The road to the Wilmington house meandered between low banks of huckleberry brush and ended a half mile later at an open field. The house, a large, rambling gray-shingled building, was situated on about fifty acres of land with a view of the ocean from a wide front porch. Elizabeth parked along with several other cars on the cropped grass, and they walked around to the front of the house and up the steps onto the porch. The door was open. To their right the front parlor hummed with quiet talk.

Scott, the eldest of the four grandchildren, greeted them. His hair and beard were neatly trimmed. "Mrs. Trumbull. Elizabeth."

"Our condolences," said Victoria. "I'm so sorry."

"Thanks, Mrs. Trumbull."

"Where are your sisters and brother?"

"They have a sort of receiving line in there. Lots of good food." He nodded toward the dining room. "Excuse me, more guests arriving."

They made their way through the crowded parlor where they'd had tea a few days ago, solemnly nodding to friends and neighbors.

Victoria greeted a stout man in his eighties with a mane of white hair and a tidy goatee. "Good morning, Fred."

"Victoria. Always good to see you. You, too, Elizabeth." Fred bit into a watercress sandwich, his pinkie extended delicately. He pressed a napkin to his lips. "I hear you were at the clinic when it happened, Victoria."

"I'm afraid so. Tragic."

"You've got police connections, Victoria. Any idea what killed her?"

"They won't know for several days," said Victoria. "The autopsy will be performed off Island."

They chatted about the neighborly turnout and then back to Mrs. Wilmington's untimely death.

Elizabeth stood silently next to her grandmother.

"Rumor has it her death was no accident. Have you heard anything?" He took another nibble.

"I wouldn't know," said Victoria. "I try not to listen to rumors." She smiled to take the sting out of the rebuke.

"Somebody stands to benefit from her death, not mentioning names, of course." He finished the rest of his sandwich and wiped his hand on the napkin he'd been holding.

Victoria said, "Elizabeth, shall we say hello to the other children?"

Fred crumpled up the napkin. "I'll wager those children are already thinking about filing a malpractice suit."

"Excuse me, Fred." Victoria turned away. "Elizabeth, I'd like to try some of those delicious-looking sandwiches."

"Ummm," said Elizabeth.

"Big money in malpractice suits," Fred said to their departing backs.

Victoria kept walking.

"What did I tell you?" said Elizabeth.

They made their way through the cluster of neighbors to the dining room, where two tall blondes and a red-haired man formed a reception line.

The redhead greeted them. "Thanks for coming, you two."

Victoria offered him her hand. "I'm so sorry, Wesley."

Wesley, at twenty-five, was the youngest of the four Wilmington grandchildren. He indicated the tall, hefty blond woman next to him. "You know Heather, of course."

"Of course."

Heather embraced her in a patchouli-scented hug, then held her off to gaze at her. "You're so sweet to come." With a napkin she'd kept from the senior-center luncheon, Victoria dabbed discreetly at her great nose to rid it of the cloying scent from the hug. She and Elizabeth moved on to Susan, the final Wilmington grandchild.

"How fortunate that you and your siblings were all here before your grandmother died," said Victoria.

"Grandmother ordered them to come for a visit and threatened to cut them off without a dime if they didn't." Susan smiled as though she was only kidding. "I visited Scott in New York the winter before last, but I haven't seen Heather or Wes since they moved out more than ten years ago." She indicated the dining room table. "People brought lots of good food. Help yourself."

Victoria looked over at the table, heaped with enough food to spoil her appetite for dinner.

"The neighbors have been most kind," said Susan.

"It's a relief to get that over with," said Elizabeth when they were on the way home. "You know, Gram, we forgot to give them the box of chocolates."

"So we did," said Victoria, reaching for the white pasteboard box.

CHAPTER 11

The day after their condolence call, Victoria sat at the kitchen table looking pensive, her hand on her jaw. It had been two days after the incident at the dental clinic.

"That tooth still, Gram?"

Victoria nodded. "I suppose I've got to do something." She got up, went to the phone, and dialed the clinic's number.

After a long pause she hung up the phone without speaking.

"Did you get the answering machine?" asked Elizabeth.

"Yes." Victoria turned and looked out the window at the distant village. The morning was so clear, she could almost read the time on the town clock in the church steeple.

"You could have left a message."

Victoria shook her head.

"What's the matter, Gram?"

"The office is closed for the morning to allow the staff to observe Vivian's death."

"Vivian? The receptionist?" Elizabeth sat suddenly. "Dead? What happened?"

That same morning, Mrs. Wilmington's grandchildren were gathered around the dining room table, eating condolence leftovers for breakfast.

Susan and Heather were wearing their short cutoffs again with

T-shirts. Heather's T-shirt was black with white print that read DON'T JUDGE A MOVIE BY ITS BOOK. Susan's was green and read BUY LOCAL.

"We need to talk about funeral arrangements," said Susan.

"We can't make any arrangements until they release her body," said Scott. As usual his slacks were neatly pressed and were topped by a black knit collared shirt. "No telling how long that will be."

"We have a family plot here in Chilmark, don't we?" asked Wesley.

"Yeah," answered Heather. She reached for a slice of ham.

"I asked you a simple question," said Wesley. "Why that tone of voice?"

"You tell him, Scott." Heather bit into the ham angrily. "Ouch!" She spit the unchewed mouthful onto her plate.

"What's the matter?" asked Susan, leaning toward her sister, who was holding a napkin against her cheek.

"A filling. Lost it last night. The fudge had nuts in it."

"I bet you can get an appointment right away with grandmother's dentist," said Wesley, grinning.

Heather moved the napkin long enough to say, "Ha, ha."

"My dentist, too," said Susan.

"*Our* dentist, before we left for greener pastures," said Scott.

"Well, I don't want to go to *our* dentist," said Heather.

"There's a clinic in Falmouth that's supposed to be pretty good," said Susan. "I'll get the number." She left the table.

"Back to the subject of burials," said Wesley. "What were you going to say, Scott?"

"We have a family plot here in Chilmark." Scott got up from the table and poured himself another cup of coffee.

"Well. Okay. That's all I wanted to know," said Wesley. "What's the big deal? I assume that's where Grandmother will be buried along with Mom and Dad."

Silence around the table. Scott returned to his seat with his coffee cup, stirred cream and sugar into it, and took a sip. Heather continued to hold the napkin against her cheek. Susan returned with an address book and sat down.

"What's the matter with you guys?" asked Wesley.

Heather rolled her eyes at Scott.

He sighed. "Our mother's buried here in Chilmark. Our father's buried near the accident site in Rahway, New Jersey."

Wesley took a moment before he spoke. "Why?"

Scott smoothed his beard. "Who knows? Mildred, our dear grandmother, blamed him for the accident."

"How come no one ever told me?" asked Wesley.

"You were too young and then everyone forgot that you hadn't been told."

"Well, hell." Wesley stood up, walked to the front door, opened it, and went out onto the porch.

The remaining three avoided one another's eyes.

Susan opened the address book. "Want me to call, Heather?"

"Please."

Scott continued to thumb through the *Island Enquirer*.

A few minutes later Susan hung up the phone. "You've got an appointment tomorrow, two o'clock at the Falmouth clinic."

"Can someone give me a ride to the ferry?" asked Heather.

Scott looked up from the newspaper. "Sure. Two o'clock appointment, you'll need to catch the noon boat."

Wesley returned from the porch and took his seat again. "Did Grandmother's obit make the paper?"

"Here. You look." Scott thrust the paper toward his brother. "If you know what boat you'll be coming back on, Heather, I'll pick you up."

"I'll call from the dentist's office."

Wesley flipped through the newspaper pages.

"There's poor cell reception here," said Susan.

Heather went into the parlor and returned with a ferry schedule. "I'll try to be on the five o'clock boat to Oak Bluffs. I don't think I can make the three forty-five."

"I'll pick you up," said Scott. "No need to call."

Wesley set the paper down. "A notice that she died, full obituary to follow. Guess we're expected to write that."

"You write it, Sue," said Heather. "You lived with her longer than we did."

Wesley got up again. The refrigerator door slammed and he returned with four glasses and a six-pack of beer.

"Isn't this kind of early to be drinking?" said Susan.

"Never too early," replied Wesley.

"I want something stronger," said Scott. "Did Mildred keep any gin? Or vodka? Scotch?"

Susan shook her head. "You know she didn't drink."

"As I recall, she kept a bottle or two for guests."

"Sorry, Scott."

"Has anybody heard when they're going to release the autopsy findings?" asked Wesley. "My creditors are getting anxious."

Scott grinned. "Worried about shots to the knees, bro?"

"They'll determine it was heart failure," said Heather.

"Everybody dies of heart failure," said Wesley. "I'm pouring beer for me. Anyone else?"

"Sure, why not," said Heather.

Wesley held up an empty glass. "Susan?"

"I'll pass."

Scott stood and stretched. "You know, people, we need to talk seriously."

"What do you have in mind?" Susan asked.

"The disposition of Mildred's estate, of course."

"Can't that wait?" said Susan. "She's not in her grave yet."

"We have decisions to make. Funeral arrangements, for one. We need to decide how to deal with her property, for another."

"You'll notify the funeral parlor, won't you, Scott?" asked Heather. "I mean, once her body is released."

"Right," said Scott.

"Does anyone know how long it's going to be before we can leave? I mean, autopsy, funeral, that kind of stuff," said Heather. "I have to get back to work."

Susan dropped the address book into a kitchen drawer and returned. "I don't see what the hurry is."

"The hurry is, we need to dispose of the property and divvy up the proceeds," said Heather. "I, for one, am dead broke."

"Grandmother didn't want the property sold," said Susan. "She was planning to put a conservation restriction on it so it could never be developed."

"Well, she didn't, did she," said Heather.

"Our father buried three hundred miles from our mother," muttered Wesley.

"Live with it, Wes," said Scott.

Heather moved the napkin away from her jaw, refolded it, and pressed it back on her jaw. "What is the house worth, does anyone know?"

Wesley laughed. "Scott knows to a penny what it's worth."

"We're talking both house and property." Scott took his phone from his shirt pocket and thumbed the small screen. "The house is valued at three million, the property, fifty acres at two hundred thousand an acre is worth another ten million. Divide that up among the four of us, less taxes, of course, and it'll go a long way toward paying our bills." Scott shook his empty beer bottle and Wesley handed him another full one. Scott twisted off the cap. "She was worth a lot, and I mean a lot."

"I knew she had money set aside," said Wesley. "I assumed it wasn't much, the way she was always economizing."

"Economizing!" said Heather. *Miserly* is the word."

"I don't know her net worth, but I'm guessing it's two million or more, plus the property at, what did I say, thirteen million?" Scott tipped his bottle and drank.

"Did she ever discuss it with you, Susan?" asked Heather.

Susan shook her head. "Of course not."

"You lived with her longest," said Heather. "Since we left."

"You know full well she never talked money with us. Never." Susan indicated the sweep of meadow and sea. "We can't sell this. We've got deep roots here."

"Taxes, Sue." Scott rubbed his thumb and third finger together. "Someone's got to pay the taxes, and we can't afford to. When a developer gets his hands on the property, he'll simply tear this imposing edifice down." He gestured at the walls around him.

Heather took a gulp of beer. "Ouch!" She held her hand to her face, dropping the bottle. It rolled, spraying a fountain of beer on the floor. Wesley picked the bottle up.

Her siblings glanced at her.

"Tooth." Heather's eyes were watering. "Sensitive."

Susan went into the kitchen, returned with paper towels, and mopped up the puddle.

"Getting back to reality, Sue," said Wesley. "We three are broke. I don't know about you."

"I've got three jobs, landscaping, house painting, and house cleaning. I get along okay."

"Don't forget, you've been living free off Mildred for the past ten years," said Scott.

"Free? Are you kidding? I wouldn't call it free. You can't begin to know what she was like," snapped Susan.

"We know exactly what Mildred was like. That's why we left," said Scott.

"And I wish you'd stop calling her Mildred. She deserves some respect."

"Not from me," said Scott.

"Or me," said Wesley.

"When will we know about the will?" asked Heather.

Wesley leaned his chair back on two legs and laughed. "You don't think we sound greedy, folks, do you?"

A helicopter droned by in the distance.

CHAPTER 12

Victoria had an afternoon appointment at the dental clinic. She was the only patient.

"Good afternoon, Mrs. Trumbull," said Tiffany, the new receptionist, a high school student Victoria had known since she was a child. "The doctor will be right with you."

Victoria took a seat. "I was sorry to hear about Vivian's death. Was it her heart?"

"Oh, no, Mrs. Trumbull. She, like, drowned!" Tiffany had a high little-girl voice.

"Drowned?"

"Yes, ma'am. They think it was suicide." Tiffany flicked her hair over her shoulder with the back of her hand. Her hair had orange and green streaks in it.

"Really!"

Tiffany nodded. "Mr. Mark was driving her home after, you know, Mrs. Wilmington passed away. He stopped at the liquor store and when he came out she was, like, in the harbor."

Victoria hardly knew what to say. "Her poor family."

"Well, she didn't really have a family," said Tiffany, clearly pleased to communicate news to Victoria Trumbull. "Her parents have, like, passed away. She wasn't married."

The phone rang. Tiffany answered, "Dental clinic, Tiffany speaking, how may I help you?"

Victoria picked up a magazine to distract herself.

Dr. Demetrios entered the reception area and Victoria set down the unread magazine. "Mrs. Trumbull. Nice to see you. We'll take care of that tooth right away and then you won't be bothered by it ever, ever again."

Victoria had never been courageous when it came to dental work. Ophelia Demetrios's words had a ghastly final ring to them. She followed her dentist into the operatory and lowered herself uneasily onto the reclining chair. Dr. Demetrios fastened the bib around her neck, donned gloves, pulled a mask over her nose and mouth, and brought forth a wicked-looking syringe. "Just a little prick, Mrs. Trumbull." Dr. Demetrios's voice was muffled.

Victoria closed her eyes. This seemed like déjà vu.

"Now we'll wait a few minutes. We want it to be nice and numb." Dr. Demetrios's voice was no longer muffled, and Victoria opened her eyes to see that her dentist had hidden the syringe out of sight and had dropped the mask below her chin. She pulled up a stool beside Victoria's place of anxiety.

Victoria said, "I was sorry to hear about Vivian's death."

"All of us, of course, were upset about Mrs. Wilmington, but we didn't realize how much Vivian was affected," said Dr. Demetrios. "Another minute or two, Mrs. Trumbull. We want it to be nice and numb."

"Ummm." Victoria clenched her toes and was immediately sorry as pain shot through her sore toe.

"After Mrs. Wilmington's episode, all our patients canceled their appointments." Dr. Demetrios rolled her large dark eyes in horror. "How are we feeling, Mrs. Trumbull?"

Victoria shook her head. She wanted to be home doing something normal like writing her weekly newspaper column.

"It was especially difficult for Dr. McBride, who was working on Mrs. Wilmington at the time," Dr. Demetrios continued. "I worry about her. Dr. McBride has excellent training, but she can be careless at times." Dr. Demetrios got up from her stool and opened drawers, took out instruments and laid them on a metal tray with an ominous clank.

Victoria cringed.

"Another minute, Mrs. Trumbull." She seated herself on the stool again. "I don't think she understands that her behavior toward Dr. Mann is highly unprofessional."

"I thought he was mawwried," said Victoria, her jaw quite numb now.

Dr. Demetrios laughed, a silvery tinkle. "Do you think that would make a difference to her? Or him? You remember the tiger I told you about?"

"Uhn," said Victoria.

"I told you the zookeepers said if he opened an eye, I should leave immediately." She put her mask back in place. "Well, Mr. Tiger opened *both* eyes. I had my hands in that big jaw of his, all full of teeth, my little pincer looking so tiny in that big jaw, and I pulled"—she demonstrated—"like this—and there you are, Mrs. Trumbull. See?" Dr. Demetrios held up Victoria's wisdom tooth.

"And what happened?" asked Victoria, concerned about the awakened tiger and almost forgetting her own jaw.

Dr. Demetrios packed gauze and cotton around the place where the tooth had been. "Well"—she drew out the word—"I pulled the tooth—a long, long eyetooth." She rolled her eyes. "And Mr. Tiger watched me with both eyes. His tail lashed. I moved back as quickly as I could until I was against the wall. He rolled off the table, looking at me—he had plenty of teeth left."

"And?" asked Victoria.

"He landed on his feet, his tail lashed back and forth, knocking bottles off the shelves in the zoo's clinic, and he paced around the table, still glaring at me, and he opened that big mouth and lifted a huge paw, and just as I thought he was about to tear me to pieces, his keepers led him away."

"Oh, my!" Victoria managed to mumble.

"I think it was a little joke on his keepers' part." Dr. Demetrios again blotted the place where Victoria's tooth had been. "Let Mr. Tiger come soooo close, until I think I am dead, clawed to death by an angry tiger, and then the keepers lead him away as though he's a nice little kitty cat." She deposited the gauze and cotton in the red bag, stripped off her gloves, and dropped them in along with the bloody gauze. She pulled off her mask, gently wiped around Victoria's mouth with a clean tissue, and said, "There we are, Mrs. Trumbull. Don't rinse your mouth for the rest of the day. Soft foods for the next day or two." She detached the paper bib and dropped that in the wastepaper basket. "I'd like to see you on Monday."

They walked together to the reception area. "Tiffany, do you need help in setting up an appointment for Mrs. Trumbull?"

"No, ma'am, thank you." Tiffany glanced up at Victoria. "Will nine thirty be convenient?"

"Fine." Victoria felt woozy and disoriented.

"Do you have someone to drive you home?" asked Dr. Demetrios.

"My granddaughter."

"There's a new issue of *Vogue* to read while you wait," said Tiffany.

But Victoria didn't have to wait. Elizabeth, dressed in her harbor uniform, was standing by the door looking concerned.

"Are you okay, Gram?"

"I'm fine," said Victoria, not feeling fine at all.

Dr. Demetrios greeted Elizabeth. "What a good little patient your grandmother is."

Ordinarily, Victoria would have snapped out a sharp reply.

Before she could, Elizabeth led her gently out of the clinic into the bright June day.

After the clinic door closed behind Victoria, Aileen McBride bustled into Ophelia Demetrios's cubicle. Her dainty freckles had turned an unattractive greenish hue. Her long auburn braid swung across her back. Her green eyes blazed.

"How could you possibly say such things to a patient!"

"My tiger story?" said Ophelia sweetly. "It's all true."

The phone was ringing when Elizabeth and Victoria came in the door and Elizabeth went into the cookroom to answer. She was scheduled to work later that afternoon at the Oak Bluffs harbor, where official boats were arriving in anticipation of the president's visit. She was wearing khaki shorts and a white short-sleeved shirt with a U.S. flag patch on the sleeve.

"I think I'll go upstairs for a few minutes and rest my eyes," said Victoria.

Elizabeth waved a hand in acknowledgment before she answered the phone with a cheerful "Good afternoon!"

"How nice for you," responded the familiar deep voice.

Elizabeth felt suddenly chilled. "Lockwood."

"So, you haven't forgotten me, Elizabeth."

She pulled a chair next to the table and plopped down. She knew she should hang up, but she couldn't. "What do you want?"

"Is that a polite way to address your husband?"

"You're no longer my husband."

"I don't know about you, but I signed on for life," said Lockwood. "Legal papers don't change that fact."

"Why are you calling?"

"I decided to pay my wife and grandmother-in-law a visit."

"You're not welcome here, Lockwood." Elizabeth leaned forward in her chair to ease the tension that had suddenly built up in her stomach.

"I know you, Elizabeth. I suggest you not hang up. I have something important to tell you."

Lockwood's voice brought back unpleasant memories. Elizabeth didn't want to ask, but did. "What's so important?"

"I'll tell you in person." Lockwood laughed.

"I'm not available." Elizabeth felt her throat constrict.

"Right-o. I'll be there in, let's say, an hour."

"What!"

"I'm on the ferry. About to leave Woods Hole."

"You can't . . ."

Lockwood had already disconnected.

She set the phone down, dazed. After her divorce, she'd come here to be with her grandmother for a brief stay. She was still here, months later.

Lockwood, a name once cherished, now frightened her.

One terrifying rainy day, Lockwood appeared, intent on taking her back to what was once their home in Washington. She'd run from him. He stalked her down the maze of sand roads that led to the Great Pond, crying out her name in a high falsetto voice. She'd hidden beneath wet oak leaves, shivering. She could still recall the eerie sound of that voice echoing through the rain-soaked woods, closer, then fading away. "Elizabeth! Elizabeth!"

She shuddered.

She glanced at her watch. An hour. She didn't want to disturb her grandmother, who'd had a rough morning at the hands of Dr. Demetrios.

She called Domingo, her boss the harbormaster, and told him she couldn't make it to work this afternoon. Then she punched in the number for the West Tisbury police station.

"Sergeant Norton speaking,"

"Elizabeth Trumbull, Junior. Is the chief available?"

"She's on the other phone right now, 'Lizbeth. Hold on. I don't think she'll be much longer."

Elizabeth could picture Junior in his pressed uniform with his crisp haircut from Bert's Barber Shop. His desk would be tidy, the pencils all sharpened and lined up just so.

The hold seemed interminable. Elizabeth watched the second hand of her watch snip off chunks of the hour before Lockwood appeared. She sketched drops of blood on the phone message pad.

"Elizabeth. What's up?" Casey answered in a brisk voice.

"Lockwood called."

"Lord!" said Casey. "When?"

"Just now. He says he's on the ferry."

"You took out a restraining order against him, didn't you?"

"You know that won't stop him," said Elizabeth, adding another drop of blood to her sketch.

"The order might not stop him, but I certainly can," muttered Casey. "Is he arriving in Oak Bluffs?"

"That's what he said."

"Where's Victoria?"

"She's lying down."

"Victoria? Lying down?"

"She had some dental work done."

"Oh," said Casey. "I'll get there as soon as I can. We're involved with security for the presidential visit so the station house is stretched thin right now."

"Same thing in the harbor," said Elizabeth.

"If Victoria's up before I get there, tell her the autopsy results on Mrs. Wilmington have come in."

"And?" asked Elizabeth.

"I'll tell her when I get there," said Casey. "Is Lockwood bringing his car over?"

"He didn't say. I didn't ask."

"Be careful, Elizabeth."

"I know, Casey. Believe me, I know."

CHAPTER 13

That same afternoon, Jane, waiting nervously for Mrs. Mann, heard a gentle rap on the door and hastened to answer it. Her first impression of the woman standing there was that she would make a good undercover agent. She was medium height, medium build, with light brown hair worn medium length and slightly waved. Everything about her was unremarkable. She was wearing gray slacks and a pink cardigan over a white blouse and she carried a large leather shoulder bag.

"Mrs. Mann?" She'd had a mental image of a more classy, elegant woman. The reality was quite different.

"Please, I'm Charlotte. You must be Jane Douglas." She put out a hand and Jane shook it.

"And I'm Jane. Thank you so much for coming. I've been wanting to meet you . . . Charlotte." It felt awkward calling Mrs. Mann by her first name. Jane stepped away from the door and her guest followed her into the house. She glanced around at the large living room and the view of the harbor. "What a lovely house."

"It was my grandparents'. I came here every summer as a child."

"Lovely. Just lovely. And it's yours now?"

"Yes. My grandmother willed it to me." Jane led the way down the wide step into the living room.

Charlotte Mann walked over to the floor-to-ceiling window and gazed at the harbor and the stretch of sandy yard leading to it.

Davina was seated in her sandbox, shoveling sand into a plastic bucket with a toy shovel. Mellow afternoon sunlight picked out highlights in her golden curls as she moved her head. Jane's heart swelled every time she caught sight of her baby daughter. How was Mrs. Mann, Charlotte, she corrected herself, going to react when she learned that Davina was the result of her husband's infidelity?

Mrs. Mann turned back with a smile. "That must be Davina. What a beautiful child." She went to the couch and sat where she could watch the little girl at play. "When I asked your nanny what I could bring she told me to bring animal crackers. So I did." She fished in her handbag and brought out a small pasteboard box shaped like a miniature circus wagon with BARNUM'S ANIMALS printed in circus-like letters on the side along with pictures of circus animals. She held the box up by its string handle and passed it over to Jane.

"Davina's favorite treat in the whole wide world. Thank you, Charlotte." Jane seated herself in the armchair set at a right angle to the couch.

A large wooden bowl on the glass-topped coffee table held a collection of whelk shells, most of them broken and showing the glistening peach-colored spiral inside the shell.

Charlotte reached toward the bowl, but before touching the shells she looked up and asked, "May I?"

"Of course. They're just shells that Davina and I picked up beachcombing. As children we always called them conchs."

"I believe that's another name for them. Both are correct." Charlotte picked one of the broken shells out of the bowl and turned it over, studying the intricate whorl. "I've never thought of displaying the broken ones like this. I'm going to copy your idea." She glanced up. "I hope you don't mind. They make a beautiful display."

"Not at all. I'm flattered."

"Abigail and I had a nice chat on the phone. I understand she's from Jamaica and has been with you for twenty-five years."

"Ever since I was born," said Jane.

"She has that lovely Jamaican accent."

"She'll be bringing out our tea things in a few minutes."

"I can't tell you how delighted I was to have you invite me to your house," said Charlotte. "Horace doesn't like to mix work and home. A matter of professionalism, he says. As a result, I know very few of the people who work with him."

"You heard about the death of one of his patients earlier this week?" Jane paused a moment, thinking about Mrs. Wilmington. "I was the technician who was helping the woman's dentist."

"Oh, my dear. How horrible for you. Something you'll never be able to forget, I imagine."

"No. Never." Jane shuddered. "Later the same day, our receptionist drowned."

"What an eerie coincidence." Charlotte ran her fingers along the smooth inside of the broken shell. "I heard about the two deaths on the local news. Not until after friends called to ask why the ambulance was at the clinic." She leaned forward and replaced the shell fragment in the bowl. "Horace keeps too much bottled up. He never said a word about the death. Two deaths." She shook her head. "Sometimes I don't understand that man."

Running through Jane's mind was the thought, how was she going to break the news to Mrs. Mann? Perhaps a glass or two of wine might help. "I know I said tea, Charlotte, but this seems like the kind of afternoon for wine. Would you care for a glass?"

Charlotte smiled, erasing the image of unremarkable with a smile that gave her warmth and a sudden beauty. "Indeed, I would."

"Red or white?"

"Either, but a slight preference for red if you have a bottle already opened."

"Red it is."

From the kitchen came Abigail's voice. "Two glasses of Merlot poured and on the way." She brought in a tray with partially filled glasses, a bottle of Napa Valley Merlot, and an assortment of tea sandwiches on dark pumpernickel, light rye, and thin white bread. She was dressed in one of her customary muumuus, this one with a print of tropical leaves and red, yellow, and blue macaws. She was barefoot.

"Cheese and ham, cream cheese and olive, watercress, tuna salad, and egg salad," said Abigail.

"Oh, my," said Charlotte, glancing up at the tray. "All favorites. You must have known I'd skipped lunch."

"Put some meat on your bones," said Abigail. Before she went back to the kitchen she looked out the wide back window. "Baby's still happy out there."

"I've been watching her play with such pleasure," said Charlotte.

"You have children, I understand." This is not the right time for the announcement, thought Jane.

"Two rambunctious boys, eight and eleven. They grow up fast."

They touched glasses and helped themselves to one sandwich after another. Their conversation ranged from the weather to Island politics and began to edge into the personal.

"I'm so glad you called." Charlotte smiled. "Rather, that Abigail called. "

"I have to apologize for not being the one to call you. I'm not good on the phone," said Jane.

"I can understand that. I feel the same way. Afraid I'll interrupt someone in the midst of dinner or a family fight or as they're rushing to catch the ferry."

Outside, Davina was running a toy truck around the railroad

ties that bordered her sandbox. She tossed the truck down and stood up.

Jane rose from her chair, but Abigail was already out of the kitchen. "I'll bring her in. Wipe the sand off her first, clean her up for company."

"She has such lovely hair. That red gold is an unusual color. Did she get that from your husband?"

This was it. "She did get it from her father," said Jane, "but I'm not married."

"Oh," said Charlotte. "I didn't mean to be insensitive."

Abigail carried Davina in. The little girl was clapping her hands together, and as she did, sand sprinkled onto the floor. "I'll give her a quick wash so she's presentable," said Abigail, heading past them and into the bathroom.

Charlotte took a sip of her wine and set the glass down. "A lot of women these days are opting to have their children without getting married. Sometimes I wish it had been that way years ago."

"Charlotte," said Jane, sitting forward in her chair. She could feel sweat trickling down her back. "I invited you because I wanted you to meet Davina."

"I'm so glad. She's lovely, Jane."

"I'm afraid I have something to tell you that's not easy for me and is going to be difficult for you."

Charlotte gazed steadily at Jane. "I have a feeling I know what you're about to tell me."

Jane swallowed. She looked down at her hands.

"You're about to tell me who fathered Davina, aren't you?"

"Yes."

"And you're afraid the news will destroy a fine friendship that has just budded."

"Yes."

"My husband, the louse, is the father, right?

"Yes."

"Well, fathering your baby is the only good thing that bastard has done lately." She turned to Jane. "You must wonder why I'm not upset."

Jane nodded.

"Or surprised," Charlotte added. "Well, I'm not. I've put up with his dalliances too long. I hurt for you and what he put you through."

Jane glanced down. "I have my Davina."

Both women stood. Charlotte went around the coffee table, her arms out to Jane.

When Abigail came in with a clean, dry Davina in a pretty flowered dress, the two were embracing.

"Mama?" said Davina, holding her arms out to both of them.

CHAPTER 14

By the time Casey arrived, Elizabeth had changed out of her uniform into jeans and T-shirt. She poured coffee and set sugar and cream on the cookroom table.

"Thanks." Casey sat and stirred sugar into her coffee. "Victoria still lying down? What did she have done?"

"Dr. Demetrios extracted a wisdom tooth this afternoon."

Casey laughed. "At ninety-two your grandmother is teething?"

Elizabeth shrugged. "Sharks grow twenty or thirty thousand teeth in a lifetime."

"Thanks for that information." Casey checked her watch. "Your ex should be here in a half hour or so."

"What do you want me to do when he gets here?"

"Nothing. Go upstairs. I'll handle Lockwood."

A half hour passed.

A helicopter whirred overhead, the sound of its rotor fading off toward the town center. Casey checked her watch. "That reminds me, I've got to get back to work before too much longer. We're going to hear a lot of noise overhead for the next several days."

Elizabeth poured more coffee.

Three-quarters of an hour passed. "Elizabeth, I gotta go. You can't believe the amount of paperwork involved in this visit."

"Yes, I can," said Elizabeth. "We're working double shifts at the harbor."

Junior called. "Any word, Chief?"

"Nothing,"

"Where is he?" Elizabeth asked.

"He's playing some kind of game." Casey stirred another spoonful of sugar into her third cup of coffee. "I'll stay another fifteen minutes, then I've got to leave."

Fifteen minutes later, as the chief was at the door about to leave, Victoria came downstairs, looking almost like herself again, and wearing her worn gray corduroy pants and the heavy Canadian sweater she liked.

"Isn't it kind of warm for that sweater?" asked Casey.

"I was a little chilly."

They started back to the cookroom.

"How's the missing tooth, Victoria?"

"It'll be fine in a day or two."

"Would you like some ice cream, Gram?" Elizabeth asked from the kitchen. "It might soothe your jaw."

"That sounds just right."

"I really gotta get back to work, Victoria, but I have some information for you." Casey set her elbows on the table and leaned forward. "Smalley faxed me the results of the autopsy."

Victoria held a hand to her swollen cheek.

"Don't you want to put ice on that?"

"In a bit. What about the autopsy?"

"Arsenic. More than enough to account for her death."

"Arsenic," said Victoria.

"Were you aware of any odor when you were at the dentist's the other day?" Casey sat back again.

"She had vomited and obviously soiled herself. Those were the prevailing odors. I'm not sure arsenic has a smell."

Elizabeth returned with the ice cream. "What about arsenic?"

"Mrs. Wilmington's death was not caused by a dental procedure," said Victoria. "It was arsenic."

Elizabeth handed her the ice cream and a cloth napkin full of crushed ice. "How does one get hold of it?"

"Easily, if you know where to look." Victoria held the ice pack against her cheek. "For instance, farmers used to put out arsenic to kill the rats in their barns, and there are still old barns around that probably have containers of arsenic. When I was a girl, stores sold it without thinking much about it. Women used products containing arsenic as a cosmetic or skin whitener."

"Did your grandmother hear about the call?" asked Casey.

Victoria readjusted the ice-pack napkin. "What call?"

"Your former grandson-in-law is back."

"Lockwood? He's on the Island?"

"He said he was on the ferry and I could expect him in an hour," said Elizabeth. "That was almost two hours ago."

Casey looked at her watch. "He's playing his games."

"I always got along well with Lockwood," said Victoria. "I feel sorry for him. He's probably just going through a difficult time. He's an intelligent, well-educated, and clever man."

"Yeah," said Casey. "Heard it all."

"Gram, he's definitely intelligent and clever. Also, he's scary." Elizabeth traced a finger around a worn spot on the tablecloth. "When we met in college he was a wonderful, bright, funny guy. He began to change shortly after we got married." She looked up. "It happened so gradually I didn't notice at first. We were broke. Had trouble paying our bills. Both of us worked. He had a job that had a lot of prestige, but didn't pay much." She looked over at her grandmother. "He started using profanity a lot. I figured he was under pressure from the job. Then he began telling me what a lousy wife I was and how stupid I was. I sort of believed him

89

because I can be kind of sloppy. Figured with all the pressure he was under, I ought to be a better wife."

"That's the way it starts," said Casey. "Did you try to get help for him?"

"He wouldn't hear of it. Everything was my problem, according to him. My fault."

Casey nodded. "Yup."

"The first time he hit me I was astonished. He wasn't brought up to be a violent man. He was terribly apologetic, talked about all the pressure he was under. I figured everything would be okay, he'd never do it again."

"Heard it all," Casey said again. "The victim accepts the apology, figures it won't happen again. Blames herself. The perp realizes he can get away with a smack or two. Even a beating. First thing you know, someone ends up dead."

"It's difficult to imagine such an intelligent man losing control like that," said Victoria.

"He doesn't lose control," said Casey. "He's definitely in control. Violence is how he stays in control."

"The second time he hit me, I left."

Victoria reached out and put a sympathetic hand over Elizabeth's.

"You said he wasn't brought up to be violent," said Casey. "What was his family like?"

"Ordinary, well-educated people. His mother and I didn't get along, but I figured that was a typical mother-in-law–daughter-in-law relationship."

"Did he like his mother?"

Elizabeth shook her head.

"Did he ever tell you why?"

Elizabeth looked down at her hands. "He told me one time when we were first dating that his mother liked to play doctor with him. She'd keep him home from school when he had the slightest sniffles."

"Whoa," said Casey. "I'm no psychologist, but a grown-up stepping over boundaries with a little kid can do a job on the kid that screws him or her up for life."

"Adults do terrible damage to children when they don't respect their personal boundaries," said Victoria. "I can only feel sorry for poor Lockwood."

"Poor Lockwood, yeah, but he's not your problem to deal with." Casey turned back to Elizabeth. "You're property. He owns you. By leaving, you stole his property. He intends to get it back."

Victoria set the ice pack aside.

"That's the way it is, Victoria. Don't go getting all sympathetic about the guy. Who knows what he has in mind now." Casey stood and hitched up her utility belt. "I've really gotta go. If he shows up, Elizabeth, give me a call. Twenty-four hours a day. I'll try to have one of my cops keep an eye on your drive, but we're short-handed."

"Lockwood and I always got along," said Victoria. "I'll be glad to talk to him."

"You're not listening to me, Victoria. No way." Casey slapped her hand on the table. "This is not a normal man with troubles. This is one bright and very scary and very sick puppy."

CHAPTER 15

On the ferry coming over to the Island Lockwood had just disconnected his call to Elizabeth, when an attractive woman stopped at
his table in the lunchroom.

"Mind if I join you?"

He looked up. "Please do." She was tall and heavier than he liked,
but attractive, wearing an interesting tunic top with an Asian
pattern in shades of yellow and brown. Lockwood graciously
moved aside the newspaper he'd been reading to make room for
whatever she intended to occupy herself with during the forty-
five-minute voyage.

He hadn't intended to converse with her. He was thinking of
Elizabeth's reaction to his call and was anticipating his next move.
He'd wait until she and Victoria left the house and then he'd plant
a small trophy in a private place that Elizabeth might not come
across for days. He'd done that before.

"I hope I'm not disturbing you?" The woman broke into his reverie. "I've been off Island for a dental appointment."

Lockwood looked up with a start but recovered rapidly. "Not
something you enjoyed, I'm sure. Don't you have an Island dentist?"

"It's a long story," she replied, looking out the window. The ferry
was passing through the channel between Woods Hole and Non-
amesset, the closest island of the Elizabeth Island chain. The green
buoy off to starboard was heeled over and bobbed in the swift cur-

rent. He could see the dazzling blue water of Vineyard Sound beyond and the unmistakable outline of Martha's Vineyard.

He belonged there. Elizabeth had stolen Martha's Vineyard from him. With an effort, he controlled the rage he felt.

"Do you live on the Island?" His voice was tight but she didn't seem to notice.

She shook her head. No makeup, thank goodness. Natural. Blond hair worn long and loose. The way Elizabeth should wear hers. Elizabeth knew he preferred long hair but she insisted on cutting it short so she looked almost like a boy. What sort of woman was that?

"No, I don't live here. I'm just visiting," said the woman. He'd forgotten that he'd asked her a question. "My grandmother died and I'm here for her funeral."

"My condolences," said Lockwood, thinking about Victoria. "Was her death unexpected?"

The woman laughed, unnerving him. "You could say that," she said. "She died in the dentist's chair. That explains why I went to an off Island dentist."

Lockwood stared at her and said the first thing that came to him. "A mistake by the dentist?" Then realized that was probably an insensitive thing to say, and added, "A heart attack I suppose."

"Arsenic," said the woman, smiling.

"I beg your pardon?"

"One of my brothers called while I was at the dentist's to tell me the autopsy results. She died of arsenic poisoning."

Lockwood almost choked. He looked down at his newspaper. Looked out the window at the whitecaps on the sound. Martha's Vineyard had gone from a blue silhouette on the horizon to a palette of greens and browns. Lighter dots marked houses.

He avoided looking at the woman. A grandmother murdered. And this woman sitting at the table with him actually smiled.

"By the way, my name is Heather," she said.

"Arsenic," said Lockwood. "Good God."

"I was supposed to return on a later boat. My older brother planned to meet me, but I haven't been able to reach him."

"How horrible," said Lockwood. "Do they know how the arsenic . . ." He paused. "Rather, do they know who was responsible for the arsenic? Something the dentist administered in error?"

"Who knows. It's possible my brothers planned the whole thing. They just might have."

"Your brothers," said Lockwood.

"Well, maybe either one of my two brothers."

"What did you say your name is?"

"Heather."

"I'm Woody." He held out his hand and she held out her plump one and they shook. "Where are you staying?"

"At my grandmother's place." She made a face that Lockwood supposed meant to indicate grief. "She owns, or owned, I guess, about fifty acres overlooking the ocean."

"Fifty acres!" Lockwood swallowed. "And you'll inherit it?"

"There are four of us. The will is being read tomorrow. Not soon enough for me. I've got to get back to work in LA."

"What kind of work do you do?"

"I work at one of the studios."

"Impressive," said Lockwood.

"Hardly." She shrugged. "I make coffee and sort through screenplays that people who think they can write submit."

They talked pleasantries until the ferry passed West Chop. Lockwood's mind was on the heiress-to-be as well as his ex-wife.

"I was headed for West Tisbury, but I'll be happy to give you a ride," he said. "Chilmark is only a few miles farther on."

"Would you? That's so nice of you." Heather fluttered her long eyelashes.

Lockwood glanced out the window. "Rounding the harbor jetty now. Might as well go down to my car. Jeep, actually." He folded his newspaper and tucked it into his briefcase.

When they both stood up she looked up at him. "Wow, I didn't realize how tall you are."

"You're tall yourself," he answered.

"Yeah. I don't usually have to look up to a guy."

They left the lunchroom, pushed open the heavy door, crossed the open deck, worked their way down the stairway to the car deck, and settled into the Jeep.

Waiting for the boat to dock, Heather said, "It's always good to get back to the Island."

"I take it you spent some time here?"

"From when I was ten until about ten years ago. My brothers and I left. My grandmother was a pain in the ass."

"Your grandmother must have quite a place," said Lockwood.

"Yeah. I guess," said Heather.

The ferry eased into the slip, deckhands ratcheted the ramp down, chains clanked, cars started up, and the lines of vehicles moved off the ferry.

Heather and Lockwood were silent for most of the drive. Lockwood was thinking how Elizabeth expected him to arrive shortly. She can worry for a while. Good discipline. He'd take his time. Go up to Chilmark with this woman. He'd like to know why she was so cavalier about her grandmother's death. In the dentist's chair. Arsenic. Murder. Yet she'd smiled. Fifty acres with a water view. However she played it, Heather was going to come into a good bit of money. Worth getting to know her.

Elizabeth tried to focus on odd jobs she hadn't planned for the rest of her unexpected day off, but every time the phone rang she started. Every time a car drove past she wondered if Lockwood was about to turn into the drive. She couldn't write, she couldn't read. She went out to weed the garden and was afraid he'd suddenly appear before she was aware of his presence. She didn't want to leave her grandmother alone in case he showed up.

In the late afternoon Victoria suggested they take a picnic supper to Menemsha and watch the sunset. "I think it's going to be a nice one," she added. "It's going to rain later tonight."

"Suppose he's keeping an eye on us and chooses then, when we're away, to hide himself in the house?"

"He wouldn't do that," said Victoria.

"Yes, he would," said Elizabeth. "He's done it before."

"We can't let fear rule us," said Victoria. "I've packed cucumber sandwiches for you, an egg custard for me, and a bottle of wine. Let's go."

CHAPTER 16

While Elizabeth was agonizing over the reappearance of her ex-husband, Dr. Aileen McBride and Scott, Mrs. Wilmington's eldest grandchild, were seated at a table in the front window of the Tidal Rip. She wore a green silk T-shirt that seemed almost fluorescent in the late-afternoon sunlight. The color matched the color of her eyes. The light picked up red highlights in her auburn hair. As though she was aware of the effect, she flicked her long braid over her shoulder with a casually graceful gesture.

Scott watched with a faint smile. He'd clasped his hands on top of the table. Although the day was not cool, he was wearing a long-sleeved plaid flannel shirt.

She reached her hand across the table and placed it on top of his. "I called you, Scott, because I wanted to meet you and tell you how awful I feel about your grandmother's death."

"Thanks for your condolences, Aileen. It's difficult for all four of us, of course. But it must have been a horrible experience for you, her dentist, with her in your chair." He withdrew his hands and reached for the drinks list. "Clearly, there was nothing you could have done to save her."

"I appreciate that, Scott." She brushed away a wisp of hair that had fallen attractively onto her forehead.

He examined the list, then looked up and studied her for a few moments. "You weren't fond of my grandmother, were you?"

Aileen flushed. "Really, Scott." She sat back.

"I didn't mean that quite the way that sounded. But knowing my grandmother, she must have been a difficult patient."

"I'm a doctor, Scott. Personalities don't enter into the doctor-patient relationship."

"Yeah, yeah." He looked down again at the list.

"I suppose we should order our drinks," Aileen said. "Since I invited you, I'm paying."

"Not necessary. I'm carrying a platinum card and I'm a gentleman." Scott shifted in his seat, withdrew his wallet from his jeans pocket, and set it on the table.

"Well," said Aileen. "Thanks."

The waitress arrived and withdrew a pencil from behind her ear. "What're you folks having?" She held her notepad ready.

"A Jameson for me," said Aileen.

Scott ordered a Sam Adams. She made a note, stuck her pencil back behind her ear, and left.

"I don't suppose they have anything to eat," said Aileen.

"Peanuts and pretzels."

"That's something, anyway. I'm starved."

Scott looked at his watch. "I'd invite you out to dinner, but I have to meet my sister on the five o'clock ferry."

"I'll take a rain check." Aileen brushed the stray curl off her forehead again. "There are some good things to recall about your grandmother."

"Like what? She was active in the Garden Club. That's the only good thing I know about her, and I'm not sure that was all good."

"She came by the clinic often."

"Oh? Some recommendation."

"I suppose a consoling factor is you'll inherit that beautiful property, not that that makes up for her sad loss."

Scott leaned forward, elbows on the table. "Look, you don't need to treat me like the grieving grandson."

The waitress returned with a glass of whiskey and a frosty mug of beer. "Anything else?"

"How about peanuts?"

"Peanuts it is." The waitress left.

Aileen lifted her glass.

He clinked his mug against it.

"Mrs. Wilmington had been my patient less than a year." She set her glass down without drinking. "She was my first patient when I joined the staff."

"The other dentists must have been glad to see you. Pass off a problem. Did you see much of her in that short time?"

"We did." Aileen rolled her eyes. "She was the dental equivalent of a hypochondriac."

"You said she came to the clinic often?"

"Every month, regular as clockwork. Not only that, but in between she stopped by occasionally with flowers or candy."

"Candy? For a dentist's office?"

Aileen shrugged. "We didn't object."

"Coming from Chilmark it was kind of going out of her way, wasn't it?"

"I think she had a thing for Dr. Mann." Aileen took a sip of her whiskey. "She took an intense and instant dislike to my assistant, Jane Douglas, for some reason."

"Do you know why?"

"Only a suspicion on my part. Dr. Mann, the head of the clinic, you know?"

He nodded.

"Dr. Mann recommended we hire Jane and he paid a lot of attention to her. Mrs. Wilmington didn't like that."

"You mean, my old granny was jealous?" Scott laughed.

"It seemed that way."

"I don't know the clinic's staff." Scott wiped the condensation off his mug with a hand.

"Of course. I wasn't thinking. Jane is new at the clinic, in her early twenties, and has platinum-colored hair."

"Was she there at the time Grandmother had the attack?"

"Yes. She was just handing me a towel when it happened." Aileen glanced out the window. "She rushed into the lavatory and threw up. She managed to avoid most of the great cleanup." She took a sip of whiskey and held the glass up in front of her with both hands. "When she finally came out she went into shock and fainted."

"It's a wonder you didn't go into shock."

"I'm a trained dentist. We don't fall apart if something happens to a patient." She took another sip, avoiding his eyes.

"I gather that you're not exactly fond of your assistant, either."

"You're perceptive, aren't you? Just wrong chemistry between Jane and me, I guess."

"How did you happen to hire her?"

"I didn't hire her. My boss, Dr. Mann, did."

"How come?"

She shrugged. "Who knows. She spent summers here. They probably met playing tennis or yachting. She's the type."

The waitress came back with a bowl of peanuts. "Sorry it took so long." She leaned forward and wiped off the table with the damp cloth she was carrying.

"No problem," Scott said.

The waitress left.

Aileen went on. "She's quiet. She's competent. Patients love her, except for your grandmother." Aileen moved her glass around in a circle. "You know, in the clinic after Mrs. Wilmington's visit, we'd joke about her. How she was always simpering over Dr. Mann."

She looked down at the glass. "I shouldn't talk about your grandmother like this to you."

"Who better?" said Scott.

That same afternoon, the regulars gathered on the porch at Alley's Store. Joe, the plumber, the first to arrive, was leaning against one of the posts that held up the roof, his cheek distended with a new chunk of Red Man. Lincoln Sibert had his back against the door frame. Sarah Germain, who was usually the first of the porch sitters, hadn't arrived yet from her job at Tribal Headquarters.

Joe yawned, pushed his faded red baseball cap back with a forefinger, and scratched his forehead. "You heard any more about Mrs. Wilmington?"

"Not me," said Lincoln. "Last I heard they figured it must be a heart attack."

Joe pulled his hat back over his forehead. "Her? Heart attack? No way. She was a tough old bird."

"She wasn't that old. Sixties?"

Joe shrugged. "Around that. Seventy, most likely."

Lincoln pulled up the sleeve of his plaid shirt and checked his watch. "Sarah's late."

Joe, who had a view looking west on South Road, said, "Here's her wheels now."

Sarah pulled into Alley's parking lot, slammed her car door shut, and hustled up the steps, face flushed, eyes bright. Her black T-shirt was emblazoned in fluorescent orange with WAMPANOAG TRIBE OF GAY HEAD (AQUINNAH).

"What's up?" asked Joe.

Sarah sat on her usual bench next to the CANNED PEAS sign. "Is someone going to buy me a Diet Coke?"

"Toss you for the honor," said Lincoln, fishing a quarter out of his pocket and flipping it. "Tails. You get it, Joe."

"Figures," said Joe, spitting off to the side of the porch.

He was back shortly with three cans of soda. "I suppose you want me to open it for you, Miz Germain?" He handed a can to Lincoln, who nodded thanks.

"That would be gentlemanly." Sarah held out her can.

Joe popped the lid. Sarah took the can back and sipped.

"Okay. Spill it. What's got you in such a tizzy?" said Joe.

Sarah took another sip. "You know about Mrs. Wilmington?"

"Everyone on the Island knows about Mrs. Wilmington," said Lincoln. "People are pulling their own teeth now. Been a run on pliers at Shirley's Hardware."

"Well, it wasn't a heart attack," said Sarah, settling back on the bench.

"Never thought it was," said Joe.

"It's always a heart attack," said Lincoln. "What else is new?"

Sarah took another sip. Joe spat again and wiped his mouth. Lincoln scratched his back on the doorframe. Sarah smiled.

"Arsenic!" she announced suddenly.

"No lie?" said Joe.

"The truth," said Sarah, holding up her right hand.

"Who administered it?" asked Lincoln.

Joe said, "One of those four grandkids of hers."

Sarah shook her head. "My bet is that Greek dentist, Dr. Demetrios."

"Yeah?" said Joe.

"Dr. Demetrios is jealous of that new dentist from Harvard." Sarah brushed an imaginary hair off her black shirt.

"How do you know?" asked Joe.

"She cleans my teeth. It's obvious."

"So, Demetrios kills Mrs. Wilmington to make McBride look bad? Come on, Sarah." Joe took off his hat again and adjusted the back band. He put the hat back on. "My bet is on one of the grand-kiddies."

"Mrs. Wilmington had money with a capital *M*." Lincoln rubbed his hands together. "What I know about the grandkids, every one of them could use some of that stuff. I'm with Joe."

"Mrs. Wilmington was practically their mother," Sarah objected.

"She wasn't their mother though, was she," said Joe. "No love lost between her and the kids. From what I hear, they're already squabbling over their inheritance. They read the will yet?"

"That's supposed to be this week," said Sarah.

"What about the girl who lived with her?"

"Woman," Sarah corrected. "What about her?"

"Works with me sometimes," said Lincoln. "Landscaping. Name's Susan."

Sarah finished her Diet Coke and set the empty can on the bench next to her. "You'd think they'd show some respect to the grandmother who raised them."

"You ever hear about cowbirds?" said Lincoln.

Joe guffawed. "Got that backward. Cowbirds lay eggs in other birds' nests and the chicks kill the other birds' chicks."

"Just what I meant," said Lincoln.

A Jeep passed by.

"Who was that?" asked Sarah.

Lincoln squinted at the disappearing vehicle. "Dunno."

"You know who it looked like," said Joe, "Miz Trumbull's ex-grandson. Some blonde with him."

"The guy has a restraining order against him," said Lincoln.

"So?" said Joe. "Never stopped me."

CHAPTER 17

Lockwood negotiated the long drive up to Heather's grandmother's house, dropped her off, and watched her climb the porch steps. A fine-looking woman if she'd lose a few pounds. At the top, she turned and waved. The breeze lifted her hair and moved the hem of her tunic.

He waved a hand in return.

He drove back to West Tisbury, where he'd booked a room at the youth hostel near Victoria's. Elizabeth would never suspect that he, who liked his comforts, would stay where he might have to contend with a group of giggling teenage bicyclists.

That night, Elizabeth couldn't sleep. The wind had backed around to the northeast bringing rain. Branches of the lilac tree next to the house scraped against the shingles, sounding as though someone was trying to climb it. Rain lashed the screen in the window. She pulled her comforter up around her neck. Wind-driven, screen-sifted rain misted her face. Her bed was on the far side of the room, which meant she'd better close the window.

This was not a simple task.

The window, dating to when the house was built, had a metal lever on one side that had to be lifted before the window could be raised to remove the screen in order to shut the window.

By the time she'd finished, her T-shirt was soaked from the waist up. She stripped it off and was about to crawl back into bed naked when she thought of Lockwood. Suppose he showed up. The last thing she wanted was to flee from him with nothing on.

Shivering, she opened her bureau drawers to find something she could escape in if that became necessary. Her hands shook. She grabbed a sweatshirt from the third drawer down, then her bikini underpants. She thought a moment and pulled on the jeans she'd shucked the night before and climbed back into bed.

Rain beat against the window. Wind rattled the ancient panes. The lilac scratched the shingles.

She couldn't sleep.

How could she get rid of Lockwood? The divorce was meant to solve her problems with him. The restraining order was to keep him away from her. For the dozenth time she thought about killing him. He was too clever to be trapped by any method she could conceive of. She wouldn't do it, of course. Couldn't. But it gave her grim satisfaction to imagine herself free of him forever.

She twisted from right side to left. She thought about turning on the bedside lamp and reading. But Lockwood could be somewhere out there, watching. She didn't touch the lamp.

She went back to imagining murder instead. Wasn't there some Greek or Roman philosopher who said something about thoughts of murder being a good way to pass a sleepless night?

The night spun into cold, wet pre-dawn blackness as she planned ways she'd like to kill him. The birds had not yet tuned up their dawn chorus. Poison was good. Poison was impersonal. She wouldn't have to touch him. Rain rattled the window.

The sky grayed. Rainwater poured down the windowpanes.

What poison could she use? And how would she obtain it? And how would she administer it? Much too complicated. She couldn't see how poisoners were able to work out the logistics of murder.

She heard her grandmother go into the bathroom next to her room and close the door.

She got up, stripped off her sweatshirt, and put on her bra and one of her BUY LOCAL T-shirts, this one moss green. The T-shirt had been manufactured in India.

Had she slept at all? Her murderous night thoughts had formed a hazy, half-remembered way to pass the long night.

Three days after the deaths of Mrs. Wilmington and Vivian, Roosevelt was still agonizing about Vivian's death. Rain began after he went to bed. The downstairs clock struck three. An hour later, four.

At the time he'd found her, he'd thought she'd committed suicide, thrown herself into the harbor. Then he thought it might have been an accident. The pale color of dawn crept up. Rain overflowed the gutters and splashed down the side of the house.

The clock struck five.

Two hours later, groggy from lack of sleep, he shrugged into his terry cloth bathrobe and joined PJ for breakfast. PJ hadn't combed his hair and dark gold strands stuck up every which way.

"I love the farm boy look," said Roosevelt. "Fetching."

His partner smiled. "You didn't sleep much last night, Rose. A lot of tossing and turning."

"I'm sorry. I didn't mean to keep you awake." Roosevelt looked down at the backs of his dark hands. His grandmother used to say his skin was good. High class. He turned his hands over and looked at his pale palms, his long, sensitive fingers. His fingers were trembling. "I just can't get her off my mind." He rubbed his eyes, scratchy from lack of sleep. "I keep seeing that flowered skirt of hers ballooning up out of the water."

PJ left the table and brought the coffeepot back. He filled Roosevelt's mug. "Are you going in to work today?"

"Not much reason to. All this week's appointments have been canceled. Even if they weren't, I'm not as sharp as I should be if I'm going to work on someone's teeth. Look at my hands."

"A bit shaky, yes." PJ returned the coffeepot to the stove and went to the window. "Wind's shifted to southwest. It'll clear up this morning." He turned back to Roosevelt. "After what you went through, Rose, I'm surprised you're as steady as you are." He returned to his seat. "You'd better get some nourishment. Stewed apples and sausages."

Roosevelt helped himself. "Thanks, Doc."

"You know Victoria Trumbull, don't you?"

"Of course." Roosevelt spoke with his mouth full. "She's a patient at the dental clinic. She was there the morning Mrs. Wilmington died, about to have a wisdom tooth extracted."

"At her age?"

"Age doesn't apply to Mrs. Trumbull," said Roosevelt. "It's not unheard of for someone of advanced years to grow a new tooth." He laid his fork on his plate. "What about her?"

"She helped me understand a badly screwed-up patient."

Roosevelt smiled for the first time that morning. "I thought they all were." He passed his empty plate to PJ, who served out the last of the apples.

"True, but Mrs. Trumbull gave me information about this patient's family that I couldn't get from him. She knows everyone on the Island and their grandparents. You should talk to her."

"What for?"

"There's something fishy about your receptionist ending up in the harbor."

"What can Mrs. Trumbull do?"

"She has insight. Talking to her will be therapeutic."

107

Roosevelt nodded at him. "I live with a therapist."

PJ shook his head. "I can't help you with this. Talk to Mrs. Trumbull."

"Okay. I'll call her." Roosevelt stood. "First, I've got to call the clinic to let them know I won't be in today."

A few minutes later he returned. "She'll see me after lunch."

CHAPTER 18

That morning the Wilmington heirs sat on the porch finishing their last cups of coffee. All four were barefoot, the two sisters in cutoff jeans, as usual, Scott in his neatly pressed chinos, and Wesley in the worn jeans that looked as though they could use laundering. Sunlight broke through rain clouds and sparkled on the wet grass and on the ocean far below.

A helicopter whirred overhead. The sound of its rotors faded away to the southwest, toward Squibnocket.

"How was the dentist yesterday, Heathe?" asked Susan.

"They took me right away. A handsome young dentist, Dr. Mc-Cloud"—Heather rolled her lovely eyes—"fixed the filling."

"Single?" asked Wesley.

"I didn't notice a wedding ring," said Heather.

Scott was stroking his beard, tugging it gently. "Doctors and dentists don't wear jewelry while they work."

"Lucky you got that ride home, Heathe, after Scott wimped out on you," said Wesley.

Scott looked over his shoulder. "I was there. I met the five o'clock boat. No Heather." He returned to the view. "You could have called."

"There was no point in trying. You know there's lousy cell reception here."

"I wasn't here in Chilmark," snapped Scott, turning to look at his sister. "I was in Oak Bluffs. How did you think I managed to call the clinic to let you know the autopsy results, stupid, carrier pigeon?"

Heather looked down at her feet. The black polish on her toenails was chipped.

"Who was he, the guy who drove you home?" asked Susan. "He didn't stick around long enough for an introduction."

"His name is Woody. I sat at his table in the lunchroom on the ferry. We got to talking, and he offered me a ride."

"You *would* hit on the lone, unattached male on the ferry," said Wesley.

"All the tables were taken," said Heather.

"Is *he* single?" asked Wesley.

"Divorced, smarty. And, yes, I gave him my cell number."

Another helicopter, flying low enough so they could read UNITED STATES OF AMERICA on its side as it passed over the house.

When the sound of the rotors died away, Heather asked, "Is that the president?"

"No," said Scott. "He's not supposed to be here until later this week. They'll fly around, checking up on what's going on down here from now until he leaves."

"Good Lord," said Wesley, "They'd better warn the president that us kids are here."

"Ha, ha," said Heather. "Very funny."

Wesley turned to Scott. "Saw you in Oak Bluffs with that hot dentist yesterday. The one who was working on Mildred."

"I'd have taken her to dinner if I'd known Heather got the earlier ferry." Scott checked his watch. "Only a few hours until the will is read."

"This afternoon"—Wesley ran his hands along his thighs—"our financial troubles will be over."

"Not so fast, Wes. Probate takes time," said Scott. "Even a simple will takes three to six months."

"Three months!" gasped Heather. "I can't wait three months."

"Three to six, I said. With the arsenic factor, it's going to take a lot longer. Did any of you think of that?"

"What do you mean?" Susan reached up and combed out her short hair with her fingers.

Heather sniffed and turned away.

"What's your problem, Heather?" asked Wesley.

"I've got to get back to LA. To my job." Heather looked at her watch.

"Don't they give you time off for a death in the family?" asked Susan.

"Sue, you have no concept of the real world. This"—Heather gestured around—"is not the real world."

"We've got to hold on to the property," said Susan.

"There's no way we can keep it." Wesley indicated the worn painted floor, the splintery wooden steps leading up to the porch, the weathered trim. "We need the money. Not one of us can afford the upkeep let alone the taxes on this mausoleum."

"Wes is right," said Heather. "We've got to sell."

"This would make a great inn," said Susan. "I mean, look at the view. It won't take much to turn it into a paying property."

"It would take a lot more money than I've got. I vote to sell." Wesley slapped his hand on the arm of his chair.

"We can't sell until the will is probated," said Scott.

"Can we get a loan based on our inheritance?" asked Heather. No one answered her.

"What time are we due at the law office?" asked Wesley.

"Two p.m. The lawyer's got a court appearance this morning," said Scott. "Sue, you know how to get to his place?"

"It's *her* place," said Susan. "Darya Blout. Her office is in Edgartown. We need at least forty-five minutes to get there."

"What's she like?" asked Wesley.

111

Heather sneered at him. "Maybe she's single, Wes. Lawyers have money."

"I've never met her. She's supposed to be very competent." Susan set her feet flat on the porch floor and stopped the swing.

"Hey!" said Heather. "I want to keep swinging."

"It's making me queasy." Susan held her feet in place. "Darya took over her grandfather's practice after he died."

"You're on a first-name basis?" asked Scott.

"Oh, for Pete's sake!" Susan sat forward and the swing tilted. "Everyone on this Island is on a first-name basis. You know how things are here."

"Yes, we certainly do," said Scott.

"Enough serious discussion for one day," said Wesley. "Why don't we all go for a swim before lunch?"

"Kinda chilly, isn't it?" Heather hugged herself.

"Bracing," said Wesley.

"It's a lot warmer in LA."

"We're not in LA now."

"I wish," said Heather.

After general agreement, they went back into the house and changed into bathing suits, gathered up towels, and headed down the pasture toward the beach.

Susan flung a towel over her shoulders. "It's turned into a perfect day."

"Not like California," said Heather. "I don't see how you can stand the winters here, Sue. I was soooo glad to get away from this place."

"Don't you miss spring and fall?" They were trailing behind their brothers, who'd raced down the hill. Sheep had cropped the grass short on the hillside.

"Not really," said Heather.

Susan stopped abruptly and looked down. "Look, Heather. Field mushrooms. Let's pick some for lunch on the way back."

"Just like Grandmother," said Heather. "Always foraging."

"Remember the gooseberry jam she made?" Susan started down the hill again. "We still have a bunch of jars in the pantry."

"Probably full of botulism by now."

"Remember finding watercress in the brook?"

"Leeches! Ugh!" said Heather.

Susan laughed. "Always the optimist."

Heather laughed, too.

They caught up with their brothers, out of breath, and passed them. At the foot of the hill they flopped down on the grass and waited.

A soft breeze brought the soothing sound of sheep bleating. Heather rolled over onto her stomach and pulled up a grass stem. She stuck it in her mouth and chewed on it.

"We had some good times," said Susan. "I miss you guys."

Heather turned onto her back, sat up, and brushed her hair out of her eyes. "It's all in the past, Sue. Grandmother failed at being a mother. She didn't even try. I'm glad we're rid of her."

Susan stared down at her feet. She'd kicked off her sandals. "She looked forward to a peaceful retirement. Then, wham! She gets stuck with four resentful teenagers."

Heather got up and adjusted her bathing suit. "She didn't have to take it out on us."

"Here they come." Susan called out, "First one in!"

"June. Brrr!" said Heather.

Lines of combers curled offshore forming sleek tunnels that arched and fell into a mass of foam. Stones tumbled in the backwash, granite, gneiss, and schist grinding together to create a beach of glittering miniature gems.

The four forgot their differences as they dived into the icy smooth curve of breakers, emerged on the back side of the wave shouting at the shock of cold water, shaking wet hair out of their eyes, laughing, and splashing each other like the children they once were. Finally, exhausted, they dropped onto the warm sand and lay there until the breeze brought them the sound of the distant noon siren in the faraway fire station.

"Lunchtime, guys!" said Heather, sitting up. "Sue found mushrooms in the pasture. How about it?"

"Wild mushrooms?" Scott frowned. "No thanks."

"You can't go wrong with field mushrooms," said Susan.

"Is that right," said Scott. "People end up in the hospital all the time after eating perfectly safe mushrooms."

"You don't have to eat any, if you feel that way," said Heather. "Let me borrow your hat."

"What for?"

"To put them in, silly!" answered Heather.

Scott yanked off his baseball cap and tossed it to her.

"Thanks, bro."

Patches of mushrooms dotted the pasture where sheep dung had nurtured them. Despite his misgivings, Scott was soon searching for the pearl-colored clumps, few enough to make a kind of treasure hunt, but after a half hour, enough to fill Scott's hat and then the kerchief Susan had knotted into a carrying bag.

Back at the house they worked together preparing lunch—a salad with raw mushrooms, hamburgers with mushroom gravy. They ate on the porch. The breeze bent the long grass that grew near the house into golden waves. At the lower end of the pasture, muted by distance, pounding surf was a steady low rumble.

"A perfect morning." Wesley forked up a chunk of rare hamburger and swept mushroom gravy onto it with a crust of bread. "Glad you recognized these were edible, Sue."

"I have to admit, that was excellent," said Scott, patting his mouth with his paper napkin. "Good job, everyone."

"I'm ready for my nap, now," said Heather, standing up and stretching. "Nothing more relaxing than a swim and a good lunch afterward. Nighty night, folks."

"Hey, sis, you're not excused from cleanup," said Wesley. "Don't forget the lawyer's appointment at two."

Heather yawned. "I'm still suffering from jet lag."

"Sure, sure," said Scott. "You wash, Heather. Wesley and I'll dry. Sue knows where everything goes. She'll put away."

Wesley snapped a dishtowel at her buttocks. "Nice try."

CHAPTER 19

Victoria was ready for Roosevelt's visit before noon. All was well and her jaw was healing nicely. She took her shoes off and set them by the door. Even though the right shoe had a hole cut into it to relieve her sore toe, it hurt today. She put the teakettle on to heat as she awaited Roosevelt's arrival. Her only contact with him had been to exchange civilities at the clinic.

Before the tea water had come to a boil, Roosevelt showed up, trim in his navy blazer and open-collared white shirt.

"Thanks for seeing me, Mrs. Trumbull," He glanced down at Victoria's shoes by the door, stooped down, and removed his own.

Victoria smiled. She poured the now boiling water over tea leaves in the blue and white teapot and Roosevelt carried it into the cookroom. She brought a plate of gingersnaps.

"You mentioned that you're uneasy about Vivian's death," said Victoria, after they were seated and the tea poured.

"I wish I'd taken her straight home."

Victoria shook her head. "If she was determined to kill herself, she'd have found another time and place."

"PJ, my partner, thinks she may not have killed herself."

"Oh?" Victoria held her mug up under her nose and breathed in the fragrant steam.

"Too many coincidences. Two deaths on the same day, two

people working in the same office, both deaths under less than normal circumstances."

"What do you think?" Victoria sipped her tea.

Roosevelt took a gingersnap and broke it in half. "I couldn't sleep last night. Kept recalling the events of that day. Mrs. Wilmington's seizure. Dr. Mann's meeting. After Vivian answered the phone, she came back, upset."

"The call was the announcement of Mrs. Wilmington's death?"

"Not an announcement." Roosevelt put one of the cookie pieces in his mouth. "The call was from a friend of Vivian's who works at the hospital." He chewed. "She'd broken an important privacy rule by telling Vivian about Mrs. Wilmington's death."

"I'm sure that was irresistible to the friend," said Victoria. "Calling Vivian with inside information."

"I thought at first that Vivian probably had committed suicide. She'd heard the news first and passed it on to the rest of us. She was the messenger, you know. Sensitive."

Victoria took another sip of her tea.

"But, lying awake last night, I thought some more. It's not easy working for the clinic." Roosevelt broke the other half of his gingersnap into smaller pieces. "A patient's death would have upset her, as it did all of us. But not enough to kill oneself."

"Could she have fallen into the harbor accidentally?"

"I thought of that, too," he said. "She might have stepped out of the car. It was windy. Water was splashing up on the bulkhead making it slippery. She was wearing a voluminous skirt that could have acted like a sail." He shook his head. "But the wind was blowing onshore from the harbor."

"Where does that leave you?" asked Victoria.

He lifted his mug and set it down again without drinking. "When Vivian came back into the office she seemed to be holding something back. What if the caller told Vivian something that might have identified Mrs. Wilmington's killer?"

"You were taking her home, I understand," said Victoria. "How long were you in the liquor store?"

"About a half hour."

"No one heard her cry out?"

"It was windy. Noisy from waves and halyards slapping masts. I don't think anyone even close by would have heard a cry." He picked up his mug again. "There were a lot of cars in the parking lot, but no people around. Everyone was in the store. Someone had won fifty bucks on a scratch card and people were making a big fuss over it. There was no one outside to see her."

"A half hour is enough time for someone to give her an unseen push," said Victoria.

"But no one could have counted on my being in the store that long. They'd be taking a big risk of being caught."

"Were you aware of anyone following you?" asked Victoria.

"No, because I was concerned about Vivian."

"The hospital's medical team was trying to save Mrs. Wilmington's life. Might she have called out something? Perhaps some word that meant nothing to anyone but Vivian."

Roosevelt shrugged. "Mrs. Wilmington calls out a word, someone passes that word to Vivian's friend, who tells Vivian, who recognizes the word as something sinister?"

"Not plausible, is it," said Victoria. "More tea?" She held up the teapot.

"Please."

Victoria poured. "Would Mrs. Wilmington have known who poisoned her? Arsenic doesn't have much taste or odor. It probably was dissolved in something she drank."

"I assume it must have been administered at the clinic," said Roosevelt. "I understand arsenic is fast acting."

"Not necessarily." Victoria glanced out the window. She could see a hawk in the distance, fleeing from several crows that were after it. She turned back to Roosevelt. "Depending on the dose it might have taken anywhere from a half hour to four or five hours before she died."

"I don't know what to think," said Roosevelt. "Somehow that phone call seems key."

Victoria said, "If the autopsy shows that Vivian was struck, knocking her into the harbor, we'll have an answer of sorts."

"Then we'll have the question of who did it and why," said Roosevelt. "And how her death is connected to Mrs. Wilmington's, that is, if it is connected."

"After Vivian informed the clinic's staff of Mrs. Wilmington's death, how long was it before the meeting adjourned?"

"Not long. I offered to take Vivian home and Arthur offered a ride to Jane Douglas."

"Which one is Jane Douglas?" asked Victoria.

"She's Dr. McBride's assistant. She was there when Mrs. Wilmington had the attack. In her mid-twenties with, I was going to say prematurely gray hair, but it's not gray, it's an extraordinary pure silver. She's quite stunning."

"What movie stars in the nineteen-thirties called 'platinum blonde.' And Arthur? Which one is he?"

"Quiet guy, works with Dr. Minnowfish. Medium height, husky build, dark hair."

"Yes, I recall him." Victoria moved her chair back. "I have to agree with PJ. Vivian had no reason to commit suicide, and it seems unlikely that she accidentally slipped and fell into the harbor. Who would have the opportunity to shove her? Who would want her dead?"

"She was an inoffensive woman. I can't think of anyone who would want to kill her."

They were silent for several minutes.

Finally, Victoria said, "The situation is so murky, I'm afraid I haven't been much help."

Roosevelt stood. "You have, Mrs. Trumbull. You've put several things into perspective for me. PJ was right."

After Roosevelt left, Victoria put her shoes back on and headed to the police station.

Casey glanced up from her paperwork. "Smalley faxed me the results of the postmortem on Vivian." She handed a sheet of paper to Victoria, who studied it.

"A bruise on the back of her head," said Victoria, looking up. "So it was murder. Someone hit her, knocking her into the harbor." She passed the paper back to Casey.

"Don't even think about investigating that one, too," said Casey. She sighed. "I know you too well, Victoria. You're not going to listen to me, no matter what I tell you."

"I listen," said Victoria.

"But you do what you want anyway." Casey shook her head. "Have you heard from Lockwood?" She opened a desk drawer and filed the paper.

"Nothing." Victoria seated herself in her usual chair in front of Casey's desk, leaned down, and untied her right shoe.

"You ought to see the doctor about that toe," said Casey. "They can fix stuff like that nowadays."

Victoria removed her shoe. "They'd probably amputate."

Casey picked up her beach-stone paperweight and tossed it from hand to hand. "Junior Norton checked with the Steamship Authority. Lockwood had a reservation on the three forty-five ferry. He was on the boat, as he said."

"Did he book a return reservation?" asked Victoria.

"No." Casey smoothed the stone. "He's playing with you."

"I'm concerned about Elizabeth, not myself," said Victoria.

"I'm concerned about both of you." Casey dropped the stone down on her papers. "No telling what he'll do next."

Victoria looked at her hands.

The phone rang. Casey answered, spoke briefly, and hung up. "The medical examiner released Mrs. Wilmington's body. Confirming what he told us earlier: arsenic."

On the Mill Pond the swans were ducking their heads underwater, dining on tender shoots below the surface.

"From what I understand," Victoria said, turning from the view of the pond, "arsenic is easily available. There's undoubtedly plenty of it around still. I believe you can order it from chemical supply houses."

"Not easily," said Casey.

"Some forms of arsenic are tasteless and odorless," said Victoria. "Someone could have given Mildred Wilmington a cup of tea with arsenic in it and she'd never have suspected. Depending on how concentrated the dose is, she wouldn't suffer serious ill effects for hours. Remember the play *Arsenic and Old Lace*?"

"Sure do," said Casey. She looked at her watch. "The Wilmington grandchildren have an appointment at the lawyer's office this afternoon. No matter how Mrs. W divvied things up, someone's going to be unhappy."

"They're civilized people," said Victoria.

"Civilization falls by the wayside when it involves inheritances. You'll see, Victoria. Someone's going to get hurt." She looked over at Victoria and grinned. "I know what you're thinking, Victoria. That since the state cops and we West Tisbury cops are flat out with the visit of the president, you're going to take on the entire investigation of Mrs. Wilmington's murder and solve it."

Victoria started to protest, but Casey held up a hand and continued.

"I can't count how many times I've told you—the state cops are responsible for solving murders, not us. Don't meddle, Victoria. I mean it!"

CHAPTER 20

That afternoon, after the lunch dishes were put away, the four Wilmington grandchildren headed for Wesley's convertible. Heather pushed the front seat aside to climb into the backseat and stopped.

"It's soaking wet back here, Wes," said Heather. "Did you wait until the rain stopped before you put the top back up?"

"A wet behind isn't going to kill you," said Wesley.

"We're going to the lawyer's, dummy. It's not like we're going to the beach."

"Okay, okay." Wesley headed to the house, returned with towels, and laid them on the wet seats. Heather and Susan climbed in, Scott took the front passenger seat, and Wesley drove.

He made a wide turn out of the pasture onto the rutted drive that led to the main road.

Scott opened the window partway. He said over his shoulder, "This too much air for you, Sue?"

"It's fine," she replied. She leaned back, folded her arms, and closed her eyes.

After the hills and stonewalls of Chilmark, they came to the gentler fields of West Tisbury. The night's rain had brought out shades of early-summer green. They passed the church, the senior center, Alley's Store. On the porch of Alley's, two men leaned against various parts of the building and a woman was seated.

Heather broke the silence. "Don't those guys ever work? They're always there, gossiping."

Wesley said over his shoulder, "They call it 'commenting on the goings on about town.'"

"One time I saw one of them move."

"Joe," said Wesley. "He spits tobacco juice every so often."

"Ugh!" said Heather.

They passed the old mill and the pond where two swans sailed on the mirror surface. They passed the tiny police station.

Heather twisted around to look behind. "Mrs. Trumbull just came out of the police station. She was at the dentist's when Grandmother died."

"Yeah, Heather. We know," said Scott.

They were quiet on the stretch of road between West Tisbury and Edgartown. The road dipped into frost bottoms, small valleys created by glacial meltwaters twenty thousand years earlier.

On the outskirts of Edgartown, they sighted the tall windmill at Morning Glory Farm.

Heather leaned over the front seat and tapped Wesley's shoulder. "Let's stop and get some fresh vegetables for supper."

"On the way back," Wesley said.

Scott turned to him. "I'm thinking we should go out for a celebratory dinner tonight. Someplace *très* upscale."

Heather glanced at Susan, who'd been silent the whole time. "Oh come off it, Sue. Stop being such a grouch."

Susan said, "We're not going on a picnic, you guys."

"Okay, okay," said Scott.

They drove without further talk down Main Street, past the Whaling Church on the left. A block before Main Street ended at the harbor they turned onto South Water Street.

"How are we doing for time?" Wesley asked.

Scott checked his watch. "Fine. It's quarter of. From what Sue says we're practically there."

The lawyer's office was in one of the restored captains' houses that lined North and South Water Street. The Wilmington grandchildren parked, crossed the road, and went up the steps onto a small open porch with built-in benches on either side.

A sign below a whale-shaped door knocker read KNOCK AND ENTER. They went in.

Inside and to the left, what was once a formal parlor had been turned into a waiting room. On the right, a downstairs bedroom was now a modern office. Its concession to the house's antiquity was the office furniture—desks, tables, chairs, and bookcases, all polished wood. State-of-the-art computers and office machines made a jarring note.

A slender woman with dark hair came out of a door beyond the office and greeted them. "Mildred Wilmington's grandchildren, I assume?"

They introduced themselves and the woman said she was Darya Blout, their grandmother's attorney.

Wesley looked her up and down. "Kind of young to be doing this, aren't you?"

Darya Blout ignored him.

Wesley flushed.

She offered her condolences on their grandmother's death. "An unfortunate way to go."

They stood solemnly, heads slightly bowed.

"Follow me, please." Darya led the way past the office to a small study where several chairs were arranged in a semicircle in front of a mahogany desk. She seated herself behind the desk. "Sit down, please. Your grandmother's will is quite simple and straight-forward, but I'm sure you'll have questions."

Scott took the chair directly in front of her and the others seated themselves on either side of him. He indicated two extra chairs. "Will someone else be joining us?"

Darya nodded. "My assistant will sit in and take notes and a stenographer will be making a word-for-word transcription of the meeting."

"Were you the lawyer who drew up our grandmother's will?" asked Wesley.

"No. My grandfather was her attorney for almost a half century. It was he who drew up the present will five years ago, superseding a previous will he'd drawn up ten years before that."

Heather looked perplexed. "Oh? What was that all about?"

Darya studied Heather before she answered. "I'm afraid I really can't tell you."

Scott said, "Fifteen years ago, Heather, is when our parents were killed and Mildred took us all in. Five years ago is long after we three moved out."

"I have no idea what transpired between your grandmother and my grandfather at either time," the lawyer said. "Even if I knew, I would not be at liberty to divulge any dealings between an attorney and his client."

Wesley gave a nervous chuckle. "There you have it, kids."

Scott shifted in his chair, tugged at the knees of his jeans as though to preserve a crease that wasn't there, and crossed his legs. "What's holding us up?" He stroked his beard.

Darya didn't answer. She had a long elegant face with prominent cheekbones and dark eyes. Her hair was pulled away from her face with combs, exposing neat ears with small pearl earrings. She was wearing a banker's gray pantsuit, the jacket buttoned halfway exposing a white silk T-shirt.

Scott uncrossed his legs and sat forward. "What's holding things up?" he said again.

Darya said, "My assistant is briefing the stenographer and getting the equipment ready."

"Equipment?" said Heather. "What for?"

"I believe you'll want a record of what is said here today."

"What's going on?" said Wesley, leaning forward. "This doesn't sound like the reading of a simple will to me."

Darya smiled. "It really is quite a simple will. Well thought out, no ambiguities. Your grandmother had all her mental faculties as did my grandfather." She looked up as a side door opened. "Here's my assistant now. Richard, these are Mrs. Wilmington's four grandchildren," and she introduced each of them.

Richard, a stout, red-faced man with thin white hair, nodded politely and sat some distance from the four, notebook in his lap.

"And this is Martha, our stenographer." Darya turned back to the four as Martha set up her recording stand. "We'll provide you with a transcript of our meeting as soon as it's available."

While the stenographer was setting up, Darya opened a leather folder and removed a document, perched a pair of reading glasses on her nose, and thumbed through the several pages.

She peered over the top of her glasses. "Martha?"

Martha nodded, adjusted her seat, and poised her hands over the stenotype machine.

Darya moved her glasses into place and glanced at the papers in front of her. She looked up briefly and stated the date and the people present. Then she began. "Mildred Wilmington, your grandmother, mentions each one of the four of you in her will. She expresses her devotion to you, wishes each of you a long, happy, and prosperous life." Darya glanced up, then back down at the papers. "To each one of you she bequeaths the sum of five thousand dollars."

Wesley half rose from his chair. "Five thousand dollars? That's all? That's all she left us? That's nothing!"

"There must be some mistake," said Scott, rubbing his beard with the palm of his hand. "Mildred was a wealthy woman."

Darya peered over her glasses. "Let me read what your grandmother says in her own words: 'Having provided for the material welfare of my four grandchildren for fifteen years, and having paid for food, clothing, entertainment, and their college education, I believe I have no further financial obligation to them. A gift of five thousand dollars to each is a token of my affection for them and my wish for each to have a long, happy, and prosperous life.' " Darya moved the document to one side, removed her glasses, and looked up.

"Token? Token?" sputtered Heather.

"Affection." Scott spit out the word. "That cold-blooded bitch didn't have an ounce of affection for anything or anyone."

The stenographer's hands typed busily.

Darya put her glasses back on. "Shall I continue?"

Silence. The stenographer paused, hands suspended.

Richard turned a page in his notebook.

"Very well, I'll continue." Darya cleared her throat. "As you supposed, your grandmother was a wealthy woman. The next item is a major bequest."

Heather glanced at Susan. Susan looked down at her hands folded in her lap. All four heirs were silent.

Darya looked down at the document. "I bequeath to Dr. Horace Mann—"

"Mann?" Scott interrupted, sitting forward. "Island Dental Clinic? Her dentist? Why, for God's sake?"

"How much does she give him?" asked Heather.

Darya removed her glasses.

"All right, we'll shut up," said Wesley.

Darya put her glasses back on. "In her words, 'To Horace Mann, who brought painless dentistry to the Island—' "

Wesley guffawed. "Hardly painless in her case, I'd say."

Darya frowned and continued, " 'I bequeath the unrestricted sum of three million dollars.' "

"Three million?" Heather gasped. "Three? Million?"

Wesley added, "To her dentist?"

Scott shook his head. "That's ironic."

"That's outrageous!" said Heather. "Three million to some dentist? And only five thousand to each of us, her own children?"

"Grandchildren," corrected Scott.

"Who gets the money if Mann dies?" asked Heather.

Darya took off her glasses again and waited.

Susan had said nothing throughout the meeting. She sat apart from her siblings and avoided looking at them. Her eyes were focused on her hands.

Scott turned to her. "Did you know about this, Sue?"

Susan shrugged.

"Well, Miz Blout, continue," said Scott. "I assume there are more surprises."

The three settled back uneasily. Susan hadn't moved.

The attorney continued. "Mildred Wilmington, your grandmother, says, 'In hopes that the house will remain in the family in perpetuity, I bequeath the house and land, and funds to maintain the property and pay the taxes, to my granddaughter Susan—' "

"What!" shrieked Heather. "What about us?"

Darya looked up again. "Your grandmother has given each of you five thousand dollars."

"But the house?" Heather insisted. "We planned to sell it."

"No, we didn't!" said Susan.

"I need the money!" said Heather.

Scott said, "I suspect we can regain possession of the house and land."

Darya said, "It's hardly a question of regaining possession. If you recall, you never owned it. Your grandmother did."

"Then we'll break the will." Scott emphasized his words by smacking his right fist into the palm of his left hand.

Darya swiveled in her chair to face the window behind her, then swiveled back again. "I don't think you understand. Your grandmother anticipated that you might threaten to contest the will." She smiled. "If any one of you should even threaten, the twenty thousand dollars—five thousand intended as a gift to each of you—is to be donated to the Island Conservation Foundation." She nodded to the stenographer who was recording every word and uttered. "I think we can consider that your remark, Scott, was not actually a threat. Or was it?"

Scott's face paled.

"For the record, you might want to retract your comment about breaking the will."

"God damn it!" said Scott.

"Shall I take that as a retraction?"

Wesley chortled. "Nice going, Scott." He pointed at the document on her desk. "Any other surprises in there?"

"I don't believe there are any other surprises. There are a few other conditions, however."

Heather pushed her chair back and rose.

"Sit down, please." Darya held up a hand.

"It's outrageous!" cried Heather. "The whole thing."

"May I continue?" Darya turned the document facedown and waited until Heather, Scott, and Wesley settled down. Susan sat impassively.

"Mrs. Wilmington understood that there might be circumstances she hadn't anticipated, so she provided a number of exception clauses. The most important for you, I believe, is that each of you has a lifetime tenancy in the house, but only on condition of Susan's approving such tenancy."

"Oh, nice," said Wesley.

"For God's sake," said Scott under his breath. "In the event that Susan predeceases us, what then?"

"You mean arsenic?" Wesley smiled.

"Stop it!" Susan stood.

Darya broke in. "I don't believe your grandmother anticipated murder, either of herself or of one of you. However, we in the firm, being lawyers, insisted that your grandmother plan for that contingency." Darya smiled. "In the case of death by other than natural causes, of your grandmother or any of her heirs, the firm holds all funds, all bequests in escrow until such time as a culprit, in the case of murder, is dealt with."

The four looked at one another.

"Does that include Dr. Mann?" asked Wesley.

"All bequests."

"That could be never," said Wesley.

Heather asked. "What are we talking about?"

Scott turned onto her. "Pretty goddamned clear, if you ask me. Nothing goes to anyone until Mildred's murderer is hanged."

"People don't get hanged anymore," said Wesley.

CHAPTER 21

On the way back to their grandmother's house from the lawyer's, the atmosphere in the car seethed with anger. Fury boiled and bubbled behind an icy silence. The other three ignored Susan. The half-hour drive was interminable. Once home, the three stalked up the porch steps without a word, slamming the front door behind them, rattling the ancient glass panes.

Susan turned away at the foot of the steps and fled to the pasture, her refuge during the years Grandmother was alive. She ran until she was out of breath, then walked, head down, kicking at the pebbly sheep dung that dotted the pasture.

Hatred. Another gift from her grandmother. She kicked at a clump of field mushrooms, scattering white fragments, unaware of the vast blue Atlantic spread out to her left. When Grandmother left her the house, she knew what she was doing to all four of them.

She came to a stand of scrub oak at the far edge of the pasture, stopped, and looked back. The house loomed like a dark hulk, silhouetted on the brow of the hill. She looked down and saw a clump of mushrooms, not field mushrooms with their smooth button caps, but a cluster with scaly bell-shaped caps. Shaggy ink caps. Fragile mushrooms that had to be eaten within a couple of hours of the time they were picked. Otherwise, they'd dissolve into an inky, unappetizing slime, hence their name. She would sauté them in olive oil when she returned and then they would keep in the refrigerator for several days. By then, her sibs would have calmed down.

Susan knew something else about the ink cap mushrooms. They were also known as Tippler's Bane. They were delicious and not classified as poisonous, but the mushrooms blocked the metabolism of alcohol. If eaten within a day or two of drinking alcoholic beverages the result was a hangover that would make one swear off liquor forever. She decided not to warn her siblings.

A few hours after the reading of Mrs. Wilmington's will, Dr. Ophelia Demetrios and Dr. Aileen McBride were seated in the reception area of the dental clinic. Both were wearing white lab coats. Dr. Demetrios was reading the newspaper, Dr. McBride was reading a magazine. No patients had been scheduled for the day.

"I don't know why we're both dressed for work," said Dr. Demetrios. "Do you expect a patient?"

Dr. McBride didn't answer.

"Three million!" Dr. Demetrios tossed the *Island Enquirer* onto the seat next to her. "Can you imagine? Three million."

Dr. McBride looked up from the May issue of *Vogue* she'd been reading. "What are you talking about, Ophelia?"

"The Island grapevine's been busy. The *Enquirer* won't have it until the end of the week." Dr. Demetrios pointed a carmine-tipped finger at the newspaper.

"I have no idea what you're hinting at." Dr. McBride went back to her magazine with some irritation.

"Mrs. Wilmington, you know, who died in your chair—"

"I know who Mrs. Wilmington is. What about her?" Dr. McBride went back to studying a photo of a slender woman holding a golden apple at eye level.

"Did you have any idea how much she was worth?"

"You just told me. Three million," said Dr. McBride, licking a finger and turning the page. "And quite frankly, Ophelia, I couldn't care less."

"You placed a wrong bet, didn't you," said Dr. Demetrios.

Dr. McBride frowned. "What do you mean by that?"

Dr. Demetrios sat back and laid her arm over the back of the chair next to her. "You've been getting cozy with Scott. Mrs. Wilmington's heir. Guessed wrong, didn't you, or were you hedging your bets, playing both Horace and Scott at the same time?"

"What!" said Dr. McBride. The copy of *Vogue* slipped off her lap and landed on the floor, splayed out. "My dear Ophelia. What are you talking about?"

"They had a reading of the will, only a few hours ago. The old lady was worth more than thirteen million." Dr. Demetrios paused. "She left five thousand dollars to each of her grandchildren."

"Five thousand." Dr. McBride bent down, picked up the magazine, and set it carefully on the seat next to her. "How did you hear that bit of news?"

"I thought that might get your attention." Dr. Demetrios stood up. "I'm sure Horace is aware of your interest in Scott."

"Oh, stop it, Ophelia. Scott and I had drinks together. What about the three million?"

Dr. Demetrios thrust a foot out in a theatrical gesture and spread her arms. "Apparently spare cash to Mrs. Wilmington."

"I've had enough of your drama, Ophelia. I'm reading." Dr. McBride picked up the magazine again.

"Ah, but Mrs. Wilmington left three million dollars to . . ." Dr. Demetrios twirled a finger in the air. "Ta-da! Dr. Horace Mann of the Martha's Vineyard Dental Clinic."

"What?" Dr. McBride set the magazine down again, carefully.

"Five thousand to her grandchildren." Dr. Demetrios smiled. "Three million to Horace."

"You're joking."

Dr. Demetrios shook her head. Her silky black hair, loose from its usual bun, swirled around her shoulders. "This will give the Island something to gossip about for months."

Dr. McBride picked up the magazine again, thumbed past the pages she'd already looked at, and stopped several pages beyond the woman with her apple. Her hands shook. "The clinic can use an infusion of cash," she said.

Abigail answered the phone in her usual careful way. "Harbor view residence."

"Abigail—"

"Dr. Mann. You know she won't speak to you."

"Please, Abigail, listen to me."

"Sorry, Dr. Mann." Abigail spoke softly. "I'm busy."

"Don't hang up, please! Things have changed. Tell her that. Things have changed. She knows I never loved my wife."

"She didn't know you had a wife until two years ago, Dr. Mann."

"I couldn't afford to leave her, that was why."

Abigail turned to check on Davina, who was playing in her sandbox. She held the phone close to her ear. "So now you can afford to buy off your wife?"

"Tell her that, Abigail. Please. I mean it."

"Sorry, Dr. Mann. After you've bought her off, you call again."

CHAPTER 22

Late that afternoon, Victoria was sorting out her bills, trying to decide which she should pay first, when a bicycle skidded to a stop by her steps and a tall, hefty young woman got off. She removed her helmet, ran fingers through her short blond hair, and leaned her bike against the railing.

By the time she'd reached the kitchen door, Victoria was waiting for her, not quite placing who the woman was. "Good afternoon. Can I help you?"

"Mrs. Trumbull, I'm Susan Wilmington."

Of course. Victoria had known Susan since she was a child and had seen her recently at her grandmother's house.

"Come in, Susan."

"Thanks, Mrs. Trumbull." Susan came into the kitchen, still holding her helmet.

"How are you and your brothers and sister holding up?"

Susan shook her head. Her lovely blue eyes were suddenly magnified by tears. "We went to the lawyer's earlier today."

"Sit down." Victoria indicated one of the gray painted kitchen chairs. She tore off a paper towel from the roll above the sink and handed it to Susan.

"I need someone to talk to, and I thought of you, Mrs. Trumbull." Susan accepted the towel and blew her nose. "You probably don't remember. When I was nine or ten I fell off my bike in front of your house and skinned my knee and you came out and comforted me. You brought me into your house and cleaned out the dirt"—she sniffed—"and put a big Band-Aid on my knee and made me feel like a wounded soldier."

Victoria smiled. "I seem to recall I told you that wounded soldiers ate graham crackers and drank hot cocoa."

"You do remember."

"You didn't fall off your bike again, did you?"

At that, Susan smiled. "Kind of."

"Graham crackers and hot cocoa, then." Victoria turned on the stove under the teakettle. She reached down the red and white box of graham crackers and handed it to Susan along with a plate. "Put some of those out, if you will."

While the water was heating, Victoria sat at the table across from Susan. "What happened at the lawyer's office?"

"Dr. Mann, you know?" Susan blotted her eyes.

"Certainly. The head of the dental clinic," said Victoria.

"Grandmother left him three million dollars." Susan stopped and looked at Victoria.

"Good heavens." Victoria couldn't think of what to say. Finally she blurted out, "I had no idea your grandmother had that kind of money."

"Neither did we." Susan crumpled the paper towel in her hands. "We knew she was well to do, but three million to her *dentist*?

"Does that include her property?" Victoria asked.

"The three million was in her bank accounts. Grandmother gave me the house along with money for upkeep and taxes."

"That seems reasonable," said Victoria. "You were the one who lived with her during the past ten or so years. But Dr. Mann? And what about your siblings?"

"She gave five thousand dollars to each of us."

"Why three million dollars to Dr. Mann?"

Susan shrugged. "No one seems to know."

"If it weren't for the three million dollars, the five thousand to the four of you would have seemed quite generous," said Victoria. "Do you know why the disparity?"

Susan nodded and wiped her nose. "Heather and Grandmother never got along. She got into a big argument with Grandmother when she was a teenager."

"You were all teenagers at the time."

Susan nodded. "Grandmother never forgave her. Scott sided with Heather and Scott moved out and Heather and Wesley moved out a year or so later."

"And you stayed."

"I stayed."

"Your grandmother never tried to resolve their differences?"

Susan shook her head.

"Didn't she understand that Heather was undoubtedly just going through a teenage phase?"

"Grandmother didn't understand kids, period. She had one daughter. Our mother. After Mom was killed, Grandmother decided she was some kind of saint." Susan looked up. "Which she wasn't."

"Of course not. But I suppose that was your grandmother's way of handling grief."

"She regarded my brothers, Scott and Wesley, as clones of our father. Grandmother blamed him for the accident."

"Your mother was her only child, I seem to recall."

"There were hints about a baby who died in infancy or something. No one ever talked about it."

Neither spoke for a while.

Susan continued. "After the accident, we were just dumped on her. She wasn't exactly easy to live with, but then when you think of it, neither were we." Susan picked at the paper towel in her hands. "But we were children."

"And you'd lost both parents."

The teakettle whistled. Victoria got up and lifted down two mugs, tore open packets of hot chocolate mix and shook them out into the mugs. Added hot water. She got two spoons out of the drawer, one for each mug. And she thought about Susan and her brothers and sister and the three million dollars willed to the dentist. She thought of the circumstances of their grandmother's death.

The tragedy of it all.

She handed a steaming mug to Susan along with a spoon. "I didn't stir it."

"Thank you, Mrs. Trumbull." Susan held the cup up and let the steam rise around her face.

"An old house like your grandmother's is both priceless and worthless. It's a burden for you."

"The other three wanted to sell it, and the will makes sure they can't. We four have always had some rivalry. I guess that's normal, but . . ."

Victoria nodded.

"You can't imagine how nasty they're being."

"This is a difficult time for all of you."

Susan set her mug on the table and folded her hands around it. "They're desperate for money. All three of them."

"And resent you because you inherited the house."

Susan nodded. "For Grandmother the house was family. The other kids never understood." She took a graham cracker and snapped it in half. "It was more important to her than we were."

"I doubt that," said Victoria.

"It's true." Susan dipped the cracker into her hot chocolate and bit off the soggy end. "Grandmother had lived in that house all her life. She knew every creaking floorboard and sticking door, and the distinctive smells of each room."

Victoria smiled. "I understand that feeling."

"Our mother was brought up in that house."

Victoria sipped her cocoa and waited for Susan to say more.

"I love that house, Mrs. Trumbull. I'd been thinking that we four could turn it into an elegant inn. It's big enough and has that glorious view." Susan paused. "Fixing it up would be a way for us to get over our differences. But now it's caused so much trouble among us, I don't want to have anything to do with them."

"I'm sure their feelings will mellow in time."

"They're desperate. Scott's ex-wife took him for everything he owned. Wesley"—Susan looked away—"gambles and owes money to some unsavory characters. Heather's run up a half-dozen charge accounts buying clothes and stuff and owes so much on them she can't keep up with the interest payments."

"Good heavens," exclaimed Victoria.

"More than thirty thousand dollars."

Victoria pushed aside her mug. "That's hard to conceive of."

Susan put her elbows on the table and her head in her hands. "Grandmother told me she was going to change her will again. That was why she wanted us all together."

"Did she tell you how she planned to change it?"

"Not exactly. Occasionally, I'd go through her papers. Not really snooping, I mean, just when I needed some information."

"You couldn't help yourself."

"She planned to give everything to the Conservation Foundation."

"Everything?"

Susan nodded. "The house, the land, her money. I'd lived with her for twenty years. Cooked for her. Did her laundry. Drove her wherever she wanted to go." Susan looked up. "I'm working three part-time jobs. Taking care of her was a full-time job. All that time she'd assured me she was leaving the house and land to me." Susan crushed the graham cracker she was holding and crumbs dropped on the floor. She didn't seem to notice. "Then to change her will like that, cutting me out completely."

Victoria felt a twinge of discomfort and said nothing.

After a long pause, Susan sighed. "I don't think you can imagine how bad life with her was, Mrs. Trumbull."

While Susan was in West Tisbury talking to Victoria, the other three Wilmington grandchildren, Scott, Wesley, and Heather, sat on their grandmother's porch, eight miles away, sharing a large bottle of Scotch. The bottle, purchased shortly after the meeting with the lawyer, stood on the wicker table next to a cooler shaped like a Grecian funerary urn. It was now half empty.

"What's the matter with Sue?" asked Wesley, holding his glass up so the fading daylight gleamed through the amber liquid.

"She'd better stay away," muttered Heather, sitting on the porch swing. She gave a vicious push with her foot. "She's always been too good to be true. The way she manipulated Grandmother. Whatever dear Sue wanted, dear Sue got."

Scott had turned his chair to face the view of the sheep pasture and the sea beyond. He rested his feet on the porch railing, ankles crossed, and was cradling his half-full glass of Scotch on his stomach. "We guessed wrong, folks."

Wesley said, "Bet on the wrong horse."

"Not funny, Wes," said Heather.

"What are the chances they can track down the source of arsenic?" asked Wesley.

"Nil." Scott took another mouthful of Scotch and held it a few seconds before swallowing it. "Nil," he repeated. "Anybody can get hold of it without leaving tracks." He looked over his shoulder at his brother. "How come you're asking?"

"Just curious."

" 'Just curious'?" Scott repeated. "I hope I put your mind at ease, then."

"I've got enough stuff on my mind without worrying about the arsenic that killed Grandmother," Wesley said, "You know about legal stuff, Scott."

Scott snorted. "Right. So the goddamned ex took me for everything I had."

"What were you going to say, Wes?" asked Heather, slowing the swing and sitting forward.

"What are the chances of breaking the will?"

Scott shook his head. "Not a chance." His voice was slightly slurred. "In the first place, where do we get the money to pay some lawyer to challenge the will? You heard that broad."

"Don't call her a broad," said Heather.

"The old lady anticipated everything. Leaves something to us so we can't say she forgot us. Invested in us. Ha!" He took another sip of his Scotch. "That lawyer recorded every word we said. Iron-clad. Forget it." He finished up the last of his drink and tossed the ice cubes over the porch railing.

"What about Sue?" asked Heather.

"What about her?" Scott passed his glass to his brother, who poured another half glass full, dropped in a couple of ice cubes from the funerary urn, and handed the drink back to Scott.

"Suppose she predeceases us?" said Heather.

"Then we lose everything, even the goddamned use of the house," said Scott. "With Grandmother taken care of, why not Sweet Sue, eh?" He glanced over his shoulder at her.

Heather ignored the innuendo. "Suppose it's a natural death and she predeceases us?"

"How do you plan to arrange that?" asked Wesley. "Reading too many screenplay submissions."

Heather smiled.

Scott stirred his drink with a finger. "I don't recall hearing natural death mentioned. How do we arrange that?"

"What are we left with?" muttered Wesley. "Lifetime tenancy in this mausoleum? Who wants to live on this Island anyway."

"Darling Wesley," said Heather, "we're welcome to come here whenever dear Sue permits us to visit. Think of what that'll be like." She handed her glass to Wesley. "Fill 'er up, bro! If Sue dies a natural death, the house and land comes to us, right?"

"Let go of it," said Wesley.

"I've got to have money." Heather stamped her foot. "Not a measly five thousand dollars."

The sun set, flaming the long clouds that hovered over the ocean with vivid shades of orange and pink. Mosquitoes hummed.

"Time to go inside," said Scott. "Any mushroom stuff left?"

"We finished it yesterday at lunchtime, but there's a container of sautéed mushrooms Sue left in the fridge."

"Where is she?" asked Wesley.

"She went off on her bike," said Heather. "Come on, I'm starved. And to hell with Sue."

CHAPTER 23

At supper that evening, Victoria and Elizabeth were dining on clam chowder made with quahogs, potatoes, onions, salt pork, and milk. Elizabeth had worked a long day at the harbor and was still dressed in her harbor uniform.

"Susan Wilmington visited me this afternoon," said Victoria.

"What was her problem?" asked Elizabeth, scooping up a spoonful of chowder.

"Her grandmother's will was read today."

Elizabeth looked up from her bowl. "Yeah?"

"Dr. Mann was bequeathed three million dollars."

"Wow!" Elizabeth said. "Three million! To Dr. Mann? How come?"

"No one seems to know. The grandchildren were bequeathed five thousand dollars each."

"Five thousand to her grandkids and three million to her dentist? She must have hated her grandkids. Who gets the house?"

"Susan does."

"At least that makes a kind of sense. What do her siblings have to say? I wouldn't want to be around those four right now."

Victoria changed the subject. "What's happened to Lockwood?"

"Please, Gram. I'm eating." Elizabeth swallowed a last spoonful of her chowder.

"Junior Norton checked with the Steamship Authority," said

Victoria. "Lockwood brought his Jeep over about the time he called you, but there's no record of his leaving."

"He's playing his game. I was sure he'd show up any minute and didn't dare leave the house and of course he didn't show." Elizabeth pushed her bowl away. "The minute I relax, he'll do something unexpected. He knows a person can't continue with that level of fear." She stood and gathered up her grandmother's and her dishes. "I have to tell you, Gram, I'm scared. I know he's going to do something."

"Such as?" asked Victoria.

"Who knows? That's what's frightening."

"I'm not worried about myself," said Victoria. "I'm worried about you."

Elizabeth shook her head. "You're on his scope as much as I am. Lockwood is convinced you're keeping me from him."

"Ridiculous."

"Gram, you're not taking this seriously. Lockwood is crazy. I'm going upstairs to change."

Elizabeth took the bowls to the kitchen and Victoria gazed absently at the baskets hanging from the beams, wondering what to do about her once-loved former grandson-in-law.

After she left Victoria's house, Susan pedaled the eight miles from West Tisbury to the house she'd called home for more than half her life. Even her grandmother's demands didn't prevent the house from providing her sanctuary. She had her hideaways where her grandmother couldn't reach her.

Her bike ride was a time to think.

She'd been in the car that night. In the backseat. It seemed like a few days ago, not twenty years.

Her mother and father were arguing, one of their endless fights about money. They were coming back from celebrating her eleventh birthday at a grown-up restaurant. Supposedly a special treat for each of their birthdays. She hated it. Her father always drank too much and got all huggy and kissy and she hated the smell of his breath and his too-tight embrace.

Susan was so involved in her thoughts, she'd scarcely noticed how far she'd ridden. She braked at the Brandy Brow junction and looked both ways, left up the hill toward Alley's Store and right toward the cemetery.

Cemetery.

Her mind went back to that night, her eleventh birthday. She had covered her ears to block out her parents' argument. She hated everything about her birthday. The waitress treated her like a child. Her parents did their make-believe lovey-dovey stuff, patting each other, her mother leaning against her father. Her father ordering more drinks to celebrate her eleventh birthday when all she wanted to do was go home.

The lovey-dovey stuff ended in the car. They started one of their usual fights. How much her mother spent and how little her father earned. Her father even blamed her, eleven-year-old Susan, for going to the fancy restaurant that cost so much and that she hadn't wanted to go to in the first place.

Even with her ears covered, she heard her mother's shrill complaints about how much things cost, and her father's gruff retorts, "I know how much things cost. You obviously don't." And her mother saying, "You arrogant prick!" and shouting, "Slow down, you fool!" And her father shouting, "I'm trying to get away from the sound of your goddamned voice." And then her mother's scream, the sound of tires skidding, horns honking, time passing slowly, then—nothing.

This memory had come back over and over again during the years since the accident, like a tune you can't block out of your

146

mind. Would she never be free of the night of her eleventh birthday?

Without noticing the landmarks around her, she reached her grandmother's house. She leaned her bicycle against the shed where the mower was kept and looked up at the house.

She'd been afraid her grandmother had changed her will, as she'd threatened, but she hadn't, thank God. Grandmother was dead. Susan wasn't sorry. The house was hers. Finally. She'd earned it. Twenty lost years, catering to her grandmother.

She started toward the house, scuffing through the long dry grass that grew around it. This part of Chilmark didn't have good soil for gardening, and even though her grandmother was a member of the Garden Club, she had never done any gardening. With compost and manure, Susan would have a garden now. A beautiful garden surrounding a quaint and expensive country inn.

She pulled up a long stem of the straw-like grass and chewed on it as she walked. Why had Grandmother bequeathed three million to the dentist? She kicked the dry earth, releasing a cloud of dust. Probably to turn her siblings against her. It would be just like her to reach out from the grave to manipulate their feelings.

She glanced down the pasture at the sea, steel blue at this time of late day. Long orange and pink clouds stretched across the horizon. Maybe she could convince her sibs that they could be partners, not equal partners, but still . . .

With this in mind, she climbed up the porch steps. When she saw the empty glasses on the porch railing, on the swing, and on the wicker table next to the empty Scotch bottle—a large bottle—she stopped.

The accident came back to her as it always did when her siblings drank. Drinking. Arguing. The screech of brakes. Death.

She turned away. No way could she take them on as partners.

And now, she couldn't stay here when they'd had too much to drink. She'd return to Mrs. Trumbull's.

First, though, she'd go up to her secret place on the hillside, rest a bit, and think. She wheeled her bike partway up the hill and leaned it against a huckleberry bush, then continued to her hideaway. From there, she could see the ocean, stretching so far away it was hard to imagine so much water. From the time she had first visited her grandmother as a little girl, she had dreamed about sailing to the horizon and beyond. How long would it take to reach land on the far side of the sea? She sat down on a cushion of soft moss. Would it take a month? More? What would it be like to see nothing but blue water stretching to the horizon surrounding you in all directions? She sighed and pulled up another grass stem to chew. She would rest a bit, then wait until darkness set in before heading off to Mrs. Trumbull's. No way could she face those drunk siblings.

As she stood up and brushed off the dried moss from the dark slacks she had worn to the lawyer's office, she had a sudden thought—the mushrooms, the ink caps she'd sautéed earlier, Tippler's Bane, they were called. If her sibs saw them in the fridge and ate them . . .

Well, it would serve them right if they did.

But if they'd drunk as much as that empty half-gallon bottle indicated, might they die? Should she warn them?

No. She shook her head. They probably hadn't eaten the mushrooms. Even if they did, they'd only have horrible hangovers. As she moved away from her hideaway, the night was pitch-black with only starlight to illuminate her path.

She retrieved her bike from the huckleberry bush. She knew every curve and dip on South Road, and once she was on it, car lights would show up a long time before a car came near.

CHAPTER 24

Wesley stumbled onto the porch and shook the sand out of his boat shoes. The bright sunset clouds had turned a deep purple and the sky was pale pink where it met the straight line of the sea. Wind picked up and the long grass next to the house rustled, scraping against the shingles. Stars began to prick holes in the sky.

He felt dizzy. The sky, the stars, the world reeled around him. He reached clumsily for the table and knocked it over. A glass fell, bounced, and rolled off the porch.

He called back into the house, "Nothing broke!" He slipped his shoes on and went back into the house. "Funny thing," he said. "I thought I saw Sue's bicycle go down the drive."

Heather swayed unsteadily. "So what?"

Scott came out of the kitchen holding a spatula in one hand. "Set a place for Sue, Wes."

"We got to eat somethin'," said Heather, bracing herself against the wall.

Wesley, equally unsteady on his feet, laid out four linen place-mats from the drawer where their grandmother always kept them. Set out in crooked lines the silverware and the linen napkins they'd used as children.

Scott, back in the kitchen, stood at the stove, stirring something in a cast-iron spider, their grandmother's frying pan. He'd tucked a dish towel into his belt.

"What's cookin'?" asked Wesley.

"Mushroom gravy." Scott continued to stir. "You capable of watching the steak, Heathe?"

Heather grunted. " 'Course."

Scott held up a bottle of Merlot. "Someone uncork this. Anyone for a glass or two?"

"Not me," said Heather, leaning against the table. "I don't feel so good."

"I'm drunk," said Wesley, dropping into a chair, his legs splayed out.

Scott gave the gravy a final stir and turned off the stove. "How's the steak coming along, Heather?"

She jumped up with a small cry and darted into the kitchen, bent down, and opened the broiler door. Smoke poured out. "Jusht right."

"Hate overdone steak," said Wesley.

"It's okay," said Scott, pulling the steak out of the broiler.

"She's inheriting a white elephant," said Wesley. "Who wants a white elephant?"

Scott passed him the carving knife.

"Not me," said Heather with a giggle. "I've got a pink elephant!"

"Sue wants a cute country inn," said Wesley. "Family run."

"Might work," said Scott, scraping the gravy out of the cast-iron pan into a china gravy boat.

"Get willed a lemon, make lemonade?" Heather giggled again.

"Does upkeep include renovation of this pile?" Wesley waved the carving knife at the walls. "I need money now." He flourished the knife at the steak. "I don't have a penny to invest in some damned renovation."

"Give me the knife," said Scott.

"I'm going to carve," said Wesley.

"I need money more than you do," said Heather. She sank back into her chair. "Can we borrow on Sue's credit?" She held her hand up as he passed the gravy boat to her. "No thanks."

"You're asking *me* for advice?" Scott pointed at his chest and laughed. "Ask my ex. She knows all the angles. Give me that knife, before you hurt someone, and let me have the Merlot, Wes."

Wesley passed the bottle to Scott, who opened it with a professional twirl. "Change your mind, anyone?"

"Brrr," said Heather, shaking her head vigorously. "If our sister predeceases us—"

"Cut that out, Heather," said Wesley.

"You've got the knife, silly. You cut it out." Heather got up unsteadily and staggered away from the table. "I'm goin' to bed."

Scott took the carving knife from Wesley and carved himself a strip of steak. "Scorched on the outside, bloodred on the inside. Cooked just right." He lifted the knife and examined the blade. "Mildred always kept her knives sharp." He set it down on the table. "Wonder if the good doctor knew in advance about the three million." He sloshed gravy over his steak, the mushrooms forming dark islands on the red meat, and held out the gravy boat to Wesley.

"I pass." Wesley touched his stomach gently and rose. "Too much to drink. Got to step outside." He made for the door.

Susan mounted her bicycle and followed the dark rutted drive the half mile to where it met South Road. She was about to turn right toward West Tisbury, when headlights flashed suddenly and a Jeep turned into the drive. The driver apparently didn't see her, because as he turned sharply into the sandy road, the rear slewed toward her and smacked into her handlebars. Her bike toppled into the underbrush by the side of the road and she landed heavily, her legs, feet, and arm tangled in the frame and spokes.

"Hey!" She cried out, but the driver was too far away to hear.

She unwound herself and got to her feet. Her arm hurt and she touched it gently. Blood oozed from a tear in her sweatshirt.

She sat on the sandy bank next to her bike. Should she go back to the house? She recalled the empty Scotch bottle. It was so unfair. Tears of self-pity welled up and she rubbed her eyes with her shoulders. And who was this Jeep driver visiting the three up at the house? The guy Heather met on the ferry? She didn't want to confront him.

And then she thought of Mrs. Trumbull. She'd remembered that long ago bicycle accident. A perfect excuse to go back to her house. Kind of full circle.

Susan got up unsteadily, slipped on the sandy bank, and came down hard on her bottom. This brought on more tears. Finally, she pulled herself together and tugged her bicycle out from the weeds. It would be just her luck to have landed in a poison ivy patch. She mounted the bike and tried to pedal. The front wheel was bent.

"Damn!"

She shoved the wrecked bike back into the undergrowth, brushed sand off herself as best she could, and limped the few feet to the side of South Road.

Within a few minutes vehicle lights approached from her left and she stuck out her thumb. The way things were going, it would probably be a serial killer who'd pick her up.

A truck stopped. She could see a light-colored dog in the passenger seat. The driver leaned over the dog and opened the window. He was wearing a faded baseball cap with lettering she couldn't make out.

"Where you heading?" he asked.

"West Tisbury?" said Susan, her voice quavering. "Mrs. Trumbull's?"

"Get in."

She opened the passenger door and climbed into the seat next to the dog.

"That's Taffy." He pointed to himself. "I'm Joe." He glanced over at her. "You one of the Wilmington kids?"

"I'm Susan." She put an arm around the dog. It was too dark to make out much about Joe. He looked familiar, though, and she realized she'd seen him on the porch at Alley's Store. "You're the plumber, aren't you?"

"That's me." Before he started up, he examined her more carefully. "Looks like you been in a fight. What did you do to deserve that?" He shifted a wad of something in his mouth.

"A car hit my bike," said Susan. "The driver didn't see me."

"Shouldn't be riding a bike this time of night. Roads are dark as death. You want to go to the hospital?"

She shook her head. "I'll be okay. Do you know where Mrs. Trumbull lives?"

"Who doesn't?" said Joe, shifting into gear.

CHAPTER 25

Lockwood had felt a slight bump when he turned onto the dirt road that led to the house of the woman he'd started to think of as "Heather the Heiress." He was glad he drove a Jeep. These sandy Island roads could be pretty rough on a car. Better slow down, though.

The road was about a half mile long, and it was pitch-black. The moon wouldn't be up for another hour or so. The house was lit up as though for a grand celebration. He smiled to himself as he parked in the pasture across from the front porch. As he went up the steps to the porch he saw the empty bottle. Yet another good sign.

He knocked on the door, waited only briefly for a response, and when none came, entered. That's how things work on the Island, he thought. People just walk into other people's houses.

Instead of the party he anticipated, he saw only a guy who was probably the older brother sitting at the dining room table alone. The table was set for four people.

"Hello!" said Lockwood cheerfully.

Scott looked up. "Hello yourself. Who in hell are you?"

"Woody. Want to offer condolences and congratulations."

"What in hell you talking about?"

"I'm the one who brought your sister home yesterday. Understood your grandmother's will was read today."

Scott glared at him.

Lockwood cleared his throat. "Also, I wanted to make sure she's okay after her dental work."

"Dental work?" said Scott looking alarmed.

"Sorry," said Lockwood, feeling, for one of the few times in his life, totally confused. "I know about your grandmother. Didn't mean to be insensitive. Your sister and I met on the ferry, and she was coming back from the dentist."

"I know, I know." Scott had both elbows on the table and was facing a plate loaded with food—steak slathered with gravy and a good-looking salad. He was eyeing a glass of red wine.

"Where's Heather?" asked Lockwood.

"She didn't feel so good. Too much to drink."

"I suppose you're all celebrating?"

"What in hell are you talking about, buddy? We have nothing to celebrate."

Lockwood was puzzled. "I thought the will was read today."

Scott emitted a short bark. "It was."

"You must be feeling pretty good about it."

Scott leaned back. "Pretty good! Pretty shitty, you mean. She cut us out."

"Completely?" asked Lockwood, pulling up a chair in front of a place setting. "Your grandmother cut you out of her will?"

"Left us five thousand bucks each." Scott looked up, bleary eyed. "I owe eighty grand. How do you think I feel?"

Lockwood didn't know what to say. He picked up the fork at the place setting and twisted it around in his hand.

"You hungry?" said Scott, suddenly. "There's plenty of steak. No one has any appetite. Mushroom gravy. Salad. You might as well help yourself."

"I guess you could use some company," said Lockwood, feeling disappointed himself.

"Want a drink?"

"No, thanks," said Lockwood.

"Well, help yourself," said Scott again, waving a hand toward the kitchen.

Lockwood went into the kitchen with the plate, carved a large slab of meat, nicely browned on the outside, rare inside, poured a generous amount of mushroom gravy, a favorite of his, over the steak, helped himself to salad, and returned to the table.

"You must be Scott," said Lockwood.

Elbows still on the table, Scott offered one of the hands with which he'd been holding his chin. "The same. And you are?"

"Woody," said Lockwood. "Food looks mighty good. You'd better dig in yourself."

"Might as well." Scott sat back and picked up his knife with his right hand, his fork with his left, and started in. He glanced up. "Help yourself to wine."

"One glass," said Lockwood. "Got to be sharp for something I've got to do tonight."

"Suit yourself."

Lockwood sliced off a chunk of steak, loaded it with gravy, and carried it to his mouth. He chewed. "This gravy is something special." He sipped his wine.

"Field mushrooms," said Scott. "My sister sautéed 'em. I made the gravy."

"I never trust wild mushrooms," said Lockwood. "But I guess even amateurs can identify the field variety." He finished up the steak he'd taken, sipped his wine, mopped up the last bit of gravy with a slice of bread, and sat back.

Scott was still working on his steak. He waved his fork at Lockwood. "Go ahead. Help yourself to more. Those two aren't going to want any."

"Two?" asked Lockwood. "Thought there were four of you."

"Sister Sue didn't show up."

Lockwood pushed his chair back and stood. "Guess I'll take you up on that. Okay if I finish up that gravy?"

"Be my guest," said Scott. "Have another glass of wine."

"Don't mind if I do," said Lockwood.

The evening was cool, and Victoria and Elizabeth were in the parlor with their evening drinks, the fire blazing cheerfully. So cheerfully that Victoria, wearing her usual gray corduroy trousers and rosebud-printed turtleneck shirt, opened the west window to let in some of the cool night air.

Someone knocked on the entry door.

Victoria checked her watch. "It's late for a caller."

"I'll see who it is." Elizabeth returned shortly with Susan Wilmington.

"Another bicycle accident?" Victoria smiled. Then she noticed Susan's torn and bloody shirt and lifted herself out of her mouse-colored wing chair. "What happened?"

"A bike accident," said Susan. "I'm back for more graham crackers and comforting."

"We'll take care of your injuries, then you can tell us what happened," Victoria said. "Follow me. There's a first-aid kit in the bathroom."

There, Susan eased her sweatshirt over her head exposing an injury that wasn't serious. Victoria poured peroxide on it, dabbed the area dry with sterile cotton, and covered it with a large Band-Aid. Elizabeth rinsed the bloodied shirt in cold water and put it in the washing machine.

"What happened to your bicycle?" asked Victoria.

Susan explained how she was sideswiped by a Jeep.

"A Jeep?" asked Elizabeth. "Could you tell what color it was?"

"It was too dark to make out the color. Dark, not light, though."

When Susan was patched up, Victoria led the way back to the parlor. "You're welcome to hot chocolate again," she said, "but perhaps you'd rather have something stronger. We're drinking cranberry juice and rum."

"Sounds better than hot chocolate," said Susan, settling herself onto the couch.

Elizabeth put another log on the fire, sending a shower of sparks up the chimney.

"What happened to your bicycle?" Victoria asked.

"The front wheel is bent. I left it in the underbrush by the side of Grandmother's road. Joe, the plumber . . . ?" She looked questioningly at Elizabeth.

Elizabeth nodded. "We know Joe."

"Well, he picked me up at the end of the drive and brought me here."

"We can take you home, when you're ready to go," said Elizabeth. "Could you tell anything about the Jeep or driver?"

"It happened so fast, I couldn't make out any numbers on the license plate, but it wasn't a Massachusetts plate."

"Have you had supper?" Victoria asked.

Susan shook her head. "I wasn't hungry."

"Is there any chowder left, Elizabeth?"

"Plenty." Elizabeth got to her feet. "I'll warm it up."

"Can I help?" asked Susan.

"Get yourself a drink," said Victoria.

Lockwood took his plate into the kitchen and left it by the sink. Scott had returned to brooding. Elbows on the table, head on his hands, his unfinished plate of food in front of him.

Lockwood paused at the table. "Anything I can do for you before I leave, old man?"

"Just leave," muttered Scott.

"Thanks for a great meal."

"Umpf," said Scott.

"Nothing like local food," said Lockwood.

Scott said nothing.

"I'll see you around, then," said Lockwood.

Scott flipped a few fingers at him in a farewell gesture.

"If there's nothing else I can do for you except eat your excellent supper, I'll be off."

Lockwood stepped out onto the porch and the crisp night. He looked up at the starry sky. He could make out stars clear to the horizon. Nothing like what he'd see in Washington. Again, he felt deprived of his share of this Island, with its stars and mushrooms. The starlight was bright enough so he could see the endless sweep of the Atlantic at the foot of the meadow. The sea was a mirrored plain that reflected millions of stars. Was it the ancient Greeks who believed the sky was a blanket with holes in it that let through starlight? He could understand. Looking up at the great Milky Way marking the edge of the galaxy, Lockwood felt as one with the universe, a sense that brought him pleasure. It was there for him and him alone.

He'd made a mistake thinking of Heather the heiress, but tomorrow was another day. He had Elizabeth to think about now.

He was reluctant to leave this majestic scene, silent except for the steady drumming of surf. From here, the sound blurred into a murmur, a throbbing he could feel in his feet. From the far side of the pasture a lamb bleated.

He started up the Jeep and turned into the rutted drive. He'd head back to West Tisbury, check on Elizabeth.

He'd lucked out again with that supper. Three helpings of steak and gravy. Those tasty wild mushrooms are nothing like the ones you buy in the store.

He headed away from the house down the drive, careful not to hit that bump again before he turned onto South Road.

CHAPTER 26

By the time Susan had finished her supper and was ready to leave, the evening had become downright chilly. Victoria closed the west window, put on her heavy sweater, and they headed for the car.

When they reached the Mill Pond, a ground fog had filled the slight valley. Streamers of mist drifted in front of them, writhing and twisting in the headlights. Elizabeth turned on the windshield wipers.

Susan, in the backseat, shivered.

Victoria turned to her. "Are you warm enough?"

"I'm fine. It's the way that mist swirls around."

"We often get fog in low places where the water is warmer than the air," said Victoria. "It makes familiar landmarks seem mysterious."

They passed out of the fog and the familiar slope of Brandy Brow was on their left. The windshield wipers squeaked and Elizabeth switched them off.

They had crossed the town line between West Tisbury and Chilmark when a Jeep came toward them.

"Lockwood!" Elizabeth said over her shoulder, "Could you tell, was that the Jeep that hit you, Susan?"

"Can't tell."

"Would he recognize our car?" asked Victoria.

"He's one of those guys who knows every make of car, who owns it, and what it cost," said Elizabeth.

"Who's Lockwood?" asked Susan.

"Elizabeth's former husband," said Victoria. "He wants to restore their relationship and that's not necessarily in Elizabeth's best interest."

"Oh." Susan sat back. Abruptly she sat forward again. "Yesterday, my sister Heather met a guy named Woody on the ferry. He gave her a ride home in his Jeep."

Elizabeth glanced in the rearview mirror where Susan was reflected. "Which ferry?"

"She got home a little after five, so it must have been the three forty-five ferry."

"Oh, my God!" said Elizabeth.

"What's the matter?" asked Susan

Victoria answered. "We were waiting for Lockwood to show up at our house and he never did."

"He will, Gram, believe me, he will."

No one spoke again until they reached the turnoff to Susan's grandmother's house.

"We might as well pick up your bike," said Elizabeth, slowing to make the turn.

"Thanks. Yes. Good idea."

Elizabeth stopped and put the top down on the convertible and they stowed the bicycle in the backseat along with Susan.

"I wonder what he was doing here this evening?" said Elizabeth.

"My sister gave him her cell phone number, but the cell reception is so poor, he probably decided to call on her."

Victoria turned in her seat and asked, "Are you warm enough back there?"

"I'm okay. It's not much farther."

They saw the lights of the house long before they reached it.

"Looks like a celebration," said Victoria.

"More like mourning," said Susan.

They maneuvered the bike out of the car, Susan thanked them for supper and the bike transport, bid them good night, and trundled the bike on its good wheel toward the barn.

Elizabeth was putting the top back up when Susan returned from putting her bike away.

"Do you need help?" she asked.

"I'm fine," said Elizabeth. "Won't take me more than a couple of minutes more."

"Well, thanks again and good night, then." Susan went up the porch steps slowly.

Elizabeth was snapping a side latch into place when Susan came dashing back down the steps.

"Wait!" she called out. "Something's wrong with Scott! A heart attack! He's flushed and gasping and can't talk. Can you call 911?"

Elizabeth reached into her pocket and brought out her phone. "I'm not getting a signal."

"What about the house phone?" asked Victoria.

"We don't have one."

Victoria moved out of the car quickly, went carefully up the porch steps, and into the house. Scott was standing outside the dining room, bent over, face twisted in agony.

"Can you talk?" she asked.

He shook his head.

Elizabeth and Susan had followed Victoria and were standing behind her.

"We'll take you to the hospital," said Victoria. "Can you walk?"

He stumbled toward her.

"Get him into the car," Victoria said. "Keep trying to get a signal on your phones, and when you do, call 911. The ambulance can meet us and get him to the hospital faster than we can."

Once Scott was in the backseat, Susan climbed in next to him. Elizabeth drove, cornering onto South Road with a screech of tires on sand, and sped down-Island. As they dipped into the valley that marked the West Tisbury town line, the car swooped and lifted as if they were about to take off into the night sky.

Scott groaned.

"I've got a signal." Susan punched in 911 and gave the operator information about Scott and their location.

When they reached the Mill Pond, they heard a distant siren and Elizabeth turned on the emergency flashers. The Tri-Town Ambulance pulled out of Old County Road, stopped in front of them, and two EMTs, a slender young man and an equally slender young woman, got out.

Elizabeth unlatched the convertible's top. "Easier to get him out with the top down."

"Right," said the man.

The lights of the ambulance swept across Scott's face. His eyes were closed.

The EMTs lifted him out of the convertible, onto a wheeled stretcher, and into the ambulance.

"One of you want to ride with him?" asked the driver.

"I do." Susan climbed into the back, and the ambulance took off.

"We needn't follow," said Victoria. "The fewer people around the better. We'll find out soon enough."

As they turned into Victoria's drive, Elizabeth said, "Everything happened so fast, it didn't occur to me until now. Where were Wesley and Heather?"

"You're right. They need to know about their brother. We'd better go back."

———

Lockwood parked his Jeep behind the youth hostel and hiked the short distance along the bike path to Victoria's house. He thought again about what he would do.

He'd recognized Elizabeth's car, of course, heading in the direction of the Wilmington's. Whether that was their destination or not, he figured he'd have time to prowl around the house a bit. By rights, his house, he told himself.

An overhanging branch brushed his face and with an angry gesture he snapped it off and flung it to the side of the path.

Victoria had trusted him. If it hadn't been for lies Elizabeth must have told her grandmother, she would have turned the house over to his care. He respected the house. He'd have taken care of Victoria.

His flashlight picked up a slight movement by the side of the path, and he shone the beam around until it picked up a black creature, the size of a cat. Two white stripes stood out, almost fluorescent in the light. A skunk. He stopped. The skunk moved its head back and forth as though looking for something, then shambled across the path only a couple of feet from him. He waited until the skunk disappeared into the undergrowth, and then continued his walk. The path dipped down into the small valley and he was almost at his goal.

The front door was always latched, he knew. A northeast wind would blow it open otherwise. The other doors were never locked. He'd enter through the south door. They wouldn't expect that. Then, and he laughed at the thought, he'd unlatch the front door and when he heard them coming, he'd exit that way. That would puzzle them, the unlatched front door.

When he was in the house he'd do something simple but baffling. Move some of Elizabeth's underwear from her bureau drawer into Victoria's.

The house was on the opposite side of the road. He crossed over and circled to the back, past the kitchen windows, still lit, apparently waiting for their return. He smelled smoke from the parlor fire and felt a flicker of anger as he thought he should be sitting by it, discussing local politics with Victoria while Elizabeth prepared supper.

A frisson of excitement ran through him as he thought about their return. Elizabeth wouldn't realize anyone had been in the house, even in her bedroom, and probably not for a day or two.

Lockwood was upstairs humming to himself when he saw the headlights of a car turn into the drive. Trapped. A surge of adrenaline kicked in. The car slowed, stopped, then continued on out of the drive and headed up-Island.

That was puzzling. Where were they going? Wherever it was, he was almost done. He'd taken three pairs of Elizabeth's cotton panties and stashed them under Victoria's more sedate underthings.

He was humming an irritating piece of music.

It would take Elizabeth a few days to discover the missing items, and Victoria a few days to find them.

He'd been listening to Ravel's *Boléro* on the Cape Cod classical music station and it had insinuated itself into his head. That's what he was humming. The repetitive theme ran through his brain, faster and faster. He hated that music. Monotonous. Why did they have to play that particular piece at this particular time?

He slipped downstairs and out the unlatched front door. He pushed it shut firmly behind him.

Dum! dum dum dum dum dum dum, Dum, dum-dum-dum!

The man must have been insane when he composed it.

CHAPTER 27

Elizabeth turned the car around in the drive and retraced their route to the Wilmington house. No streetlights marred the night's blackness. No cars approached.

"What do you think, Gram? Scott's symptoms didn't seem typical of a heart attack. That awful grimace. And vomiting? And he's my age, early thirties."

Victoria shook her head. "I don't know."

They crossed the town line, again. Their headlights picked up gray lichened stone walls on either side of the road and touched the bright leaves of beech trees. Theirs was the only car on the road. It was as though they were the only humans for miles around. In a few weeks the season would start, and things would be different.

A deer suddenly leaped the stone wall to their right and darted across the road in front of them. Victoria braced her hands on the dashboard. Elizabeth braked and the car stalled. The deer, followed by two spotted fawns, disappeared into the woods on the other side.

"That was close," said Victoria. "I'd hate to hit them."

Elizabeth started the car again. "I have trouble thinking of them as pests, but that's what they are. Mice are cute, too."

The open rolling pastures of Chilmark were dark forms in the night that blended into the darker sky. In a short time, they turned left onto the dirt road that led to the Wilmington's.

The house looked no different from the way it had when they'd rushed Scott away an hour before. Lights still blazed in the upstairs windows. The front door was open, the way they'd left it when they'd half carried him down the porch steps.

Victoria climbed the steps, holding the railing tightly, and knocked on the frame of the open door. "Hello! Anybody home?"

No answer.

Elizabeth joined her grandmother. "What now?"

"We need to make sure they're all right."

In the dining room, part of Scott's steak, bathed in congealed gravy, was still on the table. The mushrooms were unappetizing black lumps.

"I'll take his plate with us to let the doctor know what he'd been eating," said Victoria.

"Not exactly a heart-healthy meal, I guess."

"You check the parlor," said Victoria. "I'll go upstairs."

"I'll go," said Elizabeth, but Victoria was already on her way up, holding the banister firmly.

"Hello!" she called when she reached the second floor. "Anybody here?"

No answer.

She had no trouble finding her way around, since every light in the house seemed to be on. There were two open doors, one to her left, one to her right. She went into the room on the right.

The room was large and brightly lit. A king-size bed dominated the space. Heather, sprawled out in the middle, looked petite on the huge bed, although she was as well built as her sister.

"Heather?" said Victoria softly. "Heather, can you hear me?"

Heather's eyes were closed.

"Are you all right?" Victoria reached over the wide bed and took hold of Heather's wrist. The wrist was warm and Victoria could feel a steady pulse.

"Heather, wake up," Victoria said, shaking the wrist she still held. "Wake up!"

Heather mumbled, "Shouldn't've drunk so much."

"Your brother's sick. He's in the hospital. Get up!"

Heather opened her eyes a small crack and examined Victoria.

"You need to sober up. Get to the shower," Victoria ordered.

Heather edged around the bed, holding on to bedposts and chairs. "Everything's spinning around."

"Where's Wesley?"

"Over there." Heather pointed vaguely.

"Can you take a shower yourself, or must I undress you?"

"Yeah, yeah. I'll take a shower."

Elizabeth was already in the room across the hall, trying to awaken Wesley.

"He's drunk," said Elizabeth.

"We'd better take them to the hospital. The problem may be something they and their brother ate."

"I'll make coffee," said Elizabeth.

It took a half hour before the sister and brother could be settled in the backseat of Elizabeth's car. The trip to the hospital seemed endless. Elizabeth opened her window wide. "Hope you don't mind, Gram."

"Not at all," said Victoria, opening her own window.

At the Emergency Room parking lot, she looked at the two in the backseat. Wesley's head was pressed firmly against the metal brace of the convertible's top, his mouth open, and he was snoring. Heather's head rested on Wesley's shoulder. A string of drool looped from the corner of her mouth.

Victoria eased herself out of the passenger seat. "I'll go in. You wait with them."

The automatic doors of the Emergency Room made way for her. At the desk, a tall doctor with thinning blond hair was studying charts. A stethoscope hung around his neck. He looked up and grinned.

"Mrs. Trumbull. Your toe bothering you?"

She shook her head. "I've brought Scott's sister and brother. They're not in the best condition themselves."

"Same symptoms as their brother?" he asked, concerned.

"I don't know."

Susan, who'd been pacing in the waiting area, rushed over to Victoria. "I'm so glad you're here."

"We've brought Scott and Heather and the remains of their dinner, or at least his dinner, in case it turns out it's something they ate. Steak with mushroom gravy."

Susan put her hands up to her mouth. "Oh, no!"

"Is something the matter?"

Susan turned away. "I left some sautéed ink caps in the refrigerator."

"Ink caps? Tippler's Bane?" asked Victoria.

Susan didn't answer.

Chapter 28

While Victoria and Elizabeth were at the hospital with the Wilmington grandchildren, and while Lockwood was snooping around Victoria's house, Dr. Mann and Dr. McBride were seated at one of the booths at Offshore Ale. A basket of peanuts and glasses of India pale ale were on the table in front of them. She was wearing another green silk blouse that was the same color as her eyes.

"I suppose we should really be drinking champagne, Horace," said Aileen, holding up her glass in a toast.

"It would be premature to celebrate, Aileen. In a case of death by other than natural causes, like this, any bequest—"

Aileen interrupted and placed a soft hand over his. "Don't say it, Horace. It's too, too horrible to consider." She withdrew her hand and held her glass up to her lips. "I have nightmares about that horrible, horrible day. I'd heard she had a weak heart. I never realized arsenic had such an awful effect."

"What effect did you think it had?" asked Horace, setting down his glass.

"Please, don't say anything more about it." She set her own glass down. "Just tell me this. Why did Mrs. Wilmington leave you all that money?"

He smiled. "She was a great supporter of my clinic."

"There are other dentists on the Island. And I hate to say this, but some of them are better dentists than you are."

"That's why I run a clinic. I hire the best."

Aileen pouted. "Demetrios?"

"Come, now, Aileen." He reached into the basket for a peanut, snapped it open, and tossed the shells onto the floor. "Dr. Demetrios is an excellent periodontist. One of the best in New England." He flipped the peanuts into his mouth.

"She's hardly a soothing presence. She was telling poor Mrs. Trumbull how she extracted the tooth of a Bengal tiger."

Horace laughed. "Poor Mrs. Trumbull, indeed!"

Aileen moved her frosted glass around in circles in the ring of moisture on the varnished table. "I don't understand what you and Mrs. Wilmington had going between you. Three million dollars? Did you know she had that kind of money?"

Horace snapped open another peanut. "It was rumored."

Aileen opened her blue eyes wide. "You did know, didn't you? Did you know she was leaving it to you?"

"Aileen, my dear, let's order. Their hamburgers are superb."

While the doctors Horace Mann and Aileen McBride were ordering hamburgers at Offshore Ale, the doctors Ophelia Demetrios and Sam Minnowfish were dressing their hamburgers with ketchup and mustard at the Black Dog Tavern. They were seated on the enclosed porch overlooking Vineyard Haven harbor, a dark mirror reflecting lights from the departing ferry.

"Mrs. Wilmington, what was she thinking?" said Ophelia, squeezing out an angry burst of ketchup. "Three million dollars to our Horace? So much money."

Sam Minnowfish took the ketchup from her, dosed his own hamburger, and said, "Well—"

"He has the personality of, how do you say it, a turtle." She slapped the top of the bun onto her burger. "And his mind . . ." she shrugged.

"Didn't realize turtles had personalities," said Sam, around a mouthful of hamburger.

"Why?" Ophelia took back the ketchup bottle. "Why did she leave all that money to Horace?"

"Uniforms. Women go for uniforms in a big way." Sam set his burger down on the plate and took a swig of beer. He wiped his mouth on a paper napkin.

"Uniform? What do you mean?"

"That crisp white lab coat," said Minnowfish. "Girls find it sexy as hell. Why I went into dentistry."

"You mustn't talk like that, Sam." Ophelia cut her hamburger in half with sharp jabs. "The Island. He was born here?"

Sam nodded. "Born and raised here. Couple of years ahead of me at the high school."

Ophelia pushed the two halves of her hamburger apart. "His family, are they from the Island?"

"He's adopted, you know." Sam took another bite and red meat juice ran down his chin. He wiped it with a paper napkin.

"Yes. He makes no secret of it. His birth parents. Do we know who they are?"

"Nothing's secret on this Island." He wadded up the napkin and dropped it onto the table.

"You didn't answer me."

Sam shrugged.

Ophelia leaned forward. "Well, who are these people who adopted him?"

"Newcomers. Came over on the boat."

Ophelia sat back. "The way Horace acts, I thought his family came over on the *Mayflower.*"

"That's the boat." Sam grinned. "They've only been in this country a few hundred years." He thumped his chest. "Not like my family."

173

"Ah, Sam. You are a mongrel like all Americans."

"Arf! Arf!" said Sam, and took another bite of his burger.

At the hospital, orderlies wheeled Heather and Wesley into the Emergency Room. Both were protesting loudly. Heather's long blond hair was still wet from her shower. Except for that, the two looked reasonably put together, still dressed in the jeans and T-shirts they'd worn earlier.

Victoria held the plate containing the remains of Scott's dinner.

Susan rolled and unrolled a magazine she'd been reading and watched as the wheelchairs were taken into an examining room. "Where's the doctor? I suppose I should tell him about the mushrooms."

"He's in there." A tall, slim nurse wearing a blue scrub suit came out of the examining room carrying a sheaf of papers. She nodded toward the room. When she saw Victoria, she looked concerned. "Auntie Vic! What are you doing here?"

Victoria explained to her grandniece, Hope, about Scott's seizure and his brother's and sister's conditions. Hope fanned herself with her papers. "I could get high on the exhaust fumes from those two. They're drunk."

"I don't know," said Victoria. "I brought in the remains of Scott's meal." She handed the plastic-covered plate to Hope, who lifted a corner of the wrap.

"Steak?"

"Mushroom gravy," Susan said, "I'm pretty sure they used ink caps that I'd left in the fridge."

"I'll tell the doc. Did all three eat the mushrooms?"

"There were two used plates," said Victoria.

At that point, Wesley and Heather were wheeled back into the waiting area followed by Doc Yablonsky. He was the tall man in his late fifties with thinning blond hair. He nodded at Victoria. "How's your sore toe?"

"My toe is fine," she said. "I'm here with Scott's sister and brother."

"It's not Scott's heart!" Heather protested loudly. "He played football in high school."

"Ath-a-letes get ath-a-lete's foot." Wesley guffawed.

"Feet," said Heather.

"Oh, shut up," snapped Susan.

Heather pouted. "Rich bitch."

"The mushrooms in the gravy may be ink caps, what they call Tippler's Bane," said Hope. "Did they have supper?"

Dr. Yablonsky shook his head. "They had nothing to eat."

"There was a second plate," said Victoria. "Which one used it? Someone did."

The doc checked the papers on his clipboard. "Neither Heather nor Wesley had anything to eat. They overdid the cocktails and will probably have serious hangovers tomorrow."

"They were trying to drown their sorrows," said Susan.

"They almost succeeded," said Hope. "What's their problem?"

"You don't want to know."

The doctor turned to Susan. "Your brother apparently is suffering from alcohol poisoning. The mushrooms contain a substance that blocks the metabolism of alcohol."

Susan nodded and looked away.

"Do any of you know how much Scott had to drink?"

"There was an empty Scotch bottle on the porch table when I got home," Susan said. "A half gallon they bought this afternoon."

He tapped his pen on the clipboard. "The three finished off the entire bottle?"

Susan shrugged. "The Scotch bottle was empty and Scott had a half-empty bottle of wine in front of him."

"I don't know if we were able to get rid of enough alcohol. Our technician is identifying the mushrooms he ate." He looked up as a stocky woman with thick glasses strode toward them and handed a paper to the doctor.

"*Coprinopsis*," she said, and told them what they already knew about the mushroom.

Susan leaned against the desk. "What about Scott?"

"Alcohol is absorbed quickly into the bloodstream and the liver needs about an hour to metabolize alcohol in one drink," said Dr. Yablonsky. "If metabolism is blocked . . ." He didn't finish.

"Will he die?" asked Susan.

He tapped his pen against his clipboard. "It depends on how much he had to drink and how much we were able to wash out of his stomach before the alcohol got into his bloodstream."

"I knew about the mushrooms." Susan looked away. "I figured it would teach them a lesson if they ate them and drank like I knew they would." She looked down. "I didn't mean to kill them."

CHAPTER 29

At the Black Dog, Ophelia pushed the uneaten half of her hamburger aside. "This is too much. Would you like it, Sam?"

"Sure." He scooped the half burger onto his plate.

"I didn't know you'd gone to school with Horace. Such a long time ago." Ophelia set her elbows on the table and leaned her chin on her hands. "Please tell me about him."

Minnowfish took a bite, chewed, and wiped his mouth before he answered. "What's to tell?"

"You knew him in the high school here. What was he like?"

"Two years ahead of me. He was on the tennis team. That's about all I knew."

"The parents who adopted him. Who are they?" Ophelia picked up a fry from her plate, dipped it into the pool of ketchup, and nibbled it.

"Rich guy named Robert Mann. Moved to Edgartown with his wife after he'd made a bundle. No children of their own, so they adopted our Horace as a babe in arms. That's about it." He took another large bite, chewed, swallowed. "What's suddenly triggered your interest in Horace besides the fact that he's just inherited three million dollars and Aileen McBride seems to have the inside track on his affections?"

"You mustn't be so crude, Sam." Ophelia toyed with her fork.

Took a sip of her beer. Stared out the window at the lights reflected on the dark water.

Sam laughed.

Ophelia turned to him. "I don't know why you're laughing. Horace is my boss. Our boss. Of course I'm interested in knowing everything about him."

"No need to get your feathers in a tizzy."

The waiter came to their table. "Are you ready for dessert?"

"Why not," said Sam. "Blueberry pie with a scoop of vanilla ice cream for me."

"May I have coffee," said Ophelia. "Black, please."

"Regular or decaf?"

"Regular, of course."

After the waiter left with their order, Ophelia said, "What was the name of the local girl?"

"What local girl?" asked Sam, looking puzzled for an instant.

"His birth mother."

Sam laughed. "Can't let go, can you. I was imagining my blueberry pie."

Ophelia tapped her fingernails on the table. "It is of interest to me."

"Girl from Chilmark."

"Do you know who she is?"

"Look, Ophelia. I'm tired of this. You want information on Horace Mann, go to the courthouse and look it up. I want to digest my food." He took a clean napkin from the table and wiped his mouth and hands.

Ophelia continued to tap her fingernails. "You don't like Dr. Mann, do you?"

"It's not a question of like or dislike. I work for the guy. He's a reasonably good boss. I leave my work at the office. I don't fraternize with the white man, and I can see why." He wadded up the

178

paper napkin, threw it onto the table, slid off the bench, and stood. "This dinner was a mistake."

"Sit down, Sam. I'm sorry. I'll be quiet."

The waiter arrived with a large slice of blueberry pie oozing reddish-purple berries, and set it on the table.

Sam paused.

"Black Dog blueberry pie," he murmured. He sat again. "Can't waste it."

At Offshore Ale, Dr. Aileen McBride reached for a peanut, snapped it open, picked out a nut with nicely manicured fingernails, and popped it into her mouth. "Did you know that Mrs. Wilmington had that kind of money?"

Mann laughed. "Aileen, my dear, there are few secrets on this Island. When you've lived here for fifteen or twenty years, you'll understand." He helped himself to a handful of peanuts, systematically cracked them open, and brushed the shells onto the floor. "Islanders had a pretty good idea of what she was worth. Fifty acres in Chilmark?"

"It must have been wonderful living on the Vineyard as a child," said Aileen.

Mann nodded. "I was born and raised here."

"Were your parents from the Vineyard?"

He pushed the basket of peanuts toward her. "Here, I seem to be monopolizing them."

She shook her head, and the overhead light glinted on her bright hair. "I've had too many, thanks." She wiped her napkin across the table in front of her. "I read an article recently in the *Island Enquirer* about a couple named Mann, how they attended their fiftieth high school reunion in Summit, New Jersey." She looked up and met his eyes. "It said they moved to the Vineyard after he graduated from Princeton and adopted a son. Was that you?"

The waiter came to their table and set their meals in front of them. "Can I get you anything else?"

"Another ale for me," said Mann. "You, Aileen?"

"I'm fine."

The waiter took their glasses and left.

She waited for him to respond.

Mann frowned. "There's never been any secret about my being adopted." He picked up his burger and poked the tomato slice back under the bun. "My parents had no children of their own. They adopted me when I was a couple of days old. I always knew I'd been adopted." He bit into his burger.

Aileen pushed her salad around on her plate with her fork. "You must be curious about your birth parents."

"You know, Aileen, this is my private business."

"I'm sorry, Horace. I shouldn't pry." She pushed her fork into a mound of shredded green vegetables and lifted it partway to her mouth and stopped. "You know, I can't help wondering. I mean, is it possible that Mrs. Wilmington was your birth mother?"

He set his burger down carefully on his plate. "What are you talking about?"

"I know it's none of my business, but that would explain a lot. I mean, the way she was always hovering around you at the clinic." She forked the salad into her mouth and began to chew. "The three million," she said around her mouthful.

He pushed his plate away from him. "I don't like what you're suggesting."

"I don't mean to suggest anything, Horace. Don't take it personally."

"Personally! I'm not supposed to take personally this poking around you're doing into my private life?"

"I'm not poking around." She set her fork down on her plate.

"I'm simply interested. As you said, there are no secrets on the Island. Do you know who your birth father is?"

"Can't take a hint, can you." He picked up his burger again. "Enough about me." He took a bite.

"I would think you'd want to know who your real father is."

"I have a father." He chewed.

"You could have a DNA test done."

"Let's discuss you for a change, shall we?" He put the burger down, wiped his mouth, and peered closely at her hair, her eyes, her nose, her mouth. "Let's see, now. Hmmm." He tilted his head. "Yes. Your hair. You know, of course, your dark roots are showing." He leaned over the table to look more closely. "Your lips. Botox? Your nose. Inherited from your birth father? I assume you had it restructured. A botched job."

She put her hand up to her face. "Oh, stop! Stop!"

"If you recall, Aileen, I am the head of the dental clinic and you are a dentist employed by me. We have to work together." He handed her a clean napkin. "You have an advantage over me. I can't cry."

She took the napkin and blotted her eyes. "I'm sorry."

"Shall we declare a truce?" he asked softly. "Actually, your nose is just fine and your hair is beautiful."

Lockwood left Victoria's front door unlatched and headed for the hostel. She'd think she'd forgotten to slide the bolt home. Lockwood smiled. She was vain about her fine memory. It wouldn't hurt to unsettle her.

The moon had not yet risen and the night was dark.

He looked both ways before he crossed the road. No cars coming from either direction. No one to see him. He turned onto the walking path leading to the hostel. Not exactly luxurious quarters. Elizabeth would never find him there.

A swale marked the end of Victoria's property. He'd reached the bottom of the small valley when suddenly he was hit with nausea. He'd felt fine up until this moment. His mouth watered and he stepped off the path into a growth of huckleberry, poverty grass, and reindeer moss. He leaned over, hoping to clear his stomach of whatever was in it. But nothing came up. He started to sweat profusely. His heart raced. That meal he'd eaten with Scott. Steak and mushroom gravy, salad. The wine? He'd had only three glasses, a nice Merlot. He shook his head to clear it, and when he did, his head felt as though someone had struck him with a hammer. He swung his hands up to his temples to hold his head together, and then he collapsed. As he fell, he grabbed at a small bush, felt the leathery leaves. Hard unripe berries dropped off making no sound. His last thought before he hit the ground was that he was going to land in a bed of soft reindeer moss.

CHAPTER 30

The clock over the desk in the Emergency Room clicked off the time as Victoria and Elizabeth waited with Susan. Susan's sister and brother dozed some distance away, separated by several plastic chairs.

Heather had drawn two chairs together and curled her large frame into them, feet on one, head on the arm of the other.

Victoria started a sestina in the notebook she always carried, a poetry form of six stanzas with the same six words used at the end of each line, but used in a different order. Writing the poem required concentration, just what she needed right now.

Elizabeth and Susan conversed in low voices or went back to reading the magazine articles neither seemed interested in.

Doc Yablonsky left Scott's room to tend to other business, then reappeared.

"Will he die?" Susan asked.

"I doubt it." Doc Yablonsky shrugged. "Only a slim chance that alcohol poisoning will kill him. But there's a possibility that the strain on his heart might." He looked at his watch. "What is most likely is he'll have the worst hangover known to mankind, headache, queasy stomach, lasting for days."

"When will we know something definite?" Victoria asked.

"Doctor Ya-blon-sky, Doctor Ya-blon-sky," a muted voice came over the speaker system. "Please report to Intensive Care."

"Mrs. Trumbull, you and Elizabeth might as well go home. You, too, Susan. There's nothing you can do here." He looked over at Heather and Wesley. "We'll keep an eye on them."

He stopped at the desk and spoke to Hope, who nodded and left the desk to go into Scott's room.

Elizabeth stood and stretched her arms over her head. "No point in sitting here, Gram. Let's go. Although it's been nice not to worry about Lockwood." She turned to Susan, who was still seated. "We'll drive you home."

Victoria put her notebook back into her cloth bag. "Why don't you spend the rest of the night with us, Susan. We have plenty of room."

"Thanks, Mrs. Trumbull. I hate to impose."

"It's no imposition. When the hospital calls, we can go together."

They left contact numbers with Hope, who'd come out to answer the phone. Victoria glanced up at the clock. "Almost two a.m. We can get a few hours of sleep."

They drove home the back way along Barnes Road. Headlights picked up dew sparkling on the roadside grasses. As they passed the upper end of the Lagoon, the light of the half-moon shone on a sailboat riding at anchor.

Elizabeth yawned.

They stopped at the roundabout. Not a car in sight. As they passed the airport, no colored lights illuminated the runway. At the end of Barnes Road they turned onto the Edgartown Road.

A deer bounded across the road in front of them.

"I'm glad that wasn't a skunk," said Victoria. "They don't move that quickly."

"Keep a lookout, Gram. I don't want to deal with skunks."

They passed the youth hostel and the fire station and reached the brow of the valley that marked Victoria's property line. She was watching the side of the road for stray animals when she saw something that didn't belong.

"Stop, Elizabeth," she called out. "There's a large animal . . ."

Elizabeth slowed and Victoria peered out. "I think it's a person."

Elizabeth pulled to the side of the road and Victoria eased herself out.

"I'll check," said Susan, extricating herself from the backseat.

Long dry grass rustled and twigs snapped as Susan stepped over the low underbrush between the road and the bicycle path. Victoria watched her bend over, then straighten up and call out, "A man. He's alive."

Elizabeth tugged her cell phone out of her pocket and punched in 911. "A man on the bike path. We don't know his condition."

"Ambulance will be there shortly," said the dispatcher.

Susan returned. "He's alive but he's obviously in pain."

"Do you have a blanket in the car?" Victoria asked. "We should cover him."

"It's in the trunk. I'll get it," said Elizabeth.

"Someone should stay with him until the ambulance arrives," said Victoria.

"I will," said Susan.

Elizabeth slammed down the trunk lid and handed her the blanket.

Within minutes the ambulance, siren mute so as not to awaken West Tisbury's sleeping population, appeared at the brow of the valley. It made a U-turn and parked behind them, and the EMTs who'd taken Scott to the hospital a few hours earlier got out.

"Mrs. Trumbull, we meet again," said Jim, the driver. His partner, Erica, switched on a MagLite and focused it on Susan, now standing over the prone figure.

"He must have been heading to the youth hostel," said Victoria. "It's the only building around other than private homes."

A predawn breeze had sprung up and she turned up her collar. "He wasn't there when we drove past around eight. At least, I didn't notice him if he was."

The EMTs wheeled a stretcher across the narrow strip between road and path. Victoria, Elizabeth, and Susan huddled together and watched them load the stretcher and wheel it back to the ambulance. When the rear doors opened, light shone on the figure on the stretcher.

"Lockwood!" Elizabeth cried out.

"You know him?" asked Jim.

"Her ex-husband," said Victoria.

They gave him what information they could.

Jim tucked his notebook into his shirt pocket. "I know where to reach you. You better get some sleep. We'll take care of him."

He climbed back into the ambulance. Red and white lights strobed. An early-morning ground fog diffused the light and the valley was filled with a swirling pink and white cloud.

Victoria and the two young women watched until the rotating light was no longer visible.

"Was that the man in the Jeep that sideswiped me?" asked Susan.

"Yes," said Elizabeth. "Omigod!" she said suddenly. "He was in our house."

In minutes, they were home, entering by the kitchen door, as usual. "Will you be able to sleep?" Victoria asked.

"Lockwood was here," said Elizabeth. "In this house. I've got to see what he was doing." She slumped onto the parlor sofa, kicked off her shoes, put her feet up, and was asleep before Victoria could respond.

Susan yawned.

"You need to sleep as well." Victoria led her to the downstairs bedroom. Susan tugged off her shoes and, fully clothed, slipped between the sheets.

"Thanks." She breathed in the scent of sunshine-and-fresh-air-dried sheets and murmured, "Wonderful."

"The good west wind," said Victoria, turning out the light. She returned to the parlor where Elizabeth snored gently and spread a blanket over her granddaughter. After she switched off the light she went to the kitchen to brew tea.

While she was waiting for the water to heat, she thought about Lockwood. Elizabeth was right. He must have been in the house. Where was he staying? Surely not at the hostel. That wasn't like him. What was he doing on the path? Had he suffered a heart attack? Tripped over a fallen stick or a rough spot on the dark path and fallen?

The water came to a boil. She poured it over her teabag and held her hands around the mug to warm them.

Dealing with Lockwood was a job for the professionals, Casey had said. She was probably right. But professionals couldn't protect Elizabeth every minute.

In the far reaches of her mind, buried so deeply she wasn't even sure it was there, was the thought that it would be a blessing if he'd had a heart attack and died.

She felt helpless.

Not only about Elizabeth. She'd now taken responsibility for Susan, as well. Susan had a seriously ill brother, two inebriated siblings, a house full of resentment, and a murdered grandmother.

Victoria finished her tea, rinsed out the mug and left it upside down in the sink. She knew she couldn't sleep. Even though Lockwood was presumably out of commission for some time, she couldn't help feeling the need to protect her two young women.

Who had killed Susan's grandmother? All four grandchildren

needed money. Did they need it enough to kill? How ironic if they did kill and inherited only a token amount. Except Susan. The house and land was not a token amount.

She put her coat back on and went outside, closing the screen door softly. She stepped down onto the large stone step and walked through the small garden that was bounded by a low farmer's wall. She needed to be outside, to sit on the bench by the fish pond and think.

By the light of the half-moon she saw a branch that had broken off the maple tree. She bent down and picked it up. It was a large branch covered with grandfather's beard, a gray lichen. She sat on the bench beside the fish pond and snapped the branch into kindling-sized pieces while she thought. The bench was damp from night dew. The chill went through her corduroy trousers, but she scarcely noticed.

A goldfish splashed in the pond. A robin called its first chirrup of the predawn morning. And, as though the robin had lowered a conductor's baton, the air was suddenly full of birdsong. Mourning doves, a cardinal, the robin. A blue jay. Flickers and Carolina wrens and chickadees. The dawn chorus was a joyful sound and Victoria's heart lifted.

To the east, trees gradually emerged out of the darkness, silhouetted by the faint pink glow of dawn.

She stood up with her handful of sticks and headed back to the house. Everything would work out. Why had she felt doubtful?

Scott would recover, Lockwood would come to his senses, the Wilmington grandchildren would make peace, Mrs. Wilmington's murderer would be apprehended, and Dr. Mann would make good use of his three million dollars.

She got busy in the kitchen. An oven omelet, bacon, and coffee for whenever the girls woke up. And she'd bake biscuits.

Everything would work out.

CHAPTER 31

Victoria convinced herself that all would be well.

She filled the coffee maker with fresh cold well water. Why would anyone who came to the Island drink bottled water when the Island had the best water in the world? And hers was the best of the best. She fitted a coffee filter into place, dropped in five full scoops of coffee, and turned on the machine. She opened a package of bacon, laid strips on the broiler pan, and set it in the oven to cook while she mixed the omelet. The omelet would take about a half hour to bake and could be eaten cold if the girls overslept. Eggs, milk, sour cream, a sprinkling of crushed hot peppers from last year's garden, and chives from this year's cut up and sprinkled on top. She poured the egg mixture into a baking dish over a half stick of melted butter. She'd start the biscuits when she heard one of the girls moving about.

While the bacon cooked, scenting the house with its rich aroma, she went into the cookroom with her mug of coffee and a feeling of great optimism. She propped her lilac wood stick against the telephone table, fished an envelope out of the wastepaper basket, and started making notes.

The police couldn't help. Both the state police and the West Tisbury police were small units and the presidential visit was consuming all their time. She felt slighted by not being included in the security preparations for the visit.

So she was on her own to solve the murders, which she intended to do before the police were available.

That was Victoria's first note on the back of the envelope: solve the murders.

The second note to herself was to list each and every person even remotely connected with Mrs. Wilmington and Vivian. After that, she'd list possible motives. That way, she would eliminate those who most certainly were innocent.

Morning sunlight poured in through the east door and turned the wide pine floorboards a mellow gold. Catbirds sang in the lilac tree. A goldfish splashed in the fish pond. A light breeze whispered through the window screen next to her chair. There were several envelopes in the wastepaper basket that had clean backs she could write on. The bacon sizzled. Her coffee was good and strong. The timer would go off when the omelet was done.

She set to work. She would solve these murders, she would prove her worth as police deputy, and all would be right with her world.

Her list of suspects started out with Dr. Horace Mann, the head of the clinic. She'd noted the three dentists: the doctors Ophelia Demetrios, Aileen McBride, and Sam Minnowfish, and their three assistants: Jane Douglas, Roosevelt Mark, and Arthur Morgan. She'd just started on Mrs. Wilmington's four grandchildren, when she saw a blue Jeep pull up under the Norway maple at the end of her drive.

Lockwood got out slowly, one hand holding his head.

He'd been taken to the hospital, unconscious, only a few hours before. What was he doing here?

She had always liked Lockwood, and her first thought was pleasure at the idea that he had recovered and was coming to discuss the misunderstanding between him and Elizabeth. Her second thought was serious concern.

He was a tall man, perhaps six and a half feet, and he was well built. Not in the least fat, all muscle and bone. He probably weighed two-hundred-and-fifty pounds. She wasn't good at estimating heights and weights, but in her capacity as Casey's deputy, she was learning. He walked with pride. Victoria had always liked that about Lockwood, his posture. Almost military. And a flat stomach. He hadn't let himself develop a potbelly like so many men his age. He was usually meticulous about getting his thick hair trimmed, but she noticed, as he walked slowly toward the house, that a lock had fallen down over his forehead. His hair was a medium brown with gray streaks, very distinguished looking. And he'd grown a beard.

Again, she wondered why he was here. Elizabeth acted as though she was terrified of him. What was this other side of Lockwood that she, Victoria, had never seen?

He hitched up his trousers by the belt. Something heavy in the right hand pocket seemed to be dragging his pants down.

He was not what one would call handsome, but he was certainly nice looking. He and Elizabeth had made an attractive couple, both of them tall and athletic.

He wore thick horn-rimmed glasses. She couldn't see his eyes from here because the sun reflected off the lenses, but she knew his eyes were green with red and gold flecks.

He stopped halfway between the Jeep and the stone steps, leaned over slightly, put his hands on his head and held them there for a minute or two. Then he stood up straight and turned his back to the house, looking toward the village in the distance. A lovely clear day, and she could see the clock in the church steeple from her seat in the cookroom, could almost read the time. After a bit, he turned back toward her. He was wearing gray cotton work pants and a short-sleeved green and gray plaid cotton shirt.

It was such a shame that he and Elizabeth had divorced.

Lockwood was intelligent. He had a doctorate in petroleum geology, was a specialist in Russian oil at an important government agency, was well-read and witty, and could talk easily to people. What would make such an appealing man become the monster that Elizabeth and Casey described?

Of course she believed Elizabeth, but still . . .

Lockwood came up the stone steps slowly, and she rose from her chair to greet him. He rapped on the side of the open door into the kitchen.

"Come in!" greeted Victoria. "Are you all right?"

"Not really." Lockwood was holding a hand against his temple. "I've got a fierce headache."

"What happened? Please, come in. Would you like some coffee?"

"Coffee might help. Thanks, Victoria."

Lockwood was a rugged, strong, intelligent man. Perhaps Elizabeth . . .

She pushed the thought away. Both Elizabeth and Casey saw Lockwood in a different light from the way she saw him. She poured mugs of coffee for both of them, and they sat in the cookroom.

"You were about to say what happened," Victoria prompted.

He winced, closed his eyes, set his elbow on the table, and held his hand against his forehead. He was quite pale.

"You're hurting, aren't you?" said Victoria.

Without lifting his head he said, "Apparently I ate a variety of mushroom that blocks the metabolism of alcohol and I'd had some wine."

"Enough to cause such a reaction?"

"Three glasses."

Victoria was aghast. "That doesn't seem like much."

"Alcohol is poison. Normally, your liver metabolizes the poison and gets rid of it. But something in the mushroom prevents that."

the gun. It was in his lap and he was fondling it in a way that made her feel queasy. "Where is she?"

The two girls, she thought. If I upset him and he shoots me, will they come rushing in? A semiautomatic pistol means he can keep shooting. Would he kill Elizabeth? He doesn't know Susan is here. Will he kill her, too? In this most unreal situation killing was a real possibility.

"I said, where is she?" He pointed the gun at her.

Time stopped. Victoria's only weapon was her lilac wood stick. Fortunately it was within reach. He would most certainly shoot her before she could get to it, though.

She had one slim chance and took it. She half rose and looked over Lockwood's shoulder. "Oh, good morning!"

Lockwood turned for a mere instant and immediately swiveled back. "You can't trick me like that, Victoria. Ow!" He put the hand that wasn't holding the gun to his head. But in that mere instant Victoria had gotten all the way to her feet, grabbed her stick, swung it over her head, and brought it down on Lockwood's wrist with all the force she could muster. The stick landed with a horrible, sickening *thwack!* Lockwood dropped the gun and it went off with an explosion that shook the small room.

Lockwood screamed. "You goddamned witch! My hand! You've broken it!" He tried to hold his head with his hands, but his right hand was useless. "You'll pay for this!"

Victoria kicked the fallen gun across the floor.

He stood up, knocking his chair over, holding his limp wrist with his left hand. "You broke it!"

Footsteps pounded toward the cookroom. "Gram? Omigod!"

Lockwood groaned. "You're coming home with me right now, Elizabeth. Your grandmother is crazy."

Elizabeth reached for the phone and dialed.

Lockwood bent down to retrieve his gun. Victoria, adrenaline coursing through her veins, brought her stick down a second time on the back of his skull. He dropped heavily onto the leg of the overturned chair, breaking it, and impaling the right-hand pocket of his gray trousers on the snapped-off stump.

"Wow!" Elizabeth examined Lockwood from the far side of the room. "Casey's on the way." She turned to her grandmother. "Wow!" she said again.

"I hope I didn't kill him," said Victoria.

"I hope you did," said her granddaughter.

The police cruiser pulled up, siren screaming. While the vehicle was still moving, Junior leaped out, gun drawn, ran up the steps into the kitchen, skidded to a stop, and stared at the scene. Casey, gun drawn, was right behind him.

Lockwood lay slumped facedown across Victoria's overturned chair. A broken chair leg stuck out of his torn pants pocket. Victoria was sitting in her usual seat. In her right hand she held her lilac wood stick. In her left, she held the gun she'd picked up off the floor, as though she was prepared to shoot it.

She set the pistol on the table. "Would someone please check the oven? I don't want the bacon to burn."

CHAPTER 32

Jane was reading to Davina before her afternoon nap when the phone rang. Abigail answered.

"It's Mrs. Mann for you, Missy." She handed the phone to Jane. "I'll finish reading to the baby and put her down for her nap."

"Charlotte," said Jane. The two had called each other daily since their meeting the past Thursday.

"I have a wonderful idea. May I stop by in the next hour?"

"Of course. Can you stay for supper?"

"I wish I could, but my boys have a softball game tonight and I have to fix supper and go to the game. But I have a couple of free hours, if you do. And I'd like to visit your beautiful daughter again."

"She should be up from her nap by then."

An hour later, Jane answered Charlotte's knock on the door, and welcomed her into the house.

Abigail appeared. "Wine and sandwiches again, Missy?" This afternoon she wore a tan muumuu with an abstract pattern of black and white leaves.

"No sandwiches for me, thank you." Charlotte patted her stomach. "Where do you get those wonderful dresses, Abigail?"

"My niece who lives in Hilo, Hawaii, makes them." Abigail smoothed the skirt of the muumuu.

"I'd love to go there someday."

"Wine sounds good, Abigail," said Jane.

She and Charlotte went down the wide step into the living room and sat in the same seats they'd taken before, Charlotte on the couch, Jane on the chair at a right angle to her.

"What's the idea you mentioned, Charlotte?" Jane asked.

"Ever since we spoke last Thursday, I've been mulling over a way to get through to Horace. He's so wrapped up in himself he can't believe he can do anything wrong."

"He proposed marriage to me," said Jane. "I can't believe I trusted him. How could he have talked about marriage to me when he was married to you? And you have two sons." She shook her head. "I can't understand that. I believed him."

"I've been doing some research on narcissism. Let me show you something." She reached into her leather shoulder bag and brought out a paper. "These are some of the traits that define a narcissist." She handed the paper to Jane.

Jane took it and read, "'A narcissist typically has problems in sustaining satisfying relationships; problems distinguishing self from others. Will use other people without considering the cost of doing so. Has an inability to view the world from the perspective of other people. Feels no sense of remorse, shame, or gratitude.'" She looked up from the paper. "Wow."

"Describes our Horace pretty well, doesn't it."

Jane looked at the paper again. "Yes. You paid his way through dental school, I understand?"

Charlotte nodded. "Narcissists are often charming. He'd been responsible for a serious episode in college that caused his adoptive parents to disown him, but I was in love with him. I made excuses for him. I thought it was only a terrible mistake he'd made and that he'd learned from it. But no."

Abigail came in with a tray holding the bottle of Merlot, two wineglasses, and a plate of crackers and cheese.

"Thank you," said Jane.

"Baby should be waking up soon. Shall I bring her in, Missy, or you want me to put her out to play?"

Jane glanced at Charlotte. "Davina can play for a bit while we talk."

Abigail nodded and left the two women together.

"I didn't mention this when we met last Thursday." Charlotte helped herself to a cracker and spread cheese on it. She sat back and nibbled the cracker before she spoke again. "I've known for some time that Horace was having affairs, one after another."

"How could you stand it?"

"For the same reason a lot of women stay with a man—the children. Our two boys. I always believed in marriage and family and wanted our boys to grow up with a father they could look up to. But Horace has never been that."

Jane poured wine into the glasses and handed one to Charlotte.

"Lately, I've noticed the boys, young as they are, try to avoid their father whenever they can."

"How sad."

Charlotte sipped her wine. "The day after we talked, I filed for divorce."

"I don't know what to think," said Jane.

"Congratulations are in order, I believe."

Jane sat back. "Does Horace know this?"

"Not yet." Charlotte set down her glass. "I would like you to be present when I make my announcement to him."

"Whew!" said Jane. "I don't know . . ."

Abigail strode into the living room and stood, arms folded. "That's the best idea I've heard in a long time. Maybe that will get through his thick head."

"Okay?" asked Charlotte.

"Shall we meet here?" asked Jane.

"Yes," said Abigail. "Those yellow roses I rescued are still pretty. I'll put them front and center on the table."

Charlotte took another sip of wine, set her glass down, and said, "I've got to run."

At the station house that afternoon, Casey leaned across her desk. "You've got to press charges against Lockwood."

"No," said Victoria.

"Lockwood would have killed you. And Elizabeth." Casey slapped the papers she'd been holding on to on her desk in annoyance. She and Junior Norton had taken Lockwood to the County of Dukes County House of Correction in Edgartown, namely the jail. "He'd have killed everyone who got in the way."

Victoria was sitting in her usual wooden armchair in front of Casey's desk. "He didn't intend to kill anyone. He intended to threaten Elizabeth." She stroked the fine polish on her lilac wood stick.

"You know, Victoria, I can press charges without your doing so. Laws have changed with regard to domestic violence. The guy pulls out a gun and waves it around and says it's just a threat. He'll try again and again. He's got no conscience. He wants his property back, namely Elizabeth, and he wants it back even if it's dead."

"Elizabeth isn't an 'it,'" said Victoria. "I don't want you to press charges."

"Look, Victoria. Be reasonable."

Victoria sat forward in her chair. "I still care for Lockwood. He was my grandson."

"In-law," said Casey.

"He was my grandson," repeated Victoria. "He and Elizabeth have had their problems, but he and I have always gotten along. He's a troubled man and he's suffering."

Casey lifted her paperweight stone from the pile of papers it

200

held down and slapped it back onto the pile with a thunk. "Victoria, you are stubborn, misguided, and unreasonable."

"What is reasonable about incarcerating Lockwood? What good would that do? I'm the only witness to his threats. Lockwood is a respected scientist and an important government official. He's intelligent. He has no criminal record. Elizabeth never filed charges against him for assault. Would my word hold up against his? Suppose it does. Would he be locked up for a year? Two? Fined? Would he even be convicted in the first place? Then what?" She looked down at her gnarled hands, now folded on top of the stick. "He's sick, Casey. He needs treatment, not a prison term. Prison would only make him worse." She looked up. "I'd like you to recommend to the authorities that he get treatment."

"Oh, hell, Victoria. I'll do what I can." Casey swiveled around in her chair and plunked a few keys on her keyboard. The dancing cartoon pigs on the monitor screen disappeared and the screen went blank. She turned back to her deputy. "He had a license to carry. I wish to hell you'd shot him."

"I don't know how to use a gun."

"You need to learn."

On the Mill Pond the cygnets had swum away from their parents. They'd lost their fuzzy gray fluff and were sporting real feathers. Four of the seven had survived the depredations of the pond's snapping turtles.

Casey sighed and got up out of her chair. She strapped on her heavy utility belt with its array of tools. "I don't know what possessed me to name you a police deputy."

"You did it because I know almost everyone on the Island," said Victoria. "I'm related to half of them. I know where they live, I know where the bodies are buried, and I'm not afraid of anyone or anything."

"Yeah, yeah," said Casey. "I'll take you home. You can go ahead and hunt down killers while I check the guest lists of everyone in West Tisbury."

Victoria, too, stood. "If you'd invited me to help with the guest lists, I could have saved you time." She leaned on her stick. Her muscles ached from her attack on Lockwood. "Did I break his wrist?"

"Yeah, you did. He also sprained his ankle when he fell and that broken chair leg gave him a puncture wound in his side that has to be taken care of."

"That should put him out of action for a while. What about his gun?"

"I confiscated it. Don't go telling me to give it back to him." Casey headed for the door. "C'mon, Victoria. I gotta get busy with this presidential stuff. I thought looking for Mrs. Wilmington's murderer would keep you out of trouble for a while." They went out through the station house door, which, Victoria noticed with satisfaction, Casey neglected to lock. "When you nab the killer, what do you plan to do, trap and release?"

"Don't be cynical, Casey."

CHAPTER 33

———

"I'm so proud of you, Gram." Elizabeth threw her arms around her grandmother. "Without you, we might all be dead."

"He didn't intend to kill anyone. It was a threat to get you to go home with him."

"With a gun, sure." She released her grandmother and sat down. "This is home."

Victoria held up the lilac wood stick Elizabeth had carved for her and smiled. "Where's Susan?"

"While you were at the police station, the hospital called. Scott's being released along with Heather and Wesley this afternoon. Susan's in the car and we're going to pick them up."

Victoria pulled out one of the kitchen chairs and sat. She really didn't feel as peppy as she'd like. "Is Scott going to be all right?"

"Doc Yablonsky said he'll have a gargantuan headache and for a week or so will wish he was dead. Want to come with us?"

"Thank you, no. I have work to do. Besides, you don't have room in your car for six large people."

"True. Okay, we're off." Elizabeth gave her grandmother another hug. "You're a brick."

The brick hobbled into the cookroom, where she righted the broken chair and eased herself down into her armchair. Elizabeth could take the chair up to the attic where it would join a half-dozen other broken chairs. The next time her friend Mark came for a visit, he would mend it.

The two coffee mugs were still on the table, the coffee only half drunk. The morning had turned into afternoon and afternoon into early evening. Victoria realized why she felt so lethargic. All she'd had to eat since last night was a half cup of coffee. No breakfast, no lunch, and it was approaching suppertime.

And she'd had no sleep.

She eased herself up out of the chair and found the remains of the omelet in the icebox along with the bacon. As she feasted, her energy returned. She had a second helping of the omelet—it was better than delicious—and then a third, which cleaned out the baking dish. Four slices of bacon. A glass of cranberry juice.

She located the box of Chilmark Chocolates. A half-dozen pieces were left. She carried the box to her seat.

She was ready to get back to work.

The golden light of early evening streamed through the west window, casting a shadow image of the lace curtain on the far wall. Victoria picked out a chocolate truffle and nibbled a small corner, then popped the rest into her mouth.

She closed her eyes. She'd rest them for just a minute or two, then get to work.

Victoria awoke with a start, smelling the aroma of cooking. Garlic. Basil. Tomato sauce. Her mouth watered.

A light blanket was draped over her shoulders and lap, and the lights had been turned on in the cookroom.

Her granddaughter came from the kitchen with a glass of red wine, which she handed to her. "Supper will be ready in half an hour. You had quite a nap."

Victoria stood and stretched, folded the blanket, and set it on an unbroken chair. "A few minutes rest was just what I needed."

Elizabeth laughed. "It's nine o'clock."

Victoria glanced at her watch. "Do you need a hand in the kitchen? What about Susan and the others?"

"I drove them home." Elizabeth shuddered. "Pure poison. No one was talking to anyone else. Heather and Wesley have bad hangovers. Scott has a super, horrendous, gigantic hangover. He can't move without hurting. Can't even breathe without hurting."

"What about Susan?"

"Susan is disgusted with them. They all blame her for the mushrooms and their hangovers. And they resent her for inheriting the property. What a mess. I left the instant I dropped them off."

"Poor Susan."

"Don't feel too sorry for her. Wouldn't surprise me if she was the one who put the arsenic in her grandmother's tea."

"Elizabeth!" Victoria warned.

"You've got a half hour before supper, Gram." Elizabeth returned to the kitchen. She called over her shoulder, "I'll bet you can ID the killer in that time."

Victoria smiled and switched on the lamp on the telephone table.

The envelope with her list of suspects had fallen onto the floor during Lockwood's visit. Victoria retrieved it and set to work. The entire dental clinic staff. Mrs. Wilmington's four grandchildren: Scott, Susan, Heather, and Wesley. She hesitated before she wrote Susan's name. Possible motives could wait until after she'd finished listing names.

She thought about Vivian. The postmortem noted that the victim had a significant bruise on the back of her neck. Someone had knocked her into the harbor. Who? And why?

Victoria turned to the window. The village in the distance was a few bright dots of light echoing the stars she could see clear down to the horizon.

What had Vivian heard in that phone call? That seemed key.

She made a note to locate Vivian's hospital friend and find out exactly what she'd said in that phone call besides giving her the news that Mrs. Wilmington was dead.

She would need transportation. Both Casey and Elizabeth were tied up with this presidential visit preparation. She could hitch-hike, of course, but some of the people she wanted to interview lived in out-of-the-way places.

She picked up the phone and called Bill O'Malley, the owner of a fine blue dump truck.

"I'm at your disposal, Mrs. T. Anytime." He gave her his cell phone number.

Victoria hung up with a sense of renewed optimism. She crossed off her list the note "Transportation" and went back to listing motives. Money headed the list. Sex came next. She glanced out the window. Sex? Money had seemed the overwhelming motive, but when she thought of Dr. Mann, the two female dentists, and Mrs. Wilmington, perhaps she'd better give sex equal weight.

On Tuesday, Casey would drop her off at the nursing home for her weekly session of reading to the elderly. Since the nursing home was connected to the hospital, she would try to locate Vivian's friend.

CHAPTER 34

On Monday, Elizabeth dropped her grandmother off at the dental clinic on her way to work. "Call me when you're done, Gram, and I'll give you a ride home, if I can."

"I know you're busy," said Victoria. "I'll manage."

She waved an airy goodbye, and after Elizabeth drove off, she felt bad that she'd been so cool to her granddaughter. It wasn't Elizabeth's fault that she'd had to forfeit her license.

She made her way up the steps and into the clinic.

"Good morning, Mrs. Trumbull." Tiffany looked up from the issue of *M Magazine* she was reading.

"Good morning, Tiffany. Have you adjusted to the new job?"

"Not much to, like, adjust to, Mrs. Trumbull. It's pretty quiet." She set the magazine facedown, saving her place. "Is your tooth okay? I mean, you know, like, where the tooth was? We only have office hours until noon today."

"My jaw is fine, thank you. Dr. Demetrios wants to look at it, and afterward I want to talk with her."

"Yes, ma'am. I'll buzz her. Would you like a seat?"

Victoria selected one of the padded chairs and before she'd settled herself fully, Ophelia Demetrios came into the reception area, smoothing her sleek hair with a graceful hand.

"Mrs. Trumbull. How are you feeling? Let's take a look at that jaw."

Victoria returned to the reclining chair. Dr. Demetrios fastened the paper bib in place, poked around a bit, and declared that Victoria was healing nicely. "I'd like to see you in six months, Mrs. Trumbull," she said.

"I'd like to talk to you now, Dr. Demetrios." Victoria rose to her feet. "Can we go somewhere private?"

"Of course. We can sit in the garden. There's a nice bench near the bird feeder."

"It's about Mrs. Wilmington's death," Victoria said as they made their way to the garden. They sat on the bench.

"I suspected as much."

The bench was shaded by a wild cherry tree. The cherries were ripening and would be ready to pick for jelly in a few weeks. A half-dozen birds fluttered around the feeder, chickadees and finches and a female cardinal. At the base of the feeder, chipmunks filled their cheek pouches with dropped seeds.

Dr. Demetrios was wearing a long-sleeved white cotton shirt and gray slacks. She smoothed her slacks over her knees. "You were there, Mrs. Trumbull, and know as much as I do."

"I'm interested in the clinic's staff," said Victoria. "You have far more insight than I where they're concerned."

"You mean, suspects." Dr. Demetrios smiled. "I understand you have some connection with the police."

"I'd like to hear your opinions," said Victoria, "that is, if you don't feel this is an intrusion."

"Intrusion!" Ophelia flung up her hands in dismissal. "Of course not. I will be so happy when this murder is cleared up and we can get back to work."

Victoria removed her baseball cap from her cloth bag to locate the notebook and pen beneath it and set the hat between them on the bench.

Ophelia picked it up and read the gold stitching on the front.

"West Tisbury police deputy." She put the hat down again. "You are truly official, aren't you?"

Victoria smiled. She thumbed through the notebook to find a clean page. "What I hope to do, Dr. Demetrios is—"

"Please, Mrs. Trumbull. When I'm not working, I'm Ophelia."

Victoria settled more comfortably on the bench. A catbird swooped down into the birdbath near the feeder, splashed water all over himself, and flew off.

"That bird," said Ophelia. "He empties the water with his baths. We have to refill it twice a day." She turned to face Victoria. "Now, let me hear your questions."

"I'd like us to go over a list of staff members."

"Oooh, I have some strong opinions," said Ophelia. "Shall we start with Aileen McBride?"

Victoria nodded. "How did she feel about Mrs. Wilmington?"

Ophelia smiled. "She hated her. Next question?"

The catbird flew to the cherry tree and perched above them, calling out its distinctive "Meow!"

"He'll be back shortly for another bath," said Ophelia.

"Why did she hate her?" Victoria asked.

"This is between you and me?"

Victoria nodded. "Just between us."

"Mrs. Wilmington was crazy about Dr. Mann. She dropped by all the time, always giving him little gifts."

"And that upset Dr. McBride?"

"Aileen was jealous of Mrs. Wilmington. She was always flirting with Dr. Mann. Mrs. Wilmington didn't like that." Ophelia rolled her lovely almond eyes. "Mrs. Wilmington was jealous of Aileen, too. She could be quite spiteful."

"In what way?"

"She was demanding. The chair wasn't the right height. The bib was too tight. The temperature in the operatory was too chilly or

209

too warm. The light was in her eyes. Always something that was Aileen's fault, and if she couldn't blame Aileen, she blamed that poor assistant, Jane Douglas."

"That seems like reason to be annoyed with her patient, not to hate her," said Victoria.

"It was worse than that, Mrs. Trumbull. Mrs. Wilmington complained constantly to Dr. Mann. About Aileen's competence, her technique, her bedside manner, and repeatedly threatened to report her to the state certifying authorities."

"Why didn't Mrs. Wilmington change dentists?"

Ophelia shrugged. "Aileen tried to get Horace to assign Mrs. Wilmington to me or to Sam Minnowfish, but we had worked with her before, and both of us refused to work with her again after Aileen arrived. Aileen is fairly new to the clinic, and so she drew the, how do you say it, short straw? Mrs. Wilmington was determined to be near Horace."

"You mentioned Jane Douglas, Dr. McBride's assistant, and implied that Mrs. Wilmington was difficult to her, too."

"Oh my, yes. 'Get me this,' or 'Get me that.' Personal attacks like 'That outfit is unbecoming,' or 'You should color that gray hair.' Jane is the one with naturally silver hair, you know. Most women would kill for that hair."

"Would either Dr. McBride or Jane have reason to harm Mrs. Wilmington?" asked Victoria.

"On that day you heard me say that Aileen did it. Of course, we didn't know what she'd done at that point. Truly, I don't believe she killed Mrs. Wilmington, although Mrs. Wilmington certainly drove her beyond reason. I don't think Aileen has the courage, quite frankly."

"But she had motive and opportunity?"

"Yes, and she certainly had the means. It's easy for a dentist to obtain something like arsenic."

"I understand there were problems between Dr. McBride and Jane Douglas, as well," said Victoria.

Ophelia rolled her eyes again and patted her hair. "All about Horace," she said. "Everything revolves around Horace. Aileen lusts after him. She hungers after him. I don't know what she sees in him. But she sees Jane as competition."

"Dr. Mann is married, isn't he?"

Ophelia laughed. "Not for long. According to the Island grapevine, Jane Douglas invited him to drop by her house. His wife was there. She informed him to take a flying leap and the divorce lawyers would handle the details."

Victoria sat back absorbing this latest development.

"Back to the history as reported on that efficient grapevine. Aileen was jealous of poor little Jane. She didn't know Jane had a daughter by Horace. For that matter, neither did I." Ophelia ran her hand over her hair again. "I don't think anyone else knew, either. That prim and proper girl"—Ophelia glanced at Victoria—"what else was she hiding? Horace insisted that Aileen take Jane on as her assistant." Ophelia leaned closer to Victoria. "This something going on between Horace and little Jane, Aileen was not happy about it. Little did she know."

"Certainly an awkward situation."

The catbird fluttered from the tree to the birdbath, perched on the edge for a moment, then hopped into the water and splashed vigorously. Victoria wrote in her notebook.

"You see what I mean about that bird?" said Ophelia.

Victoria watched, thinking about the role Dr. Mann had played. A not terribly attractive man with women squabbling over him. She glanced at Ophelia. And a murder that might well have been because of him.

And then she thought of the four Wilmington grandchildren. Too many suspects.

The catbird shook its wings, scattering water droplets, and flew off again.

Victoria checked her list. "What about Dr. Minnowfish?"

"Sam?" Ophelia tossed her head back. "He has pretentions about his Wampanoag heritage. He and Horace both went to high school here on the Island. Sam was a year or two behind Horace. They get along, but they're not as close as you'd think they'd be, since both have Island roots." She paused and Victoria waited. "Actually, Horace was adopted. Did you know that?"

"So I'd heard. Who are his adoptive parents?"

"People with money and a long genealogy. Longtime summer visitors who moved here permanently and adopted Horace. He had all the privileges. Sailing, tennis, that crowd. That would explain why his world and Sam's didn't intersect."

"Are Dr. Mann's birth parents from the Island?"

"Who knows?" said Ophelia. "I found out about the adoption from Sam just the other day."

"What about Sam's relationship with Mrs. Wilmington?"

"Both Sam and I were happy to pass Mrs. Wilmington on to Aileen. I refused to work with her and so did Sam. We avoided her when she came to the clinic. I can't think of any reason why Sam would even care whether Mrs. Wilmington lived or died."

"How much did Dr. Mann know in advance about his inheritance?"

"Horace? We've all been speculating about that. He wants to expand the clinic, but can't until he acquires a larger building and some expensive equipment. Not an answer to your question."

"Expectation of inheriting a large sum would be a strong motive," said Victoria.

"And getting rid of Mrs. Wilmington would restore some peace in his clinic," said Ophelia.

"It sounds as though he'd still have problems." Victoria thought about the friction between her own dentist and Dr. McBride, Mrs. Wilmington's dentist.

Ophelia snorted. "If you mean Horace, he loves having women fight over him." She leaned back on the bench and looked up at the ripening cherries. "Who shall we tear apart next?"

"I don't really want to tear anyone apart, but what about Arthur Morgan? Who does he work for?"

"Arthur and Roosevelt Mark are technicians and are not assigned to any one person the way Jane Douglas is."

"Tell me about Arthur."

"Quiet. A hard worker, competent, smart. He has the hots for Jane, but doesn't push things, at least not in the clinic. He's got a master's from Boston University in software or something. I don't know anything about his personal life except he's single and has a dog named Dog."

Victoria looked down at her notebook. "Morgan is an Island name. Is Arthur from the Vineyard?"

"I believe so. He went to high school here."

"Anything else you can say about him?" asked Victoria.

"Patients like him. I don't socialize with him." Ophelia was quiet for a moment, watching the bird. "Arthur is a nice man. He'd do anything for you. If you break something, he'll fix it for you without making a big deal of it. But, I don't know, there's something about him that makes me uncomfortable."

"Can you pin that feeling down more?"

Ophelia shook her head. "I'm being unfair to him. He's just unsophisticated, kind of raw, in a way. A sort of natural man, I suppose. Next person."

"The only person left is Roosevelt Mark," said Victoria.

"He found Vivian's body, you know."

Victoria nodded. "I heard he dived in, hoping to save her."

213

"He's got a Ph.D. in art history, but he can't use a degree like that on the Island. He's married to a psychiatrist."

"The Island has the most highly educated workforce in the world," said Victoria.

"Roosevelt's way overqualified for the job. He's so nice. He was always pleasant to Vivian. The rest of us hardly knew she was alive." Ophelia watched the birds flutter around the feeder. "I feel bad about that, now. I know nothing about Vivian or her personal life. In fact, I scarcely remember what she looked like, except that she needed to lose weight."

"Can you think of anyone who might harm her?"

Ophelia shook her head. "None of us even knew she was alive. She answered the phone, made appointments."

"Is there anything else you can think of that might help?"

"I don't think I've given you any help at all," said Ophelia.

"It's difficult to know what will help, at this point," said Victoria. "Putting pieces together will come later." She stood. "Thank you. Are any other staff members here today?"

"I'm the only one here. We will not have many patients until the murderer is caught." Ophelia went over to the birdbath. "You see? I've got to fill it again." She turned back to Victoria. "I'm sure you've met Mrs. Wilmington's grandchildren." They walked to the door and she added, "I'd look for the killer among them."

Chapter 35

Victoria stood on the clinic's steps deciding what to do. She was reluctant to call her granddaughter, knowing how busy she was.

"Mrs. Trumbull!" Ophelia came out of the clinic. "Sam called and will be here shortly. I told him you'd like to talk to him."

"Yes, I would. Thank you." Victoria went back inside.

Sam Minnowfish arrived a few minutes later.

"I don't have time to answer questions," he said. "I've got a date with some bluefish and just dropped by to check up on things." He doffed his long-billed fisherman's cap.

"Where do you plan to go fishing?" Victoria asked.

"Quansoo. I need to find someone who has a gate key."

"If you'll give me a ride home, answer a few questions, and provide me with some fish, you're welcome to borrow mine."

"I'll catch them, all right," said Sam with confidence. "A deal."

A red Jeep in the parking lot sported a half dozen surf rods in a roof rack. "I'll wait in your Jeep."

A few minutes later, Sam joined her.

He started up the engine and shifted into gear. "Good fishing last couple of days." He backed out of his spot and headed away from the clinic. "I suppose you want to talk about the murders. Fasten your seat belt, by the way."

Victoria obliged. "I'd like your thoughts about staff members. You went to high school with Dr. Mann?"

"Two grades ahead of me. Big difference when you're sixteen and he's eighteen."

"What was he like?"

Sam lifted his shoulders. "Never socialized with him. He was on the tennis team," he said, as though that explained it all. "Girls were all over him for some reason. Never could figure why. He's not what you'd call handsome. Carrot hair and freckles, skinny, prominent Adam's apple. Zilch for personality."

"I've just learned he was adopted. Do you know anything about his birth parents?"

"Rumors," said Sam. "I don't hold much with rumors."

"This is hardly a formal inquiry," said Victoria.

Sam came to the end of Barnes Road, waited at the stop sign for two police cars to pass, and turned right. "Every cop car on the Island is out patrolling."

"I suppose they have to be ready for any emergency with the president coming. The rumors?"

"Well"—Sam set his hands high on the steering wheel—"everybody figured his mother was a married Island girl who wasn't as careful as she should have been."

"Why not claim the baby was fathered by her husband?"

Sam glanced at her. "Rumor was the baby's father was a Wampanoag. Member of the Tribe, you know. Dark skin, hooked nose, kinky hair." He pointed at himself. "Look at me."

"Dr. Mann hardly fits that description."

"Look at me closely, Mrs. Trumbull." He faced her and opened his eyes wide. Pale hazel. He turned back to the road and lifted his hat. His short tightly curled hair was a light reddish brown. "Not a carrot top like our friend, but close."

"You're quite handsome, Sam."

"Thank you."

"Are hazel eyes and reddish hair tribal characteristics?"

"Describes a lot of us."

"What about his birth mother?" asked Victoria. "Surely there were rumors about her."

"Don't you wonder why Mrs. Wilmington left Horace three million dollars?"

Victoria sat back and thought for a moment. "One of her grand-daughters told me about a baby who'd died in infancy."

"That was the story, all right," said Sam. "'Course, this was before my time. But folks said she went off Island to have the baby and came back without it. Few weeks later, this rich Mann couple appeared with a new baby they'd adopted."

"So Dr. Mann could be Mrs. Wilmington's son by an unknown Wampanoag."

"That's the rumor." Sam grinned. "A Wampanoag brave."

"That would explain Mrs. Wilmington's frequent visits to the clinic. I suppose she felt remorse at abandoning her child. Did Dr. Mann suspect that she might be his mother?"

"Who knows what Mann thinks. He plays his cards pretty close. He was polite to her. She was a patient, after all, and a wealthy one. But it was obvious he despised that woman."

"I suppose he would resent her abandonment of him."

Sam shrugged. "Who knows," he said again.

"Would he have known she was leaving him a fortune?"

"Mann's not stupid."

"Have you ever talked to him about these rumors?"

"Good God, no," said Sam. "Why should I? The Tribe financed my dental degree. We're from different worlds. His adoptive parents are rich. He went to the best schools. Married a nice girl who paid his way through dental school."

"I thought you said his adoptive parents were rich?"

"They had some kind of falling out when he was in college. Rumor was"—he glanced at Victoria with a half smile—"he got a girl in trouble, insisted she get an abortion, backroom kind of deal. Girl died. His parents found out about it and disowned him."

"Well." Victoria sat back. "I don't know what to think."

"All rumors, Mrs. Trumbull."

Victoria was quiet.

They passed the youth hostel and the fire station.

"My house is just after this little valley."

"I know where you live, Mrs. Trumbull."

He turned into her drive and parked under the Norway maple and walked with her to the house. "Who would you like to talk about next? Got seven more people to analyze."

"Seven?"

"Three assistants, Jane, Arthur, and Roosevelt. Two dentists, Ophelia, and Aileen. Mann, the boss. And Vivian."

"Vivian is a victim, hardly a suspect," said Victoria.

"Who knows? She may hold the key to Mrs. Wilmington's death as well as her own."

"Speaking of keys, here you are." Victoria unhooked the Quansoo key from the entry wall and handed it to him. "When you return with the fish, I'd like to talk more." She was already planning her supper based on his yet-to-be-caught bluefish and didn't want to keep him waiting.

"Won't be back until after the tide turns, but I'll have your fish."

Victoria went back to work. The only new information Sam had provided was the rumor about Dr. Mann's heritage. Although she professed to discount rumors, this one, that Mrs. Wilmington had given birth to Dr. Mann, seemed worth following up.

But how?

She brewed a cup of tea and sat at the cookroom table with her list and added to it questions that she needed to answer.

The antagonism between Aileen McBride and Ophelia Demetrios: Was it professional jealousy or their respective interests in Dr. Mann? Or something else? How could she find out?

Aileen McBride had ingratiated herself to both Horace Mann and Scott Wilmington. Was it because one of them might inherit a vast sum? As Mrs. Wilmington's dentist she might have been privy to information about her patient's bequests.

Roosevelt Mark seemed almost too decent. Why would such a well-educated man settle for a dental technician job? Since he hadn't found a position in his own field, he could easily have found a higher paying position elsewhere. He was the last person to speak to Vivian. It seemed unlikely that he'd killed her, but then everything in this mess was unlikely.

So much seemed to cycle back to Vivian. Victoria made a note to find out more about her, especially that call that was so upsetting.

Then there was Jane. Victoria remembered her from the clinic, a tall, slender, refined woman with the silver hair everyone commented on. Why was she working there? Aileen McBride, her boss, clearly didn't like her and nor did Jane seem to like Aileen. Odd. From everything she'd discovered, Jane was a private person. She'd spent all her youthful summers at her grandparents' house on the Vineyard Haven harbor and had inherited the house after her grandmother's death. Active in the tennis and yacht clubs. Not exactly a background leading to a lowly position in a dental clinic. Dr. Demetrios and Sam Minnowfish had both hinted at tension between Jane and Dr. Mann and had told her about their child.

It was easy to overlook Arthur Morgan, but he could be important for that very reason. Pleasant, respected by the clinic's staff, well educated. Like many Islanders who'd not mingled with visitors from off Island or who'd not spent much time off Island themselves, he was socially inept. Victoria knew little about his family except that his father had left when he was quite young and he'd been brought up by his mother.

And there was her own dentist, Ophelia Demetrios. Victoria was unwilling to see her dentist as killer. She put her name on the bottom of the list along with Roosevelt Mark's.

She would need to talk with Dr. Mann. She would invite him for drinks. That way, he'd be in her territory with her rules. Victoria was pleased with the thought.

She transferred her notes from the back of the envelope to her notebook and got up stiffly, having sat for too long. Time to go out to the garden.

The three bloodroot plants she'd ordered would be shipped from the nursery in the fall. She'd prepare a bed for them now so it would be ready for them when they arrived.

While she was carrying her kneeler out to the shade garden, thinking about the delicate white flowers of the plants she'd put here, she laughed suddenly. How oddly her bloodroot seemed to echo murder in a dental clinic.

She pulled on her gloves to protect her fingers from the wicked thorns of the wild blackberry vines that grew everywhere and searched for just the right spot for the bloodroot. She found it and positioned the kneeler, lowered herself slowly onto it, and scratched away at the vines and weeds with her long-handled weeder.

Overhead, the catbird warned, "Cat! Cat! Cat!"

McCavity, Victoria's marmalade cat, stalked around a shrub and sat next to her on his haunches, his tail curled gracefully around him.

While she worked she thought about the Wilmington grandchildren and, another echo, their blood roots. The three who had come to visit were desperate for money. Susan had admitted that she knew her grandmother was about to cut her completely out of her will. Had the four gotten together and plotted to kill their grandmother? Was their hostility to Susan simply a pretense?

Digging in the dirt was a way to clear her mind. In a short time she'd excavated a patch about a foot long, almost as wide, and about five inches deep. She levered herself up by the handles of the kneeler, wincing at the ache in her knees. McCavity arose, stretched, and settled himself in the hole, eyes closed.

Victoria gathered up the vines and weeds she'd cleared, carried them to the far compost bin, and arranged them on top of the grass clippings that had already begun to heat up.

The mushroom poisoning troubled her. Susan had told her she was the one who'd picked the ink cap mushrooms after they'd returned from the lawyer's office. She had sautéed them to preserve them for a few days. She knew, too, that the mushrooms blocked the metabolism of alcohol and her brothers and sister had bought a large bottle of Scotch and would undoubtedly drink too much. What was she thinking? Was she trying to kill them? That would seem to be an overreaction to their hostility to her inheritance. As far as Victoria knew, no one had ever died from eating *Coprinopsis* mushrooms, although those who'd combined them with liquor often wished they were dead.

Then it occurred to Victoria that since the property Susan had inherited was worth more than thirteen million dollars, were her siblings reacting to her inheritance by plotting a "natural" death for her?

After she'd piled the weeds and vines onto the compost heap, she turned to the bin next to it, where the compost was ready. It seemed magical, this transition from thorny vines, coffee grounds, grass clippings, eggshells, and other kitchen scraps into this soft, fluffy, sweet smelling earth that would nurture any plant she chose to put into it.

She dug out a pailful and returned to her excavation where Mc-Cavity lay, curled up, orange tail to pink nose.

"Sorry, Cavvy," she said as he protested when she shoved him out of the hole, which she then filled with rich compost. The bed would be ready when the bloodroot arrived in the fall.

She'd done enough for now.

On the way back to the house she thought of Casey, going over guest lists, making sure no suspicious persons had been invited to West Tisbury at the time of the presidential visit. She could help with those lists. She knew everyone in the village and had written about most of their guests in her column. But she hadn't been asked to help. Casey should be solving the murders and *she* should be going over the guest lists.

She'd talk to Casey about that again.

Right now, though, clearing up the mystery of Vivian's phone call might answer a few questions. Tuesday was the day she usually read to the elderly at the nursing home connected to the hospital. It would be simple to find out who made the call to Vivian.

CHAPTER 36

On Tuesday morning, Casey picked up Victoria for her weekly reading. "There's an all-Island police chiefs' meeting, Victoria, so I may be late picking you up."

"No problem," said Victoria. "I have business at the hospital. I need to learn who called Vivian."

Casey sighed. "I should be investigating. You should be checking my guest list."

"Why didn't you ask me?"

"Requires a security clearance."

"Ridiculous," said Victoria.

"I agree." They pulled up to the nursing home's main entrance and Victoria got out. "Good luck, Deputy."

Victoria touched her fingers to her forehead in a kind of salute and went inside.

She read to her small group of patients for about an hour. Her volunteer stint at the nursing home always left her feeling depressed, and after she'd shaken hands with her audience and said goodbye, she walked slowly down the corridor that joined the two buildings. It didn't matter what she read, the patients were glad to have someone talking to break the monotony of their days. The home, not really a home, was like a fancy hotel. Lovely caring nurses. A beautiful setting. Excellent food. A daily routine.

She sat down on one of the benches in the corridor.

That was just it. Routine. Grandchildren and great-grandchildren didn't tear in and out, slamming doors, laughing, crying, shouting, arguing, playing, asking to be read to and snuggling up at one's feet, thumb in mouth, hugging a favorite bear. People dropping by with town gossip and a dish. People dropping by with petitions to sign. Life and liveliness and vigor.

"Hi, Auntie Vic!"

Victoria looked up from her reverie. Hope, her grandniece, was striding down the corridor toward her. "I thought I might catch up to you. I heard about the chiefs' meeting and figured you might have time to grab a bite to eat."

Victoria brightened at the sight of her much-loved grandniece. "That's exactly what I need."

"Everything's crazy with all the construction going on. They've moved the cafeteria."

They hiked down the long corridor with its wide windows and view of the harbor and launched into the usual Island chatter about the president's visit.

"We've been practicing drills for every emergency you can think of."

"I suppose that means no beach time?" asked Victoria.

Hope shook her head and her long hair swirled around her face. "Not until he's safely back home. What have you got planned for this afternoon, Auntie Vic?"

"You might be able to help me with some research."

"Sure thing." Hope steered them toward the cafeteria door. "After you. Best food on the Island."

Victoria loaded up her tray with a chicken potpie, an avocado and tomato salad, a roll, and, reaching far back into the food display, the largest slice of blueberry pie.

"Ice cream on top, Mrs. Trumbull?" asked the counter woman.

"Coffee ice cream," said Victoria. She reached into her wallet. "I'm paying for both of us."

"I'll bring your pie and ice cream to you when it's time for dessert."

They carried their trays to a table near the window and ate and talked. More about the president's visit. Security at the hospital. Backgrounds checked. Specialists on call. Helicopters parked on the pad behind the hospital with pilots housed where they would be only seconds away from takeoff.

"Pretty exciting," Hope concluded. "Now," she said, changing the subject, "how's Lockwood? Safely in jail, I hope."

Victoria shook her head. "I didn't press charges."

Hope frowned. "The guy's a loose cannon."

"Imprisonment wouldn't do any good," said Victoria.

"I guess you know what you're doing. So tell me what you need from me." She stood up. "First, I'll get your pie."

"Here it comes now," said Victoria, seeing the counter woman bringing her dessert.

Hope sat again. "Okay, what can I do for you, Aunty Vic?"

"Do you know anything about the woman who called Dr. Mann's office the day Mrs. Wilmington died?" Victoria turned the plate so the pointed end of the pie faced her.

"Do I! What a furor that call of hers caused." Hope leaned her elbows on the table. "The hospital fired her on the spot. Giving out patient information is a huge no-no."

Victoria cut off the point with her fork. "Do you know anything about the woman?"

"Yeah, sure. Vivian was her friend. A close personal friend, as in spouse."

"Ah," said Victoria, referring to the piece of pie she'd just eaten. "Wonderful pie."

"Good food at the hospital," said Hope.

"Do you know where they lived?"

"I can find out. It'll only take a couple of minutes." Hope got up from the table. "How about a cup of coffee?"

"That would hit the spot. Regular, not decaf. Black."

She had finished her pie and was still savoring her coffee, watching the birds at the birdfeeder in the small garden and thinking about Vivian when her grandniece returned.

Hope sat down and handed Victoria a paper with names, addresses, and phone numbers. "Her name is Pace Pacheco, lives in Oak Bluffs off Wing Road. She and Vivian were a pair for a long time, several years, anyway."

"Did Pace find another job after she was fired?"

"I have no idea, Auntie Vic. Why?"

"I want to stop by her place on my way home and talk to her."

"Can't hurt. Can I do anything else for you?"

Victoria held up the paper with the address. "This is what I needed. Thank you."

Hope checked her watch and stood. "Gotta run. Thanks for lunch, and good luck with the detective work."

"I can't spare more that fifteen minutes, max," said Casey, when Victoria asked her to stop at the small house on Wing Road. "I have to go over the invitation list for someone who's getting married. Why'd they have to pick the same date as the visit?"

"They probably set the date before the president did. I'll volunteer an hour to go over the list."

"You don't have clearance," muttered Casey.

"Sign your name to my work."

Casey laughed. "Wish I'd thought of that two weeks ago."

"I might have saved you several days."

"Yeah, yeah, Victoria. Don't rub it in."

The house was a gray-shingled cabin with red trim, the size and shape of a trailer. It was surrounded by scrub oak and pine and had a small vegetable and flower garden out front, with tomato plants and lettuce, daisies and early roses. Casey parked by the side of the road, and Victoria went up to the house.

Her knock was answered by a motherly middle-aged woman wearing a smock spotted with daubs of paint. She smelled of turpentine and was holding a long, narrow paint brush wet with yellow paint in one hand.

"Can I help you?" She did a sort of double take. "You're Victoria Trumbull. I love your poetry. I'm Pace."

"Thank you," said Victoria. "I wanted to offer my condolences on Vivian's death. I understand you and she were close."

"Omigod"—Pace's expression became grave—"come in, won't you? Sorry about the mess."

To Victoria, the mess looked considerably neater than her own house.

"You can sit wherever there's a place. I've got to put this brush in turpentine."

"I don't want to interrupt your work," said Victoria.

Pace thought a moment. "Come on into my studio, then. That's what Vivian called it. It's a corner of our bedroom."

Victoria followed her the few steps. "I'm so sorry you lost both your job and your partner all at once."

"That's not all, Mrs. Trumbull." She took a deep breath and let it out. "I'll show you what I'm working on."

The bedroom took up almost half of the small house. In one corner was a queen-size bed, a bureau, and two bedside tables. The other two-thirds of the room was taken up by Pace's easel and a large deal table covered with tubes of paint and jars of brushes. Paintings were stacked against the legs of the table.

Pace took another deep breath and straightened her shoulders. "Here." She turned the easel so it faced Victoria. A portrait of Vivian.

"It's beautiful," said Victoria, meaning it. "You've given her a quality we never saw at the clinic, almost ethereal."

"That's how she was, Mrs. Trumbull. She was so inoffensive. Kind. Shy. Sweet. Why her?"

"I'm so sorry."

"The job loss, well that's okay, I guess. I'll get unemployment. I'm painting, and I've got a few job possibilities lined up." She glanced at the painting, tipped her head to one side, and examined it. "You don't mind if I keep working?"

"Please do. Tell me about the call."

"Stupid of me. But I'd just been diagnosed with breast cancer and that was why I called. To tell Vivian. I didn't realize she'd freak out the way she did. I mean, it's not a death sentence anymore. It's something unpleasant that you have to deal with." She dipped her brush into a swirl of blue and green paint and touched it to the side of Vivian's face. The hint of color suddenly gave the face a three-dimensional quality. "I know chemo will be tough. I expected that. When she freaked out, I changed the subject to the first thing that came into my mind: Mrs. Wilmington's death. Someone must have overheard me." She worked silently at the painting for a few minutes. "Committing suicide is something I have trouble living with, Mrs. Trumbull. I should have waited until we were home and having a glass of wine before breaking the news."

"She didn't commit suicide," said Victoria.

Pace stepped away from her painting, brush still in the air, and looked at Victoria. "What?"

"Someone apparently struck her on the back of the head, knocking her into the harbor."

Pace sat on the foot of the bed. "Murdered?"

"You weren't the cause of her death."

"Who was?"

"We don't know yet." Victoria stood up.

"Oh, dear God!" Pace held her hand up to her forehead.

"Are you all right?"

"Yes. Yes, I'll be fine."

"What you've just told me may help us find her killer," said Victoria.

Pace glanced down at her paint-smeared hands, still holding the brush.

"I don't like to leave you alone after that," said Victoria, "but someone is waiting for me."

Pace, too, stood. "You've brought bad news, Mrs. Trumbull, but you've also eased my guilt. Let me see you to the door."

In the police cruiser, Victoria fastened her seat belt and sat back, looking straight ahead.

"Okay, Victoria. What happened in there?"

"We thought that phone call had upset Vivian because she heard something to do with Mrs. Wilmington's murder."

"Oh?" Casey started the engine.

"Her killer must have thought so, too."

Casey checked the rearview mirror and pulled away from the side of the road. "Care to explain?"

Victoria nodded. "Pace had been diagnosed with breast cancer. That's what upset Vivian."

"Yikes," said Casey. "If Vivian's killer thought she knew something, he was waaaay off."

"Waste. Such a terrible, terrible waste," said Victoria.

Back home, Victoria called the dental clinic. "Good afternoon, Tiffany. Is Dr. Mann in?"

"No, ma'am. Can I help you?"

"Do you know where to reach him?"

"Yes, ma'am. I've got his cell number." Papers shuffled and she came back on the phone with the number.

"Thank you," said Victoria, disconnected, and dialed again.

He answered after the first ring.

"I want to offer my condolences, again," said Victoria. "Such sad losses of both Mrs. Wilmington and Vivian."

Mann cleared his throat. "Tragic. Both of them."

"Would you care to stop by my house this afternoon for a cup of tea or a drink? I'd like to talk to you."

"Is this something we can clear up on the phone?"

"It would be more pleasant over a drink. I've got Scotch, bourbon, and wine."

"A social matter, not a police matter, then?"

"Both, but we'll start with social."

"All right. I was going to say I'm busy, but I'm not. What time?"

"Would four thirty be convenient?"

"I'll see you then."

"You know where I live?"

"Of course, Mrs. Trumbull. An Island landmark."

CHAPTER 37

Victoria laid out crackers and cheese on the coffee table in the parlor, thinking the more formal setting would be to her advantage. The cookroom with its baskets hanging from the beams and its red-checked tablecloth might put him too much at ease. She didn't know what his preferred drink was, so she brought out a bottle of Scotch and a bottle of bourbon along with the ice bucket and a pitcher of water.

Dr. Mann drove up at precisely four thirty and she met him at the door.

He was wearing an open-collared blue shirt with the sleeves rolled up, pressed khaki trousers, and boat shoes with no socks. Victoria was accustomed to seeing him in a white lab coat over a dress shirt and tie. Now, he looked young and vulnerable and she could see his appeal to women.

"This is the first time I've been inside your house, Mrs. Trumbull. I drive past it all the time and have for years. It's"—he paused—"authentic."

"Thank you." Victoria smiled. "I'm glad you agreed to come."

She went into the parlor and he followed her. She sat in her usual mouse-colored wing chair and Mann perched on the stiff sofa with its elaborately carved back.

"You'll have to help yourself," Victoria said. "I'm not good at mixing drinks and I don't know which you prefer."

"You, first, Mrs. Trumbull. What's your preference?"

"Bourbon," said Victoria.

He reached for the bourbon bottle. "How do you like it?"

She indicated a half inch with thumb and forefinger. "With plenty of water."

He poured hers, added water and ice, then poured bourbon for himself. "Cheers, Mrs. Trumbull." He held up his glass.

"Cheers," said Victoria.

"Down to business?" he asked. "Or shall we relax first?"

"The latter sounds good," said Victoria. "Congratulations, by the way, on the three million dollar bequest. That's going to be a big help for the clinic, isn't it."

"We can use an infusion of cash, quite frankly. Came at a good time."

"Did you have any idea Mrs. Wilmington planned to bequeath you that?"

"I knew she was wealthy. I didn't realize just how wealthy she was. You know, when I opened the clinic she and all four grand-children were my first patients."

He hadn't answered her question. But this was their social time. Victoria tried to think of something that didn't hit a hot button, but everything seemed fraught with meaning.

Fishing would be a safe topic. Almost everyone was a fisherman and those who weren't liked to make fun of those who were.

"Do you like to fish, Dr. Mann?"

"Horace," he corrected her. "No, but I enjoy eating what others catch."

"The other day Sam Minnowfish caught several bluefish at Quansoo and brought me some nice fillets."

"Sam is quite a fisherman," said Mann.

"I baked them with mayonnaise and fresh dill," said Victoria.

"Sounds delicious," said Mann, toying with his glass.

The conversation lagged. Victoria decided to plunge right in and ask her questions. "How did Vivian happen to be working for you?"

"She answered an ad in the *Island Enquirer*. One of three people, and I hired her."

"I'm surprised you got so few responses to the ad."

"I offered a minimal wage with few benefits." He smiled suddenly. "Free dental care." He sipped his drink, put the glass down, and checked the bottle. "Maker's Mark. Good bourbon."

"I'm glad you enjoy it." Victoria took a small sip of her own. "Patients seemed to like Vivian."

"She wasn't good with the chitchat that patients need. Otherwise, she was adequate. Conscientious."

"Do you have any thoughts on what might have upset her so much in that last phone call, aside from the death of Mrs. Wilmington?"

"No idea at all. The caller was completely out of line divulging patient information. There are strict rules about privacy." Mann's voice had become tight. "A death, compounded by the fact that the patient's family hadn't yet been notified. I called the hospital immediately to report her and I understand she was fired. As she should have been." He picked up his glass and took a swig of the bourbon. "Mrs. Wilmington's granddaughter, Susan, was there at the time of Mrs. Wilmington's seizure."

"I know. I was there, too."

"Of course. Apparently a grandson came by earlier but left."

"Which grandson was that?"

"I didn't see him. Aileen mentioned that Mrs. Wilmington's grandson had stopped by, didn't say which one. Maybe both."

Victoria made a mental note to check on that. So it was Horace Mann who had notified the hospital about the call. "The caller probably told her something pertaining to Mrs. Wilmington's

death or her last words," said Mann. "I blame the caller for caus-
ing Vivian's suicide."

She changed the subject. "Tell me about Dr. McBride's assistant,
Jane Douglas. She seems out of place in the clinic."

Mann glanced at her sharply. "What do you mean?"

Victoria wasn't sure what she meant. "I suppose it's because she
seems so refined, so, I don't know."

"She answered an ad I placed for a dental assistant," said Mann.

"I got the impression that Dr. McBride was not enthusiastic
about Jane working for her."

"Aileen recognizes Jane is competent and that patients are fond
of her."

"Apparently she came with high recommendations from you,"
said Victoria, turning her glass around in circles to avoid looking
directly at him. "Had you known Jane for some time?"

"Jane was a summer girl. Our paths crossed at the yacht club
and tennis club. Yes, I knew of her."

"She seems delightful, very gracious."

"Yes," said Mann. "She is."

"Mrs. Wilmington seems to have had issues with her. Do you
know why?"

"I hadn't noticed," he said.

"I knew Mrs. Wilmington socially, but not well. She could be
abrasive." Victoria took a small sip of her drink. It was too early in
the day for her to enjoy a cocktail. "Almost every time I came to the
clinic, she was there."

Mann got up from the sofa and began to pace. He glanced at
the portrait of the woman that hung above the sofa. "That woman
looks half drowned."

"She does, doesn't she." Victoria thought about Vivian, drowning. "She also looks like Jane, at the clinic, except the woman in
the portrait has dark hair."

"Yes. A bit." He paced to the west window and back and looked up at the portrait as he passed it. "Her eyes follow me wherever I go."

"When we were children, we'd crouch down or stand on tip-toe to find a place where the woman wasn't watching us. We were afraid to fib, because we were sure she'd know and tell our mother."

"It's an eerie portrait. I should think you'd be uncomfortable with her watching over you like that."

Victoria smiled. "I suppose that's why I like it so much."

Mann turned back to Victoria. "You know, Mrs. Trumbull, there've been a lot of rumors flying around."

"I've heard a great many rumors. Which ones do you mean?"

"About my heritage."

"I knew you were adopted. I didn't think that was rumor."

Mann sat down on the sofa, his back to the portrait. "No, not that. My parents, the Manns, adopted me when I was only a few days old. They were my true parents."

"What were the rumors?" Victoria prompted.

"For as long as I can remember the identity of my birth mother has been a matter of speculation. A summer girl? An Island girl? A married woman? No one actually said anything to me, but I knew about the rumors and I could hear the whispers."

"That must have been difficult, especially when you were a child."

"I didn't understand what the gossip was about until I was old enough to learn about sex and then I got curious. Wanted to find my birth mother. Who was she? Who did she couple with to pro-duce me? Why was she so eager to get rid of me?" He sat forward, hands clasped between his knees. "I imagined her as a beautiful, innocent presence who'd been taken advantage of. I imagined she was hunting for me and it was taking years because she'd been hospitalized. Or been in prison for a crime she hadn't committed. Or had been kidnapped. Tall, slender, golden haired."

Victoria listened, her own drink forgotten.

Mann picked up his glass, took a gulp, put the glass down, wiped his mouth with the back of his hand. "In my dreams, she was always backlit, her face indistinct. Her hair was a golden halo, reddish gold, coppery like mine. She was always running toward me, wearing a long gauzy dress, her arms outstretched to me." He reached over and lifted the bourbon bottle. Nodded at Victoria, who shook her head. She'd hardly touched hers and his was still almost full. He topped off his glass anyway.

"And?" asked Victoria.

"And then, Mrs. Wilmington came into my life." He sat back, arms folded over his chest. "When I opened the clinic, as I said, she was my first patient along with the four grandchildren. I'd heard rumors that she'd borne a child out of wedlock, but didn't connect the rumors with me. At least, not at first."

"How did you learn of the rumors connecting you with her?" Victoria took another sip of her drink to keep her hands occupied.

"Sam Minnowfish was kidding around with Arthur after one of Mrs. Wilmington's first visits and I overheard them. Arthur said something like, guess we're stuck with her. Sam said something about keeping track of her baby boy. That was enough to trigger my curiosity."

"Were you able to talk to her about your suspicions?"

"Good Lord, no."

He got up and paced again, hands thrust into his pockets. He stopped in front of the portrait. "While I was sitting there, that lady's eyes were boring a hole in my back." He continued to pace. "A couple of months ago, I told Mrs. Wilmington I had a test I needed to do and took a buccal swab."

"I don't know what that is."

"It's a way to get a sample of cells for DNA analysis."

"DNA analysis? I thought that was not only prohibitively expensive, but time consuming."

He stopped pacing. "Not anymore. Anyone can purchase a kit on the Internet. You rub a cotton swab on the inside of someone's cheek to collect buccal cells, send it off to a lab for analysis, and get the results in a couple of weeks." He began pacing again. "Since buccal cells are on the inside of the cheek a dental patient doesn't question having her dentist swab the inside of her mouth." He stopped again in front of the portrait. "I sent off a swab of my own at the same time."

Victoria waited.

He jabbed a finger at his chest. "I'm the son of that goddamned bitch."

"Not the gentle sylphlike image you'd dreamed about," said Victoria.

"The bitch didn't want hubby to know about me."

"Why not simply claim he was the father?"

"The rumor was that she'd fornicated with a Wampanoag brave. Afraid my looks would give her away."

"The Island's Wampanoags don't look distinctively Indian. Look at Sam Minnowfish."

"We could pass for brothers, right? I guess that was what she was afraid of. So she gave me away." He snapped his fingers. "Just like that. Never acknowledged me."

"Do you have any idea at all who your birth father is?"

He gave a brittle laugh. "One of these days I'll get Minnowfish to check his DNA. Maybe we *are* brothers. Wouldn't that be ironic."

He reached for his glass and took a mouthful of his drink. He swallowed and began pacing again.

Victoria said nothing.

"What in hell was she thinking when she came to my clinic

when I first opened it? She wanted to come every week to look at me?" He thrust his hands into his pockets. "She made this cute hint about helping to support the clinic one of these days."

He stopped. Walked to the west window and glanced out. His back turned to her. "When I told you the infusion of cash would be welcome, I should have said I was desperate. I decided to kill her and I planned it in detail." He turned and bowed to the portrait. "There you have it, Madam Inquisitor."

"Did you?" Victoria asked.

"Did I?" He swiveled around to face her and grinned. "You think maybe?" He looked at his watch and picked up the tray with its bottles and still-full glasses. "I'm certainly the number one suspect, don't you think?"

CHAPTER 38

Victoria needed fresh air. After Mann left, she emptied their glasses into the sink, put the bottles back in the cupboard, then hiked to the police station.

She breathed deeply to rid her system of Mann's visit. Even this late in the day, Casey would be busy.

"What were you thinking, Victoria? Alone with that cold-blooded guy who might have murdered that woman and you ask him point blank if he did it?"

"He never answered seriously." Victoria settled herself into the armchair in front of Casey's desk. "In fact, I don't think he did kill her. He doesn't have the strength of character a killer needs." She folded her hands on top of her lilac wood stick. The stick had several scars along its polished length, one fresh.

"You never learn, do you." Casey sighed and sorted papers into piles on her desk. "Speaking of would-be murderers, what's happening with Lockwood?"

"We haven't heard from him since he hurt his wrist."

"You mean, since you broke it. He's probably hiding in a cave somewhere, licking his wounds." Casey shoved one of the piles toward Victoria. "Here's the guest list. Anything you can do to help identify these people will be much appreciated. I'll sign off on them."

It took Victoria less than an hour to go over the list. She had known most of the wedding guests for years and had mentioned all of them in her weekly column.

"Can't believe I didn't think of signing off on your work," said Casey as she drove Victoria home again. "Thank you, Victoria."

The following day Victoria got Jane Douglas's phone number from Tiffany at the dental clinic.

Jane answered on the first ring.

"Mrs. Trumbull, I'm so glad you called," Jane said. "When you came to the clinic I wanted so much to meet you—"

"But too much was happening," Victoria finished. "I'd like to talk to you today if possible. Can we meet in some convenient place?"

"Of course. Do you mind coming to my house? It's my nanny's day off."

Elizabeth dropped her grandmother off at the foot of the long hill that ended at the Vineyard Haven harbor. Jane's house was tucked in among low trees and overlooked the harbor. Victoria tapped on the sliding glass of the front door. She could see through the house's open plan to the harbor beyond, sparkling in the late-afternoon sun, dotted with boats of every description.

Jane came to the door holding a small child. "Come in, Mrs. Trumbull. This is my daughter, Davina. She's almost two."

Davina, thumb in her mouth, ducked her head into her mother's shoulder.

"You're very pretty, Davina," said Victoria. "I have a cat who has fur almost exactly the color of your hair."

Davina took her thumb out of her mouth. "Kitty cat?"

"Yes. His name is McCavity. He's a marmalade cat and I call him Cavvy for short."

"Shall we go into the living room?" asked Jane. "I have some lemonade and cookies."

"Cookies," said Davina.

"I just recently heard you had a daughter," said Victoria, seating herself in an armchair where she had a view of the harbor.

"I like my privacy," said Jane. "It's not easy on the Island where everyone seems to know everyone else's business."

Victoria smiled. "True. That's what makes people behave themselves."

At that, Jane smiled, too. "I wish." She got up from the couch holding her daughter. "I'll take her out to her sandbox to play. Be right back." She slid open the door that faced the harbor and deposited the baby in the sand patch bounded by landscaping ties. She dusted sand off her hands and returned to the living room, leaving the door open, and sat on the couch at right angles to Victoria. "I assume you want to talk about Mrs. Wilmington."

"I'm trying to get some picture of the staff and the dynamics involved." Victoria said.

Jane nodded. "I'm relatively new at the clinic. I applied for a dental assistant job that Dr. Mann advertised."

Victoria nodded. "You have a college degree, don't you?"

"Yes, in art history."

"That's Roosevelt's field, too."

"We have art in common, but he has a Ph.D. I don't."

"Why did you choose Dr. Mann's clinic? There are other Island dentists."

"I'd known Horace for many years." Jane's smile seemed forced. "I wanted to work for him."

"Dr. Mann told me that you and he were active in the tennis and yacht clubs during summer," said Victoria. "That must have been quite a romantic time."

Jane nodded. "It was. I spent summers with my grandmother here in this very house. We teenagers went sailing and swimming, played tennis. Those were golden times."

"Not far back from what I see. You're hardly out of your teens."

Jane glanced out the window at her daughter, who was running a toy dump truck along the wooden borders of her sandbox. "Davina is Horace's daughter," she said suddenly.

Victoria nodded.

Jane went on. "I didn't know he was already married."

Victoria waited.

"I said earlier that everyone on the Island knows everyone else's business. But I was a summer kid and had no knowledge of anything that went on outside the tennis and yacht clubs. That was my world." She stood and went to the open door, watched Davina for a moment, then returned to her seat. "Horace had two worlds, the world of the working Islander and the moneyed world of his Mann parents." She looked up at Victoria.

"He wanted me to have an abortion, too. I didn't understand why he was so insistent. I know, now."

"This was before you went to work for him."

Jane smiled again. "Working for him is my way of getting back at him. He sees me every day, knows I am rearing the child he wanted me to abort."

"Isn't that difficult for you, working in such a hostile environment? I know Dr. McBride is an uncomfortable boss."

"Dr. McBride has her eyes on Horace, Mrs. Trumbull. Especially now that three million dollars is involved. It's hardly a secret. In his mind, Horace is irresistible to women. Some of us are stupid enough to fall for his"—she made quotation marks in the air—" 'sincerity.' Bullshit. All bullshit."

"I don't know what to say," said Victoria.

"I don't blame you. Horace came by the other day, wanting to bond with 'his' daughter." Again, she glanced out the window at Davina, who was now pouring sand out of a bucket onto her legs. "I don't want my baby to have anything to do with him. He had

242

the gall, the audacity, the temerity to send me a dozen yellow roses." She looked at Victoria. "You know the traditional meaning of yellow roses, don't you?"

Victoria shook her head.

"Well"—Jane smiled—"yellow roses mean infidelity. What do you think of that?"

Victoria didn't know what to think and said nothing.

"Last week I met with his wife, Charlotte. I wanted her to meet my baby. I thought she should know."

"Good for you," said Victoria. "That was exactly the right thing to do. How did she respond?"

"We're friends. I wasn't Horace's first conquest and Charlotte was aware of what he was doing to their sons. She's filed for divorce."

Victoria nodded. She waited a moment and then asked, "Did you have any idea Mrs. Wilmington was bequeathing Dr. Mann such a large sum?"

"Mrs. Wilmington hinted that she had money and someday some of it might go to the clinic. None of us believed her. Well, maybe Aileen did." Jane stood again, went to the floor-to-ceiling windows and the open door, and watched her daughter.

Victoria waited. She could hear Davina singing to herself.

Jane turned back again. "The way Mrs. Wilmington kept pestering him, the staff suspected she was Horace's mother."

"Did Dr. McBride have a special dislike of Mrs. Wilmington?"

"Aileen? She hated her. But to give Aileen credit she never was anything other than professional when it came to treating that woman." Jane returned to her seat on the couch. "You know, it would have been easy for any of us, after one insult too many, to administer arsenic to Mrs. Wilmington. In Aileen's case, I can imagine her thinking it would not only get rid of the worst possible thorn in her flesh, but would help Horace." She stood again. "Would you like a cup of tea? I'm getting one for myself."

"That would be lovely."

While Jane was in the kitchen, Victoria tried to absorb all the information she was getting.

When Jane returned with a tray and tea things, Victoria asked, "Tell me about the other staff members, Ophelia Demetrios, Sam Minnowfish, and the two technicians, Arthur Morgan and Roosevelt Mark."

"I don't really know Ophelia." Jane poured tea into delicate cups and handed one to Victoria. "Sam likes to flaunt his Wampanoag heritage. He's a good dentist. He doesn't like Horace, but tries not to show it. Arthur"—she hesitated—"he's competent. Patients like him. Roosevelt and I talk about art when we're not busy. He's very knowledgeable."

"You seem to have some doubts about Arthur?"

Jane picked up her own cup but didn't drink. "It's embarrassing. He has a schoolboy crush on me. He's careful not to show it in the office, but the day Mrs. Wilmington . . ." Jane stopped.

"The day of her death," prompted Victoria.

"The day of her death, Arthur drove me home. I've tried to keep my life and my daughter private. But Arthur knew where I lived and that I have a daughter. It felt as though he was stalking me."

"We were saying the Island has few secrets," said Victoria.

"You're right. I just felt uncomfortable on the drive home. He invited me to have lunch with him. Lunch was the last thing I wanted after, well . . ."

"Understandable," said Victoria.

"It sounds silly now. He's a nice man, but he's not my type. I suppose I was being overly sensitive." Jane glanced again at her daughter.

"Do you know anything about Arthur's background? Or his relationship to Mrs. Wilmington?"

"Just that he's from the Island and he felt the same way about

Mrs. Wilmington that all the rest of us did. The staff, except for Dr. Mann, would compare what we called our 'Wilmington notes' after she left and make jokes about her." She sipped her tea and set the cup down in its saucer. "Except Roosevelt. He never took part in the discussions."

"Had Arthur worked with her?"

"Before I was hired, he was the dental technician who helped whichever dentist was assigned to Mrs. Wilmington. When Aileen came, they dumped Mrs. Wilmington on her. Before I arrived, Arthur worked with Aileen."

"What did you think of Mrs. Wilmington?" asked Victoria.

"Don't ask!" Jane laughed. "You have no idea how awful that woman was. Pretending she was coming to the clinic for treatment, when she was spying on her son. I have no sympathy for Horace, but I can see where he's coming from."

"What about her treatment of you?" asked Victoria.

"Belittling, demanding, ugly, nasty, vain, egocentric."

"Why, do you suppose?"

"She probably suspected a connection between Horace and me and didn't like that one bit."

"And how did she treat Dr. McBride?"

"Mrs. Wilmington was more or less civil to Aileen, but she was awfully picky and demanding. After all, Aileen was the one who jabbed her with needles and stuck her hands in her mouth."

There was a knock on the door and Victoria looked up to see Elizabeth, who'd come to pick her up.

"Come in," said Jane, getting up from the couch to greet her. "You're Mrs. Trumbull's granddaughter, I know. Would you care for some tea?"

"I'd love some, but can't stop. The harbor is crazy busy."

"The presidential visit. At least spare a minute. I'd like your grandmother to autograph my copies of her poetry books."

Elizabeth smiled. "I can wait for that."

In the convertible, Elizabeth shifted into gear and started up the long hill to Main Street. "Did you learn anything new?"

"I've been getting a picture of Mrs. Wilmington. She was not popular."

Elizabeth slowed at the top of the hill and waited for a car to pass, then turned left onto upper Main Street. "That's just the clinic staff's reaction. Think of her grandchildren."

"I have been," said Victoria. "I have a feeling the grandchildren disliked her even more."

"What about Dr. Mann?"

"I'm increasingly losing respect for our Dr. Mann."

"You think he killed her?" Elizabeth asked with surprise.

"I don't think he has the pluck to kill anyone."

Elizabeth slowed as they approached the library where Main Street became one way against them and turned right onto Greenwood.

"What next?" asked Elizabeth.

"I haven't talked to Arthur Morgan, but from what everyone has said about him, I don't think I'll learn anything new."

"I can't give you a ride tomorrow," said Elizabeth.

"I knew you'd be busy. Bill O'Malley is giving me a ride," said Victoria. "In his dump truck."

CHAPTER 39

Bill O'Malley drove up to Victoria's house in his blue dump truck the next afternoon. He set a milk crate by the passenger door for her to step up into the high passenger seat.

"Where to, Victoria?"

"Snake Hollow Road." Victoria hoisted herself up into the truck with O'Malley's help. "I don't know the house number, but it's on the right with a dog pen next to it."

"Shouldn't be a problem," said O'Malley, shifting into gear. "How's Elizabeth?"

"Busy," said Victoria, thinking that Bill O'Malley was not only single, but was just the right age for Elizabeth. He was attractive in his red plaid shirt and worn jeans. And the owner of a fine dump truck with air-conditioning and music.

"I moved my boat to Tashmoo," he said, apparently unaware of Victoria's assessment of him. "The Oak Bluffs harbor is crawling with official vessels. I figured there'd be a lot of activity there for the next week or so."

"Have you heard when the president is scheduled to arrive?"

"Later this week." O'Malley turned left onto Edgartown Road and then right onto Old County. "Who's this guy you're visiting?"

"Arthur Morgan. He's a dental technician at the clinic. Do you know him?"

"Lot of Morgans on the Island. If he's who I'm thinking of, he's got a huge dog named Dog."

"He's the one. Do you know anything about him?"

"Just know him by sight."

They drove past the elementary school and Whippoorwill Farm's stand and when Old County ended, right onto State Road. Snake Hollow was just before the Tashmoo Overlook and O'Malley turned onto it.

"Does this guy know you're coming?"

"I left a message on his cell phone," said Victoria.

They drove past several turnoffs, each of which led up a steep hillside, and eventually came to a narrow dirt road marked with a sign that read MORGAN AND DOG. They drove up the steep slope until they were within sight of a small cabin with a dog pen next to it. A large dog lay in the middle, chewing on something that appeared to be a ham bone. The dog looked up. The access road narrowed.

"I'm not sure I can get much closer," said O'Malley.

"It's only a short walk," said Victoria. "Drop me off here."

"I'll pick you in a half hour then. Will that give you enough time?"

"That should be plenty."

He set down the milk crate again and helped Victoria out of her seat. She glanced up at the cabin and was glad she'd brought her lilac wood stick, as the way up looked quite steep.

"I'll walk you up to the cabin," said O'Malley.

"That's not necessary. I'll see you in a half hour."

But the narrow drive, even though it was short, was steeper than she'd realized and she had to pause partway up to catch her breath. The dog watched her approach, dropped his bone, stood, and barked.

"Hello, Dog." Victoria rested again, leaning on her stick.

The dog stopped barking.

Arthur, apparently alerted by Dog, came to the door. "Mrs. Trumbull, greetings. My drive is kind of rough walking." He hurried down the steps.

Victoria took his offered arm. "I hope you got the message that I was coming."

"Sure did," said Arthur. "Made some iced tea in case you'd like a glass."

"That sounds delightful." They went up the steps onto the porch, Victoria holding Arthur's arm with one hand, her stick with the other. At the top, she bent over to catch her breath.

"You okay?" he asked.

"I'm fine. Just a bit out of shape."

She was several inches taller than Arthur, and when she stood up straight, he had to look up to her. Victoria had only seen him before at the clinic, where he was usually dressed in khaki slacks and a white cotton uniform jacket. Now he had on jeans and a T-shirt that fit tightly across his broad chest and exposed hairy, muscular arms with fading tattoos. If it weren't for the unfortunate scars that pitted his face, he'd have been quite handsome with his wavy dark hair and bright blue eyes.

"Come on in, Mrs. Trumbull. Not much of a place, but it suits me."

"I wish more people knew how delightful a small house can be. Mine is much too large."

"Takes a lot of maintenance to keep up an old house like yours." He stepped aside so she could enter.

The interior was an open area, a combination of living room, dining room, and kitchen. A counter separated the kitchen area from the rest. A stove, refrigerator, and sink were to her right, and directly ahead of her, the living room had a large floor-to-ceiling window with a view of the hillside beyond, almost blocked by a large flowering rhododendron.

"This is it," said Arthur, spreading his arms to encompass his domain. "That door goes to the bathroom. My bedroom is behind this curtain." He pulled it aside to show a room just big enough for a single bed and a bureau. "I built the house myself."

"Wonderful," said Victoria. "I'm quite envious."

"Have a seat," said Arthur. "The couch is pretty comfortable." He indicated a battered leather couch pushed against the wall ahead and to the right.

Victoria settled onto it. When she turned slightly she could see the mass of shell-pink rhododendron blossoms. Light filtered through them giving the room a warm glow.

"Such a lovely sight," said Victoria.

"You know, I got that rhododendron plant about five years ago." Arthur moved into the kitchen area and poured tea into glasses. "On sale, end of season." He set the pitcher down. "Only about so big." He held his hands a foot apart. "It's pretty happy there. Acid soil. You take sugar in your iced tea, Mrs. Trumbull?"

"Just plain, thank you." Victoria moved slightly to a more comfortable part of the couch.

He set the tray with the glasses of tea on the wooden crate that served as a coffee table. "Here you are, Mrs. Trumbull." He handed one of the glasses to her.

"Thank you." Victoria took a sip. "That hits the spot."

An easy chair with worn green upholstery faced the couch where she was seated. "Dog's place," said Arthur, brushing dog hairs off a striped Mexican blanket that covered the seat. He sat down and lifted his own glass as a kind of toast. "You said you wanted to talk to me. About Mrs. Wilmington, I guess."

"I was interested in your impressions of the clinic's staff," said

Victoria. "And their reactions. Apparently Mrs. Wilmington wasn't well liked."

He nodded. "You got that right."

"You worked with her before Dr. McBride arrived. What sort of person was she?"

Arthur leaned back in the chair, his fingers laced over his stomach. "You know, before Dr. McBride was hired the other two dentists, Ophelia and Sam, had to work with her. I was always the tech she asked for. She didn't like Roosevelt."

Out in the yard, Dog started to bark.

Arthur stood. "Mind if I let him in? He's a good dog."

"Please do. I like dogs," said Victoria.

Dog bounded in, stopped by Victoria and sniffed her outstretched hand. She patted his head and he lifted a paw.

"He likes you," said Arthur.

"He's a nice dog," said Victoria. "Well behaved."

"Thanks." Dog settled himself next to the chair with his head on his forepaws. "You wanted to know about Mrs. Wilmington. She was definitely a pain in the . . ." He paused. "A real pain."

"Was she especially disliked by anyone on the staff? Dr. Mann, for instance."

Arthur laughed. "She was especially disliked by everyone." Dog lifted his head and Arthur bent down and scratched it. "She was always bugging Dr. Mann."

"In what way?" Victoria picked up her glass of iced tea.

"She'd drop by the clinic every week like clockwork. On her way to go shopping, you know. She usually brought a present of some kind, cookies or a box of candy."

"That doesn't sound too bad." She took a sip and waited.

He stopped scratching Dog's head. "It was disruptive. Dr. Mann had to stop what he was doing and butter her up, you know. Had to be polite. She was a patient, after all." Dog lifted a paw and

Arthur scratched his head again. "Patients sit there, uncomfortable, you know. Dental appointments are no fun."

Victoria nodded, thinking about her last few visits.

"I understand she willed him a large sum. Do you know why?"

"Well, it was rumored that she'd had a baby and the baby died. This was before my time. You know how Island stories are."

"I do indeed."

Dog's eyes were closing and Arthur continued to scratch his head. "Once she hinted she'd leave the clinic something when she died."

"That's a powerful motive for him to wish her dead."

"Yeah, I guess."

"How did the other staff members relate to her?"

"Well, starting with Roosevelt, the other tech, she didn't want him to work on her because, you know, of his skin color. So he was lucky."

"Oh?"

"He's a quiet guy. Got a good education. He didn't care. The staff would talk about her and he'd listen and smile."

"What about the dentists—Ophelia, Sam, and Aileen?"

"Well, before Horace hired Aileen McBride, Sam and Ophelia had to work on Mrs. W. I was their tech whenever. She wasn't too bad with Sam, kind of picky was all. But with Ophelia, nothing was right." He lifted his glass, took a couple of sips, and set it down again. "The light was too bright, the place was too cold, the bib wasn't large enough, that kind of stuff. Sometimes she got personal, criticized her hair, whatever."

"That must have been unpleasant."

"Well, we'd sit around later and tear her to pieces. Except for Roosevelt, like I said."

"When Dr. McBride was hired, did things get better?"

"Yes and no.

"Mrs. W was just as bad to McBride, and still worse to Jane Douglas. Jane came on board just a few months ago."

"Tell me about her," said Victoria.

Arthur colored slightly. "She's pretty classy."

Victoria nodded. "She told me how much she appreciated your taking her home." She picked up her glass and took a sip.

Arthur looked down into his own glass. "She was sure upset that day."

"With good reason. She was there when Mrs. Wilmington collapsed. Why was Mrs. Wilmington so hard on her?"

He shrugged. "Got no idea. I have to tell you, Mrs. Trumbull, the abuse Jane put up with, anyone else would have killed that woman a lot sooner."

"You're not implying that Jane . . . ?" Victoria left the sentence unfinished.

Arthur looked startled. "You mean, do I think Jane killed her?"

"I haven't ruled out anyone," said Victoria.

"Oh, no, Mrs. Trumbull. No, no, no. Not Jane."

From her seat on the couch, Victoria could hear the murmur of bees mining the blossoms. A breeze moved the rhododendron's branches against the big window. Inside, the soft pink light quivered.

Victoria thought it wise to change the subject. "I assume you know Mrs. Wilmington died of arsenic poisoning. How difficult is it for someone working at the clinic to obtain arsenic?"

"I wouldn't know. I'm just a tech. I suppose any of the docs could get it by contacting a chemical supply house and giving them his or her credentials."

"I would think it might be hard to administer it to a patient."

"Well"—he paused—"arsenic has no taste, you know, so you can mix it with something the patient is going to drink."

Victoria watched the bees at work and was quiet for a few

moments. She hadn't really learned anything she didn't already know. After a bit she said, "Such a shame about Vivian drowning on the same day."

"Yeah. I guess she couldn't take it."

Obviously, the police had not released the fact that Vivian had been struck on the back of her head.

Arthur stood, took his glass to the counter, and poured himself more tea. He turned to Victoria. "You want more?"

"I'm fine," said Victoria, who still had an almost-full glass. "Were you at the meeting when she got the phone call?"

"Everyone was there." He reached down a sugar bowl from a shelf above the counter, dumped several spoonfuls of sugar into his tea, and stirred vigorously. "She wasn't very bright." He shrugged. "I guess Mrs. Wilmington's death was too much for her."

Victoria looked at her watch. "I believe my ride will be here shortly." She took a few more sips of her tea. "You've been most helpful." She set her glass down. "I visited Jane yesterday and we had a nice chat."

Arthur returned to his seat and Dog snuggled up to him again. "Did she say anything about me?"

"She told me how kind you'd been to her that day."

"She's a very nice lady."

"Have you met her daughter?"

"I've seen her. You heard about the tragedy?"

"Tragedy?" Victoria wondered where this was leading.

"Her husband was a pilot and died in a plane crash."

Recalling her conversation with Jane, Victoria wasn't quite sure what to say. "I didn't know she'd been married."

"Of course she was married. She has a daughter. The father never knew their child."

Victoria, who'd been feeling comfortable up until now, felt relief when she heard the rumble of Bill O'Malley's dump truck climbing the narrow access road.

"Guess your ride is here," said Arthur, standing. "Don't know how much help I've been."

"You've given me a great deal to think about," said Victoria.

CHAPTER 40

"How did your interview go, Mrs. Trumbull?" asked O'Malley once he'd backed down the steep drive and could relax a bit.

"I learned nothing new until just before you showed up."

"Did I spoil things?" They'd reached the beginning of Snake Hollow Road where it met State Road. O'Malley looked both ways and waited for a pickup and two cars to pass.

"I believe you saved me some embarrassment. If you hadn't come when you did, I'd have challenged something Arthur said. It would have been the wrong thing to do."

O'Malley turned onto the paved road and the dump truck picked up speed. "Care to elaborate?"

She'd been delighting in the new bright foliage of the beech trees on either side of the road, but turned to O'Malley. "Perhaps you can clarify my thinking." She looked down at her hands, folded in her lap. "Yesterday I met with Jane Douglas, the dental technician who was with Dr. McBride when Mrs. Wilmington died. At one point she told me her baby daughter was fathered by Dr. Mann, the head of the clinic."

"Is that common knowledge?" He glanced at her.

"Definitely not. Dr. Mann has a wife of twenty-something years."

"Oh," said O'Malley. "Awkward. How does this relate to Arthur?"

"Arthur is smitten with Jane, who doesn't reciprocate. In the last few minutes I was talking to him before you showed up, he insisted that Jane had been married and that the father of her daughter was killed in a plane crash." She looked up from her hands.

"What's your take on that?" he asked.

"I don't see any reason for Jane to lie. I met her baby daughter, who bears a striking resemblance to Dr. Mann."

"And Arthur?"

"He's apparently been stalking her and she didn't realize it until he said something about her cute baby girl. She's been extremely protective of the baby. I'm not sure many others even know she has a child."

O'Malley nodded. "Where their beloved objects are concerned, stalkers lead a fantasy life."

"It was unsettling to hear him state so positively, 'Of course she'd been married. She has a daughter.'"

"Ah, yes. Nice girls don't bear children unless they're married, and Jane is a nice girl."

"What's likely to happen when he learns the truth?"

"Nothing good, Victoria."

She was quiet until they reached the West Tisbury town line. She settled back into the comfortable seat. The same warm feeling washed over her that she'd had as a child riding in her grandfather's horse-drawn truck wagon, almost home.

O'Malley, who'd crossed from Tisbury into West Tisbury with Victoria many times, reassured her, "Almost home, Victoria."

She smiled, acknowledging his remark. "I came awfully close to blurting out that Horace Mann was the baby's father."

"Lucky I showed up when I did. Not a good idea to disabuse a stalker of his fantasy. On the other hand, he probably wouldn't have believed you."

Over drinks that evening, Victoria recounted her afternoon's visit with Arthur. They were sitting in the parlor, Victoria in her wing chair, Elizabeth on the sofa, drinking their usual cranberry juice and rum, munching on crackers and cheese. The fire simmered with a comforting low blaze, flaring up occasionally as it reached a pocket of gas in a log.

"You're a brick, Gram. It would never have worked to prosecute Lockwood. He's got credentials and connections and money. He's popular with his colleagues. He'd never be convicted, never." She took a sip of her drink. "And whether he got convicted or not"— she shuddered—"once he was out, he'd seek revenge for sure. He's smart, a lot smarter than I am. If Casey recommends psychological counseling . . . well, who knows. That might help."

They sat quietly for a while.

"I was sure, at first, that the killer must be someone from the clinic," Victoria said. "Assuming the two deaths are connected, I didn't see how anyone but a staff member could be aware of that key fact—the phone call that upset Vivian. I didn't realize the entire Wilmington family, Mrs. Wilmington and her four grandchildren, had been clinic patients." She reached for a cracker. "Susan was there the day Mrs. Wilmington died."

"Susan, who hated that woman's guts and inherited the property." Elizabeth pushed the cracker plate closer to her grandmother.

Victoria selected a chunk of cheese. "Dr. Mann told me that, according to Dr. McBride, one or both of the grandsons stopped by the same day."

"This complicates things, doesn't it."

Victoria nodded. "Furthermore, even though three of the grandchildren had been away from home for a decade, one or two of them kept in touch with some of the staff."

"Are you going to talk to the grandkids, and if so, what on earth are you going to ask them?" She lowered her voice in an imitation of her grandmother. "'Did you children kill your grandmother?'"

Victoria laughed. "Do I sound like that?"

"I wouldn't know where to begin," said Elizabeth, ignoring the question.

"I don't know myself, but if I'm quiet and wait, people sometimes divulge things they didn't intend to."

"Like fishing," said Elizabeth.

Victoria glanced up at the portrait hanging above the sofa. "Our friend in the painting unnerved Dr. Mann, who said far more than he should have."

"Take the painting with you to the Wilmington's."

"Better than that. I intend to invite them here," said Victoria. "My turf."

"All four of them?"

"I think so."

Before Victoria had a chance to call the Wilmington heirs, an opportunity to talk with Dr. Aileen McBride came up the next day and she took it.

Elizabeth had dropped her off at State Road Cronig's Market on her way to work, and Victoria assured her she would get a ride home with no problem.

She had pushed her grocery cart as far as the pet food aisle when she saw Dr. McBride, who was checking out cans of cat food.

"Good morning, Aileen," Victoria greeted her. "I'm never sure what my cat will eat from day to day."

Aileen laughed. "Mine brings home his disgusting latest catch, half eaten, but turns up his nose at chicken-liver treats."

"I'm glad I ran into you. I wanted to talk to you. Would you be available in the next day or two?"

"Of course, Mrs. Trumbull. We're not exactly busy at the clinic right now. I can stop by after I've finished shopping, if that's convenient. Actually, why don't I give you a ride home and then we can talk."

"Thank you," said Victoria. "I'll meet you at the checkout after I've found something McCavity won't turn up his nose at."

They moved away with their carts and a short time later met at the registers.

The checker smiled at Victoria. "Good morning, Mrs. Trumbull. Did you bring your bags?"

Victoria unloaded two cloth bags from her cart and in a few minutes her full bags were loaded into her cart. Aileen was waiting for her.

Aileen's car was a new Honda SUV. She loaded Victoria's bags into the back along with her own.

On the way to West Tisbury, Aileen said, "I've heard you're investigating both deaths. Did I understand you're with the West Tisbury police force?"

"I'm a deputy. Chief O'Neill is involved with the presidential visit, so I'm doing what I can to help."

"Well, ask me whatever you want."

"We can talk over a cup of tea or a glass of wine, if you have time."

"Wine sounds lovely. I've always wanted to see your home."

Once there, she carried Victoria's groceries into the kitchen, set the bags down on kitchen chairs, and looked around. "This must have looked much the same way back in the seventeen hundreds."

"Except that even up to the nineteen fifties, we had oil lamps, drew water from the well, and the stove was a woodstove."

"Really! That wasn't so long ago."

"The Gay Head Lighthouse had no electricity until around nineteen fifty-four. It was lighted by kerosene."

Aileen turned around examining the room. "The kitchen has six doors. You don't have a lot of wall space."

"Old houses had a lot of doors for ventilation, but also to make sure the inhabitants could escape in case of fire. A house fire was quite likely in the early days. I'll put my groceries away later. Let's have our wine."

They carried their glasses into the cookroom and sat at the table with its checked tablecloth.

Aileen touched her glass to Victoria's. "How would you like to start?"

"You came to work at the clinic only a few months ago. What was it like when you arrived?"

"It's been almost a year. It's hard to believe. So much has happened."

"Tell me what it was like when you first arrived."

Sunlight poured through the windows. Aileen turned her wineglass around watching the moving reflections of the wine on the tablecloth.

"I married right after college but the marriage didn't last, so I decided to get my dental degree. I was older than most students. Right after graduation, I read an ad in one of the journals that Dr. Mann was hiring a dentist, so I applied, and he hired me." She smiled. "It was just that easy. I'd spent summers on the Vineyard as a child and thought it would be fun to live here. My first patient was Mrs. Wilmington." She picked up her glass.

"Certainly a difficult patient to have as your first. What was she like?"

"Picky. Demanding. Critical. Insensitive. She was always coming to the clinic with some imagined problem. I felt more like her psychiatrist than her dentist."

"Did you attempt to have her switched to another dentist?"

"Both Ophelia and Sam had worked on her. My turn, they insisted."

"In addition to dealing with Mrs. Wilmington, I understand Dr. Demetrios gives you a hard time."

Aileen set her glass down. "We've never gotten along. Professional jealousy, I suppose. I graduated from Harvard Dental School, she didn't."

"And then you got Jane as an assistant, and that's not working out."

"It sounds as though I'm the odd one out, doesn't it." She shook her head and her long braid swung. "I'm not, really. With Jane, the chemistry is wrong. She's competent, I can depend on her, but I just don't like her."

"I wonder why?"

Aileen thought for a few moments, turning her undrunk glass of wine around and around. "She's condescending. She's only a tech, but she thinks she's better than anyone else. She doesn't socialize with anyone. She's a loner. And she treats Dr. Mann, who's the one who recommended that we hire her, as though he's some kind of dirt under her feet."

"I see," said Victoria. "You admire Dr. Mann?"

Aileen looked down at her glass. "I do. Professionally, certainly." She looked up. "And it's more than that, Mrs. Trumbull. He has a magnetic appeal. He cares so much about all of us on the staff and wants us to be a big, happy family."

"Do you know anything about his personal life?"

"His personal life is here at the clinic. He puts all his time and energy into making the clinic what it is." She leaned forward. "I was too young when I married. I've matured. Now I wouldn't mind marrying the right man."

"You knew he was adopted?"

"We all knew. He was entirely open about that. I imagine that's why we're his family, since he has none of his own."

Victoria toyed with her own wineglass, wondering how much she should divulge about Dr. Mann's marital status. She decided she might eke out new information by doing so.

She glanced over at Aileen. "He *is* married, you know."

"What do you mean?" Aileen sat back in her chair.

"He's married to his college sweetheart. They have two lovely children."

Aileen stared at Victoria with parted lips. "Surely you're mistaken, Mrs. Trumbull. He doesn't act like a married man."

"Had he indicated that he's available?" asked Victoria.

"He acts single. The way he lets Ophelia and me wrangle over him he definitely acts available." She looked up. "He doesn't wear a wedding ring."

"He's been married for twenty-something years."

Aileen picked up her glass and set it down again. "Twenty years?"

Victoria nodded.

"I don't know what to say. I don't know what to think. I had the impression that our relationship was really going somewhere."

"I suspect Ophelia is under the same impression," said Victoria.

"What a waste." Aileen turned so she could look out the window. "Three million dollars."

CHAPTER 41

"What did she mean by saying 'What a waste'? Do you think Dr. McBride killed Mrs. Wilmington?" asked Elizabeth. They were preparing supper that evening. "McBride was working on her. She could easily have gotten the arsenic, being a dentist. And she could easily have fed the arsenic to her."

"It's much too obvious," said Victoria. "I suspect her comment had more to do with the time she'd put in hoping to make a fine marital catch." She lifted the heavy cast iron spider from the hook above the stove, put a large pat of butter in it, and set it on the burner. "Aileen had no reason to suppose getting rid of Mrs. Trumbull would land her a marriage proposal from Dr. Mann. Nor could she guess that Dr. Mann would inherit such a fortune after Mrs. Wilmington's death."

Elizabeth had peeled three large onions and was chopping them. "Want these in the pan?"

"When the butter melts, yes."

Elizabeth continued to chop. "The more I hear about Dr. Mann the more I think he's a skunk." When the butter melted she transferred the chopped onions into the pan.

"Male skunks breed promiscuously and leave the females to take care of the resulting offspring." Victoria stirred the onions. "You couldn't have picked a more apt comparison."

"That's our Dr. Mann. I'm glad I'm not still married."

"Speaking of that, have you heard from Lockwood?"

"Nothing, and that's fine with me. I hope you put him out of commission permanently, although I doubt it."

The onions were turning a rich golden color and Victoria continued to stir. "Pass me the flour, please."

"What are we making, exactly?" asked Elizabeth.

"A recipe our friend John gave me. Pasta with onion sauce."

"Which John is that?" asked Elizabeth.

"John W. Beal. He's the one in the Coast Guard,"

"Oh, sure. I remember him. Tall, handsome guy. I had a huge crush on him in high school." Elizabeth went over to the sink. "I'll put the water on to boil. When are the Wilmington four coming to talk with you?"

"If their phone is working, I'll invite them for tomorrow."

"Wine and cheese?" asked Elizabeth.

"I believe something stronger is called for."

"Bet none of them will drink it," said Elizabeth.

The following afternoon, the four Wilmington grandchildren arrived at Victoria's house in the same car. Elizabeth had come home on a brief break from harbor activities and was standing at the window watching as they got out of their car.

"They don't look happy," she said.

Victoria, too, watched as the group approached.

Scott, Heather, and Wesley, the three who'd inherited five thousand dollars each, were ignoring Susan, the one who'd inherited the house and land, and were striding along ahead of her.

All four had fixed grim expressions, and all four marched as though they were part of an alien army invading enemy territory.

"How did you get them to agree to meet with you?" asked Elizabeth, turning away from the window.

"I suggested that the only way any of them can receive even a mere pittance of a bequest is to help solve the murders."

"Suppose one of them is the murderer?"

"If you were the murderer, you would want to be present when someone promises to identify the killer, wouldn't you?"

"I don't think so, Gram. I'd get a plane ticket to South America instead."

"I'd better greet them," said Victoria.

"I'll make myself scarce," said Elizabeth. "Not too scarce, though, in the unlikely case you need help."

When the four reached the stone steps that led to the west door, Scott, who'd been leading the group, moved aside politely to let Heather go first and followed her in. Wesley stepped aside to let Susan go before him.

Victoria watched. The hostility among them was palpable.

"Welcome," she said. "We have drinks ready in the parlor."

"Not for me," said Scott. "I'm on the wagon."

"I hope you're on the road to recovery," said Victoria.

"I'm told it will be at least a week before I'll feel like living again," said Scott.

"I'm sorry to call you out for this get-together," Victoria said. They were walking through the dining room on the way to the parlor. "But the sooner we solve the murders, the sooner everyone will be able to return to normal."

Heather was right behind her. "Normal? Hardly," she said.

Victoria settled herself in her mouse-colored wing chair. The others stood.

"Would anyone like a drink?" Victoria asked. "I know Scott would prefer not to."

"No, thank you, Mrs. Trumbull," said Heather.

"Nor I," said Wesley.

Susan shook her head.

Victoria pointed to the armchair her grandfather had called the throne. "Scott, why don't you take that chair." She indicated seats for the others. "I want to start by saying how sorry I am about your grandmother's death," said Victoria. "I know she was a difficult person, but she was, after all, your grandmother and your only living relative."

"Thank you, Mrs. Trumbull," said Scott.

The others were looking anywhere but at Victoria.

Wesley glanced up at the portrait above the couch. "Is that an ancestor?"

"No," said Victoria. "It was a picture my grandmother had in her cabin during a five-year whaling voyage."

"She's looking right at me," he said.

"At me, too," said Heather. "She's creepy."

"We're here to help you in any way we can, Mrs. Trumbull," said Scott. "Where would you like to start?"

"We need to address several questions," she said. "One, of course, is who had motive. The second is who had intent, and the third is who had the opportunity."

"This sounds like a criminal proceeding," said Wesley.

"Let Mrs. Trumbull finish," Scott said.

"Thank you. Let's talk openly about all three questions," she said. "I don't mean to cast suspicion on any of you, but your comments may shed light on the identity of the killer."

"You want us to comment just on our thoughts or on anyone we think of?" asked Heather.

"Anything you can contribute will be worthwhile," Victoria responded.

"Let's start," said Scott. "To be quite candid, Mrs. Trumbull, every one of us had motive. Revenge and money. The two most powerful motives there are. For years I've passed pleasant hours visualizing how I'd get that woman out of my life permanently."

He sat forward with his elbows on the chair arms. "The old lady's treatment of us as kids was shameful. She thrived on tormenting us. Four kids who'd been orphaned. Can you imagine? She knew our weaknesses and how to make each of us feel like shit, if you'll pardon the expression. Revenge is a powerful motive." He sat back again. "When she insisted that we four come for the first visit in a decade, we knew it was to tell us something unpleasant."

"That was grandmother," agreed Wesley.

Victoria sat quietly.

"The other most powerful motive is money. We all have money problems. Definitely a motive." Scott glanced up at the portrait. "Our grandmother was secretive about money, but the old lady had money and we knew it. Every one of us is desperate for money. Desperate enough to kill?" He shifted his gaze back to Victoria. "I doubt it. Of course the main deterrent was the likelihood of getting caught." He turned to his brother, who was sitting to his left. "You want to say anything, Wes?"

Wesley nodded. "Since I was the youngest, my brother and sisters shielded me to some extent." He glanced around at his siblings. "On the other hand, I was such a little kid at the time, I was helpless." He paused for a moment. "I came to this reunion, or whatever she called it, because I planned to ask her for a loan."

"Yeah, sure," said Heather. "Fat chance."

Victoria felt growing pity as they talked about their grandmother. She felt sorry for the four grandchildren, and she felt sorry for their dead grandmother. The grandparent relationship was, or could be, so rewarding.

"None of you seemed to feel great affection toward her."

"That's for sure," said Heather.

"What about you, Susan. You lived with her."

The other three stared at Susan, who had been sitting with

her head bowed, her knees together, and her hands clasped tightly in her lap.

Without looking up, Susan said, "I knew she intended to change her will."

"How did you get that bit of information? She tell you?" asked Wesley.

Susan glanced over at him. "I saw some papers on her desk."

"You were prying?" said Heather.

Susan shrugged. "I cleaned her house. I couldn't help seeing her papers."

"Yeah, yeah," said Heather. "I suppose she was leaving us fifty dollars each. A token of her affection."

"I'd be interested in knowing what the change would have been," said Scott.

"She planned to leave five thousand to each of us and the house and property to the Island Conservation Foundation."

"Cutting you out, too," exclaimed Heather. "That's a laugh. What did you do to deserve that?"

Susan flushed. "I deserved the property, Heather. For twenty years, I worked like a slave for that woman. Cooked, cleaned house, did laundry, put up with her insults and complaints. You know what she was like. You three escaped." She pointed to herself. "I earned that house and land."

"Bitch," muttered Heather.

"Let Mrs. Trumbull move us on," said Scott.

"I think I'll change my mind about a drink," Victoria said. "Would you mind pouring me a light bourbon and water, Scott?"

"My pleasure," said Scott, getting unsteadily to his feet. "I'll try not to breathe in when I pour."

"Thank you, Scott," said Victoria, picking up her glass. "I'm sorry you hurt."

"Susan's fault," said Heather. "She did that cute mushroom

thing on purpose. She knew how the mushrooms acted and she knew we had that bottle of Scotch."

"Stop it!" said Susan.

Victoria cleared her throat. "What about you, Wesley?"

"I lost track of the question," said Wesley.

"Revenge," said Scott. "Money. Motive."

Wesley leaned back in his chair. "I made some unwise investments. My creditors are after me."

Scott laughed. "He's an addicted gambler, Mrs. Trumbull. His creditors intend to get their money."

"Grandmother had a soft spot for me," Wesley said.

"Yeah, a soft spot like cast iron," said Heather.

"I figured I could talk her into lending me what I needed."

"Had you asked her?" asked Victoria.

"I did. No dice."

"So to speak," said Scott.

Victoria turned to Susan. "Did you know when the change in the will was to go in effect?"

"She had an appointment to meet with her lawyer on what turned out to be the day the will was read."

Wesley said, "Old ice maiden?"

"If you mean Darya, yes."

"That's why we were able to get an appointment," said Wesley. "Ironic, no?"

"What about your financial problem, Heather?" asked Victoria.

"Champagne taste, peanut butter budget," Heather said.

"Nicely mixed metaphor," said Wesley.

"That wasn't a metaphor, dummy. I ran up bills on my credit cards that I haven't been able to pay. I thought Grandmother might just possibly lend me the pearl necklace that belonged to our mother for a film festival I'd thought of attending."

"You wouldn't sell our mother's pearl necklace?" said Susan.

"Of course I would."

"That was to go to both of us."

"You got the entire house and land. What do you care about a necklace?"

"That's stealing."

"No it's not. Our father gave that necklace to our mother, not to *her.*"

Victoria took a long sip of her drink.

"Brrr," said Scott, turning away.

Victoria set her glass down and after a pause said, "Did you talk to each other about murder?"

They looked at one another.

"Yes," said Scott.

"Oh, shut up, Scott," said Heather.

Wesley said, "People contemplate murders they never intend to commit all the time. We were no exception."

"What were your thoughts on how you might kill her?" asked Victoria.

"Do we need this?" cried Susan. "That's not getting us any-where."

"I hope you'll bear with me. I have reasons for asking."

"I seem to be the spokesman," said Scott, "so I'll speak. Three of us, Heather, Wesley, and I—Susan wasn't in on the discussions because she was usually with Grandmother—talked about guns, knives, bludgeons, poisons, throttlings, and hangings, and we talked about them in some detail. How they might work, where we would stage the murder, how we might escape detection."

"We even thought about a staged suicide," said Wesley, with a smile.

"Come on, you guys," said Heather.

Susan said nothing.

Scott added, "We ruled out the obvious methods. Guns, knives,

271

blunt instruments, strangling, and hanging. None of us had the money to buy a gun, and the rest were too intimate. That left poison."

"Which is how she was killed," said Wesley with a shrug.

"Does that answer your question, Mrs. Trumbull?"

"What I'm trying to learn," said Victoria, trying not to show her exasperation, "is what might have been going through the mind of the actual murderer. He or she undoubtedly went through the same thought processes."

"Pretty obvious," said Wesley.

"How would you determine what poison to use and how would you obtain it?"

"We never got that far," said Heather. "We talked about arsenic, because that's what the elderly aunts use in the play *Arsenic and Old Lace*. I don't know how you'd get it. Google it, I suppose."

Victoria glanced around at the four, but Heather seemed to have spoken for them.

"Did any of you know Vivian, the clinic's receptionist?"

"I did," said Susan. "A quiet, mousy person."

"What did you think of her?"

"I didn't think anything about her. She answered the phone and made reservations. She was okay. No pleasantries or anything like that. She always seemed like a scared rabbit with a hawk soaring overhead."

"What about the rest of you?"

They looked at each other and shrugged.

"You were all patients at the clinic at some time, weren't you?"

"I still am. I get annual checkups and Dr. Minnowfish has been my dentist ever since we moved to the Island," said Susan.

"And you accompanied your grandmother on her trips to the clinic?"

"Not usually. The day she died, though, I was there."

"I recall seeing you. Not a pleasant occasion for you." Victoria turned to the others. "You all became patients when Dr. Mann first opened the clinic, didn't you?"

"Mann had opened the clinic several months before we arrived. I don't know how long before," Scott answered. "Dr. Minnowfish and Dr. Demetrios were with him when we first went, along with the two technicians who are still there, Roosevelt Mark and Arthur Morgan."

"Did you keep in touch with any of the clinic's staff after you left the Island?"

"Sam Minnowfish had been my dentist. He was a big influence on me, kind of a father figure," said Scott. "I wrote to him occasionally. Later, kept in touch on Facebook. You did, too, right, Wes?"

"I was a lot younger," said Wesley. "I was crazy about cowboys and Indians. Dr. Minnowfish was an Indian and I thought he was God."

"And he capitalized on that," said Heather. "I remember he'd say, 'How!' when we went for our checkups and hold up his hand like some movie Indian."

"A good way to keep a child from being afraid to go to the dentist," said Victoria. She turned to Scott. "Did you or Wesley drop by the clinic for a visit when you came back?"

"I did," said Scott. "Guess you did, too, right, Wes?"

Wesley nodded.

"What about you, Heather?"

"When I lost a filling earlier I went off Island to have it fixed." Heather glanced over at Victoria. "Does that answer your question?"

"I think it does."

"My dentist was Dr. Demetrios. She was kind of scary with that

273

sleek dark hair pulled back tight and her accent. I can imagine her poisoning someone."

Inwardly, Victoria winced. But she recovered and asked, "Did you keep in touch with her?"

"No way." Heather shook her head.

CHAPTER 42

The phone rang while Victoria was eating her supper. Elizabeth had gone back to the harbor. It was Casey.

"Are you at work?" asked Victoria. "It's Saturday."

"You forget. The president is coming. Just called to ask how things are going."

"I talked to the four Wilmington grandchildren this afternoon and I'm not sure I learned much. They all disliked their grandmother, and they had talked together about killing her."

"They told you that?"

"Fantasies, I suspect," said Victoria. "All had been patients at the clinic and knew their way around."

Victoria pushed her plate with her half-eaten meal aside.

"Any connections to Vivian?"

"The only person who seemed to know Vivian was Susan, who thought she was an adequate receptionist, but called her mousy."

"Have you ruled them out?"

"No," said Victoria. "They have strong motives for killing their grandmother and were careful about not letting me know too much."

"Do you think they might have worked together?"

Victoria thought about it. "If they did, it was the three who'd moved off Island who worked together. They're hostile to Susan, especially after learning she inherited the property."

"What about Susan?"

"Much as I like Susan, I can't rule her out."

"No?"

"She'd poked around in her grandmother's papers and found that her grandmother intended to change her will to cut Susan out of inheriting the house and property."

"Whew. That would do it."

"Susan knows the clinic and its staff and knew Vivian. The others didn't seem to know her, although I'm not sure they weren't playing dumb."

"Are you busy now?" Casey asked.

"You mean, right now? I'm eating my supper."

"I could use some help on another batch of names that just came in. Care to help me vet them?"

"Of course."

"I'll give you fifteen minutes to finish supper, and then I'll come by."

"Come right now and I'll give you a cup of coffee."

"I'd love to, but I honestly don't have time. See you shortly. Bye." Casey hung up.

The batch of names took Victoria an hour to go through and identify. Included in the names was Lockwood's. She pointed this out to Casey.

"Yeah, I saw his name. You're not the one doing this, remember? I am. I'll put a notation next to his name. Don't worry about it, Victoria."

"Does anyone know where he is now?"

"He was staying at the hostel, but I checked and they told me he'd left. I've alerted the other five police departments to watch out for him. I don't think he's a threat to the president, but who knows?

If the president of the United States gets in the way of Lockwood, it's a concern for sure. We need to locate him."

"I'll keep ears and eyes open," said Victoria.

The next day after church, Victoria went through her notes. On her list of everyone even remotely connected with the clinic, she checked off the most likely suspects.

Dr. Mann, certainly. She put a check next to his name. He resented this odious woman who turned out to be his birth mother. He needed money to support the clinic, and Mrs. Wilmington had indicated that she was leaving him a sizable amount. It was he who had reported to the hospital the phone call Vivian had received. He was her number one suspect. The only drawback was that he was too obvious a suspect. If he was found guilty, that was the end of his clinic and his hopes to acquire Mrs. Wilmington's fortune.

On the clinic staff, the second most likely was Dr. McBride, Mrs. Wilmington's dentist, and she put a check next to her name. McBride had hoped to capture the attentions of Dr. Mann, who'd managed to keep his marriage a secret from most of his staff. She, too, was too obvious a suspect.

Dr. Minnowfish, Dr. Demetrios, Roosevelt Mark, she crossed out. She thought about Jane Douglas and put a faint pencil line through her name. Why should she doubt Jane's innocence? She thought about that and erased the pencil line. She decided she felt uneasy about the way Jane was willing to join the clinic staff in order to get even with Dr. Mann. Was she cold-blooded enough to be able to kill Mrs. Wilmington and lay the blame on Dr. Mann or Dr. McBride? She thought about Jane's baby and put back the faint pencil line she'd erased.

Arthur Morgan she would have to talk to again. How would he react when he was faced with the fact that the father of Jane's baby was actually Dr. Mann? Victoria had put a light pencil line through his name the first time through, but erased it. She would talk to him again. Besides, she would like to see that magnificent rhododendron again before it finished blooming.

She put a check next to Susan's name as not only likely, but the one with motive and opportunity. Arsenic, Victoria was convinced, was more easily available than Casey suggested.

It was quite possible that the other three Wilmington grandchildren had collaborated in killing their grandmother. The three had made no secret of their feelings about their grandmother. When she'd met with them, she'd had the sense that the three were a bit too complaisant in playing their game of imagined murder.

The call to Vivian announcing Mrs. Wilmington's death was key. The killings were connected, she felt sure, and the killer had to have known about the call. Would any of the grandchildren have heard about it?

Elizabeth came home late that evening, exhausted, cranky, and hungry. She went upstairs to take a shower. By the time she came downstairs again, Victoria had cooked spinach, scrambled two eggs, made toast, and had a pot of tea waiting for her.

"Exactly what I needed, Gram. Thank you."

They sat at the cookroom table and while Elizabeth ate she told her grandmother about the preparations going on in the harbor. "You know how tiny the harbormaster's shack is?"

Victoria nodded.

"Five Secret Service guys were in there getting in our way and keeping us from getting anything done."

"In what way?"

"We'd get a radio call from a boat asking about accommodations in the harbor and these macho guys insisted on taking the call and

278

checking the caller out, sure it was some terrorist hoping to bring his sailboat into the harbor with a load of explosives."

"I thought the harbor was closed for the week around the visit."

"It is. I wanted to tell the caller the harbor is closed and suggest they go to Falmouth. But no, every radio call had to be checked out."

"I'm sure they can't be too careful. After all, it is the president."

"Then why don't they just take over and let the rest of us go home?" Elizabeth took a ferocious bite of her toast. "They might as well. They're keeping us from doing anything useful. There isn't room enough in the shack for all those huge guys plus us."

"It will all be over soon," Victoria assured her.

Elizabeth scraped up the last morsel of eggs. "Sorry for piling my bitching on your shoulders, Gram. Actually, it's pretty exciting to be part of a presidential visit." She pushed her chair back and was about to stand. "Here I am, talking about my day. How was yours?" She sat again. "Any progress? I had to leave before you finished talking to the grand-heirs. Anything come of your meeting?"

"It's difficult to know," said Victoria. "I want to talk to Arthur again. I'm curious to know what his reaction will be when he learns that Dr. Mann is the father of Jane's baby daughter."

"Why?" asked Elizabeth.

"He's fixated on Jane Douglas, seems to see her as a kind of Madonna-like figure. He's convinced she's a grieving widow, but Jane has never been married."

"You're not going to tell him, are you?"

"I think Arthur knows something he hasn't told anyone, hoping to protect Jane. Hearing that her daughter is Dr. Mann's, he may divulge some critical information."

"I don't think that's a great idea," said Elizabeth. "Let someone else be the one to tell him."

279

"Who would be better than I?" asked Victoria with some asperity.

"Gram, you're right. You are the best." She reached over and patted her grandmother's shoulder. "Would you like me to take you to Snake Hollow?"

Victoria was not mollified. "Thank you for offering, but I'll get a ride with Bill O'Malley."

"Sure, Victoria," said Bill O'Malley when she called him that night. "Let me know when you plan to meet with Morgan and I'll be happy to chauffeur you."

CHAPTER 43

Victoria awoke the next morning to a brilliant day. She'd called Arthur Morgan, who seemed pleased to hear from her. He'd be delighted to have her visit again that afternoon, he said. She lined up her ride with Bill O'Malley.

O'Malley parked the dump truck at the upper reaches of the narrow drive and this time walked Victoria the rest of the way up the hill. Arthur met them at the foot of his steps with Dog by his side. Dog was wagging his tail, his tongue hanging out, dripping.

"Howdy," said O'Malley in his good-old-boy persona. He held out his hand and he and Arthur shook. "Nice to meet you."

Arthur nodded at the dump truck parked some distance down the hill. "Great vehicle you have there."

"Not so great on Vineyard access roads, though. Got to get back to work. See you in an hour or so, Mrs. Trumbull?"

Victoria smiled at the sudden formality.

Arthur held the door for her. "Come on in, Mrs. Trumbull. You got a friend here in Dog. I made iced tea again."

"I couldn't resist returning to see your beautiful rhododendron."

"Well, then you can sit in the same place you did the other day where you get a good view."

281

After exchanging pleasantries about the rhododendron, the beautiful weather, O'Malley's superb dump truck, and Dog's appreciation of her, they sat for a few minutes, drinking iced tea.

Victoria was wondering how to broach the subject of Jane's daughter, when Arthur brought it up first.

He was sitting across from her on Dog's chair. He leaned forward. "You said you visited Jane the other day and met her daughter."

"What a delightful baby. She seems very bright."

"I've only seen her from a distance. Jane is a good mother."

"She certainly seems to be," said Victoria.

"It's tough having to work when she ought to be with her daughter."

Victoria reached for her glass of tea. "Fortunately, she has her wonderful nanny to watch the baby."

"I saw someone at the house, figured it was a babysitter."

"More than that," said Victoria. "I believe Abigail was Jane's nanny when she was a little girl."

"Is that right? I had no idea." He fiddled with his own drink.

Victoria, still wondering how to bring up the subject of the baby's father, decided to keep the conversation going and see what happened. Arthur clearly liked talking about Jane. "The house belonged to Jane's grandparents and Jane came here every summer as a child." She continued to hold her glass and took a few sips of iced tea.

"I saw her around summers," said Arthur. "Classy lady even as a teen." He drank from his glass and set it down on the crate table. "She told me she inherited the house. High-rent district, right on the harbor like that. Taxes must be astronomical."

"It's a shame that family houses have gotten so valuable family members can't afford to keep them," said Victoria. "I don't think she makes a very good salary at the clinic."

"That's for sure. Minimum wage. She's a well-educated lady, too. She should be working someplace where they appreciate her."

"I'm sure they appreciate her at the clinic."

"Not hardly."

"What do you mean?"

"Well, Dr. McBride, her boss, makes it clear she doesn't like her. She's doesn't treat her bad or anything. Just aloof."

Victoria nodded. "Yes, I could sense that."

"And Mrs. Wilmington, she was vicious."

"In what way?"

"Well, always belittling Jane, putting her down, nothing Jane did was right. Always picking on her."

"Why?"

"Who knows. You could tell Dr. Mann liked Jane and that seemed to bother Mrs. Wilmington."

"And you think that's why she picked on Jane?"

"Sure. It was unfair, because Jane wouldn't have anything to do with Dr. Mann. She was all business. Totally professional." He looked over at Dog, who was dozing by the window, stretched out in the warm pink light filtering through the blossoms. "But all Mrs. Wilmington could see was Dr. Mann trying to make up to Jane. She was a nasty one, Mrs. Wilmington was. Good riddance, I say. Life is a lot easier for Jane now she's gone."

"You told me the other day that Jane's husband was killed in a plane crash. When did that happen?"

"Well, it must have been before her daughter was born, so I guess that would be about two years ago."

"How did you learn about him and the plane crash?"

He scratched his head. "I don't know."

"Do you know his name?"

He shook his head. "I assumed it was Douglas." He stopped. "Come to think of it, that was her name when she summered here."

"Did you know her then?"

"I knew who she was, all right. But I didn't travel in her circles, that's for sure."

Victoria decided this was the opportunity to set things straight. "When I met with Jane, she told me she'd never been married."

He set down his glass. "That's not so, Mrs. Trumbull. She has a daughter. You must be mistaken."

Victoria suddenly felt as though she was trespassing into swampy territory. She turned toward the window. "You've done marvels with that rhododendron in just a few years. Do you fertilize it?" She turned to him.

He was staring at her. "She told you she never married?"

Victoria nodded, feeling increasingly uneasy about the way Arthur was staring at her.

He stood up. "Jane told you that? Herself?"

"Yes."

He continued to stare at her.

Victoria could hear the hum of bees working, could see them bustling in and out gathering nectar. The blossoms quivered with their activity. His stare was disconcerting her. She'd probably learned all she could for now.

He said, "I wonder why she said that to you." He took a step toward her. Victoria looked at her watch. "I think it's time for me to go now."

Arthur looked at his own watch. "Your driver won't be here for another quarter hour." He sat down again. Then got up and paced the room.

"Jane wouldn't lie."

"I think you're right," said Victoria. "She wouldn't."

"She's such a saint. So pure."

"You know, Arthur, many people have children these days

without marrying. There's no longer a stigma attached to unwed parents."

He sat down again and rested his forearms on his knees. Over by the window, Dog lifted his head and looked over at his master. He got up, stretched, padded across the room, and laid his head on Arthur's knee. Whined. Arthur patted him absently.

"I'm afraid I've given you news you didn't want," said Victoria. "It's not bad news, Arthur. Jane is still the same person you've always cared about."

"No, she's not," said Arthur.

"Yes, she is," said Victoria.

"Who was the father? Does she know?"

"Of course she knows."

"Who was it? Did she tell you?"

"I don't think it's a secret." Victoria thought for a few moments about what she should divulge and how she should do it. "The baby is the very image of her father."

"Someone I know?" demanded Arthur.

"I believe it explains Mrs. Wilmington's attitude toward Jane."

"What are you talking about, Mrs. Trumbull?"

Victoria shifted to a more comfortable position on the lumpy couch. Why had she gotten herself into this conversational predicament? She looked at the pink blossoms. She watched the bees. She could see in the distance beyond, a hawk soaring. She turned back to Arthur.

"I'm sure she suspected Jane had a daughter."

"Jane tried to keep her private life private, but it's hard to do that on this Island." He patted Dog's head. "So why should the old bitch, excuse me, give a damn?"

"Didn't the clinic's staff speculate that Mrs. Wilmington was the birth mother of Dr. Mann?"

"Yeah. Well . . . Oh my God!" He stood pressing his hands to his forehead. "Mann!" He turned back to Victoria. "Jane and Mann?"

Victoria nodded.

He returned to his chair and slumped back into it, hands still pressing his forehead. "What a fool I am."

"I'm so sorry, Arthur. I shouldn't have told you."

"Yes. Yes, you should." He slapped his hands against his forehead. "What a fool I am. I suppose everyone knows but me."

"I don't think anyone else knows. Just you and me."

"And Dr. Mann and Mrs. Wilmington and Sam and all the rest of them."

"Dr. Mann, yes. But Jane's a private person, Arthur, as you know." Victoria searched for the right thing to say. She hadn't done too well so far. "You mustn't take it so hard, Arthur."

"After all I did for her."

"She appreciated how kind you were giving her the ride home that day."

"No, no, Mrs. Trumbull. You don't understand."

Suddenly, Victoria did understand. "Mrs. Wilmington?" she asked gently.

He laid his head in his hands and nodded. She couldn't see his face.

"You did that for Jane. Took care that Mrs. Wilmington would never torment her again."

He nodded.

"Arsenic," Victoria said. "It was easy to put it in the relaxant Dr. McBride gave her to drink."

He nodded.

"How did you make sure that only Mrs. Wilmington, no one else, would drink it?"

He mumbled, head still in his hands. Victoria could barely make out what he was saying. "Sealed bottle. Dr. McBride had drawers

286

marked for each of her patients. She had a drawer marked for Mrs. Wilmington."

"I suppose you sealed it up again before Dr. McBride gave it to her to drink?"

"I sealed it again, yes."

"When the lab was cleaned, you were able to discard the bottle."

"Yes."

"Where did you get the arsenic?"

He looked up. "You remember Gifford's store?"

"I do. It was where we got our kerosene."

"When their grandkids cleared out the store I bought a lot of old stuff."

"Including arsenic. I see. I can remember my grandfather used to buy arsenic to kill rats in the barn. It was sold quite commonly when I was a girl and a young woman."

Victoria felt as though she was in a dream. Should she be afraid of this man who'd just confessed to murder? She wasn't. She felt pity for him. Was he likely to kill her now that he'd confessed? She didn't think so.

"It must be a great load off your mind to tell me this," she said. "You thought you were doing the right thing for Jane."

He leaned forward, head down, hands dangling between his knees.

"Did you think she heard something in that phone call?"

He repeated it. "She heard something in that phone call."

"Did you think the caller told Vivian you had poisoned Mrs. Wilmington?"

"I know Vivian knew, from the way she was acting."

"Did you think she would tell someone what happened?"

"I knew she would."

Victoria took a deep breath. "How did you know where to find Vivian?"

"After I took Jane home . . . Jane!" Hands to his face.

"Did you go back to the clinic?"

He spoke as though in a trance. "I drove along the harbor, thinking of Jane. Her baby . . ." He looked up.

"And?" prompted Victoria.

"When I came to the liquor store I saw Vivian's car."

"Was she in the car?"

"No. She was standing by the harbor, that skirt of hers blowing up around her, looking off into the distance." He stopped.

"And you grabbed something and hit her on the back of the head."

"My rifle. From the gun rack in my pickup." He glanced up at Victoria. "She never knew what hit her."

Suddenly he stood. "I did it for Jane." He swung around. "Jane, the whore!" He stumbled to the door, shoved it open, stepped off the porch, climbed into his truck, and slammed the door behind him. The truck started up, backed around, and sped down the dirt track spewing sand, gravel, grass, and oily smoke behind it.

He'd killed twice. Jane was in danger and she had to warn her. She had to find a phone. As she was searching, a familiar blue Jeep pulled up in front of the cabin. It had to be Lockwood. What was he doing here? She felt a surge of relief. He could help her. She would ask him to follow Arthur, who most certainly was headed to Jane.

Lockwood got out of the Jeep, limped around to the front, and leaned against the hood. His right arm was in a cast that went from his thumb partway to his elbow. His right eye was swollen almost shut.

Victoria charged down the steps and clambered into the Jeep. "Thank heaven you're here. How did you find me?"

Lockwood stared at her. "Where is she? Where are you hiding her?"

Victoria, forgetting her granddaughter and thinking only about Jane, said, "Arthur is after her. We've got to get to her, right away. Hurry!"

"Arthur? What are you talking about?" Lockwood limped around to the driver's side.

"She in that house?"

"No, we've got to get to her."

He climbed in, grimacing with pain. "Where is she?"

Victoria was out of breath from rushing down the steps. "Main Street, Vineyard Haven. No time to explain."

"There'd better be a good explanation."

"Hurry!" said Victoria. "He's going to kill her!"

Lockwood, jarred into action, started up the Jeep, shifted into gear left-handed, and tore down the hill, sideswiping O'Malley's blue dump truck, which was about to turn up into the drive.

"Don't stop!" Victoria waved at O'Malley and in the side rear-view mirror saw the dump truck back up into a dirt entry road side road and turn to follow them.

"This better be good, Victoria." Lockwood hunched over the wheel, steering with his left hand. "Who's Arthur?"

"Can't talk."

"I saw you get into that damned dump truck and I followed you here. Where is she?"

"Hurry!"

"Damnation, Victoria, I'm going sixty-five in a forty-five mile zone. You want to get stopped for speeding?"

The dump truck was on their tail.

Victoria clung to the door handle. "Left onto Main Street." Her short white hair blew about her face. Her eyes watered. Wind streaked tears down her cheeks. Traffic was backed up from the Bunch of Grapes Bookstore.

"Do something!" said Victoria.

Lockwood snapped at her. "Want to get out and walk?"

Victoria let go of the handle and brushed hair out of her eyes, the tear streaks off her cheeks. "It's my fault if anything happens to her. I pushed him too far."

"Are you losing your mind, Victoria?"

A car backed out of a parking place. Another car pulled into it from the line of traffic. Traffic moved again. Lockwood shifted awkwardly into gear. Pedestrians stared at the blue dump truck on his tail. They passed the library.

"Turn right," said Victoria. "Down the hill."

Arthur's truck was at the bottom of the hill, heat waves rising from the hood.

Lockwood stopped behind the truck. "That his?"

"The house on the left," said Victoria.

Lockwood limped toward the house. Victoria, right behind him, glanced over her shoulder.

The dump truck had ground to a stop behind the Jeep. O'Malley hiked up his jeans, ran a hand through his hair, grinned, and gave Victoria a thumbs-up.

"Better be an explanation for all this," muttered Lockwood.

"Pray we're not too late," said Victoria.

CHAPTER 44

Jane was bathing Davina in the bathtub, sloshing warm water over the baby's golden hair and holding a hand against her forehead to keep water out of her eyes when someone pounded on the door.

"Can you get it, Abigail?" Jane called out.

Davina said, "Ducky?"

Jane fished the duck out from behind a wall of bubbles. "Here's your duck, honey."

More pounding.

"Just a minute," Abigail shouted. "Keep your shirt on! Got something on the stove."

More pounding, then the crash of breaking glass.

"Abigail?" Jane cried out. She lifted Davina from the tub into a towel.

Davina started to cry. "Ducky?"

"Just a moment, honey."

Abigail flew past the bathroom door with a butcher knife in her hand, fire in her eyes, muttering, "That Mann has gone too far this time."

Shouts. Curses. Confusion. A wet and sobbing baby. Jane wrapped the towel tightly around Davina and crept into the adjoining bedroom. More voices. It sounded as though an army was at her door. All Jane could think about was her daughter, and she held her so tightly, Davina cried out between sobs.

"I'm so sorry, honey. It's all right." She had no idea what was all right. Horace must have cracked up. Abigail had called out his name. She opened the closet door thinking she and the baby could hide there, then thought that would be a place from which she couldn't retreat, and, still holding Davina tightly wrapped in the towel, opened the glass door that led out to the beach. Or up the hill to the gazebo. Someone would be out there to help.

Abigail had dialed 911 before she grabbed the butcher knife. She skidded to a stop, the knife held out in front of her like a lance. The man in front of her wasn't the man she expected and she stopped short.

"Who you think you are?" she demanded, the knife pointed at Arthur's stomach. Abigail, who normally spoke pure English with a British accent, lapsed into street talk.

"Where is she?" demanded Arthur.

"You take one step more, mon, an' I'll gut you," said Abigail.

Arthur backed up and backed into Lockwood.

"What do you think you're doing?" demanded Lockwood. "Where is she?"

"She's in there, all right," said Arthur. He faced Abigail. "Let me by."

"Hell I will." The blade of the nicely honed butcher knife glistened. "And who you think you are?" to Lockwood.

"I've come to take her home with me."

"What you talkin' about, mon?"

"She's my wife," said Lockwood, with dignity.

"*Your* wife?" said Arthur, turning to stare at him.

"She ain't nobody's wife, mon."

"She's my wife and I'm taking her home," said Lockwood.

"Whore!" Arthur cried out.

"Don't you call my wife a whore, you runty bastard," said Lockwood, lifting his hands as though to throttle Arthur.

Victoria emerged from behind Lockwood.

Abigail, eyebrows raised high, said, "Miz Trumbull?"

Arthur moved forward and Abigail ticked his shirt with the point of the knife. Arthur backed up.

Without moving, Abigail said, "An' who's that?" as O'Malley lined up behind Victoria.

O'Malley held up both hands in surrender. "Just an onlooker."

"God damn it, where is she?" demanded Lockwood.

Abigail's eyes glittered. "Someone care to tell me what's goin' on?"

"I'm gonna kill her, that's what," muttered Arthur.

"Hell you will." Abigail pricked his shirt, drawing blood. Arthur looked down and backed up some more.

"Where's the phone?" asked Victoria. "I'll call the police."

"Already on the way," said Abigail.

"Let me by," said Arthur.

"She's my wife," said Lockwood.

"That baby of hers . . . ," said Arthur.

"What baby!" said Lockwood.

"Y'all shut up," said Abigail. "Stand right there until the po-lice come, an' straighten this mess out."

Jane, holding Davina in the damp towel, crept around through the bayberry bushes and wild roses at the side of the house until she reached the small gazebo that overlooked the harbor.

"Mama play?"

"Yes, honey, we're playing a game."

Davina stuck her thumb in her mouth and snuggled against her mother. Jane, holding her tightly, sat on the bench that ran around the inside of the gazebo where she could see the front door of her house.

At least five people were gathered there. Sweat had dripped into her eyes, and it took her a moment to focus. When she did, she could make out Abigail. The blade of her butcher knife glittered and so did her eyes. Victoria Trumbull? What was she doing here? She made out Arthur, and Abigail was pointing her knife at him. There were two men Jane didn't recognize. Her cell phone was in the house. She had no idea what was going on. She had expected to see Horace, not this.

She watched for several minutes, trying to sort things out.

Two police cars, one marked TISBURY POLICE, the other marked WEST TISBURY POLICE, arrived, sirens screaming, red and blue lights flashing. They screeched to a stop behind the dump truck. Four police officers got out, guns drawn. One she recognized as West Tisbury's chief of police,

Davina pulled her thumb out of her mouth. "Mama play?"

"Yes, honey. It's all a game."

When the police finished, Arthur sat in handcuffs in the backseat of the Tisbury cruiser, headed for the County of Dukes County House of Correction. The state police would meet him there.

Casey shook her head. "Don't know how you do it, Victoria."

Abigail went into the kitchen with her knife and Victoria heard her singing as she stroked the blade on a whetstone.

Junior Norton walked up the hill to fetch Jane and returned, holding the baby in one arm, Jane's hand in his.

Lockwood saw Jane. "That's who you were protecting?"

"Yes," said Victoria.

"Where's Elizabeth?"

"She's with the president's security people."

"You, Victoria!" He jabbed a finger of his left hand at her. "You've made a fool of me!"

He started to limp away but turned abruptly, slamming his bandaged ankle into a large rock.

"Ouch! Owww!" He lifted his injured foot a few inches off the ground. Tears of pain streamed down his cheeks. "Now look what you've done, you . . . you . . ." He lowered his foot gingerly. "You and that granddaughter of yours . . . you haven't heard the last of me . . . I'll be back!"

Casey was standing next to Victoria, her hand on the butt of her gun. "We'll be waiting for you."

He turned away in disgust, carefully this time, and limped back to his Jeep. He climbed in slowly and slammed the door shut.

"Crazy, both of them," Victoria heard him mutter. "Ought to institutionalize both of them."

He started up the engine and headed up the hill in the direction of the Steamship Authority dock. From Jane's living room window, Victoria could see the ferry rounding the jetty. He'd be able to make it.

Junior climbed into the backseat of the police cruiser and Victoria sat in the shotgun seat.

Casey settled herself in the driver's seat. "If he tries any funny business, I'm putting that loony away permanently. You'll have nothing to say about it, Victoria."

She backed the vehicle around and headed up the hill. "Well, you've done it again." At the top of the hill she turned onto Upper Main Street. "I was sure the grandkids had killed Mrs. Wilmington. Once the president had come and gone, I planned to focus on them."

"Did the guest lists get approval from the authorities?" asked Victoria.

"I got congratulated by some guy in the Secret Service for a thorough job of knowing and vetting the people of my village and their guests. They're giving me a letter of commendation." She glanced at Victoria.

Victoria patted her hair and smiled.

Two nights later, Victoria and Elizabeth were in the parlor. Victoria was holding her glass of cranberry juice and rum up so she could watch the firelight flicker through the ruby red drink, when there was a knock on the kitchen door. She set her glass down and Susan came into the parlor.

"I heard the news, Mrs. Trumbull, that Arthur admitted to both killings."

"Yes."

"I was sure my brothers and sister were responsible."

"Let me fix you a drink," said Elizabeth, and left, returning shortly with a glass in hand. "Has Scott recovered from the mushroom episode?"

"I knew they'd been drinking and I was sure they'd eat the sautéed mushrooms I left in the fridge." Susan sipped her drink. "I'm ashamed of setting them up like that. I knew if any of them ate those mushrooms they'd be sick. I didn't realize how sick. At least Heather and Wesley didn't eat them."

"It was fortunate that Lockwood did," said Victoria. "If he hadn't been suffering from a horrendous headache, I'd never have been able to distract him long enough to make him drop his gun."

"Well, Scott swears he'll never touch another drop of liquor as long as he lives. He's having dinner tonight with that dentist, Dr. McBride." Susan sipped some more of her drink and watched the flickering firelight. "You know, Mrs. Trumbull, I'm definitely turning Grandmother's house into a country inn. If my sibs want to partner with me, fine. If not, well, that's fine, too."